PRAISE FOR *THE FINAL SIX*

"I sat down to read a bit before bed and then it was two a.m. and the book was half gone. This is a space competition of epic proportions, loaded with disturbing hidden secrets and intense action. Your eyes will be glued to the page."
—KENDARE BLAKE, #1 *New York Times* bestselling author of *Three Dark Crowns*

"A breathtakingly real look at love, loss, and the dangers of space, *The Final Six* skyrockets into twists and turns I never saw coming!"
—BETH REVIS, *New York Times* bestselling author of the Across the Universe series

"Compelling, cinematic, and fascinating. I can't wait to read what happens next in the mission to Europa!"
—ROMINA RUSSELL, *New York Times* bestselling author of the Zodiac series

"An ingenious thrill ride of a novel with memorable, diverse characters, *The Final Six* is a five-star read."
—ALYSON NOËL, #1 *New York Times* bestselling author of the Immortals series

"This novel is YA sci-fi grounded in a very plausible, only-just-in-the-future version of our world, with two relatable, compelling MCs and a relentless thriller pace. Read it!"
—BARNES & NOBLE TEEN BLOG

"*The Final Six* is a mixture of Space Camp + Climate Change + Political Thriller. I highly recommend this book."
—KAREN JANSEN, Teen Librarian Toolbox

"A stunning new take on the dystopian novel."
—PAPERBACK PARIS

ALEXANDRA MONIR

THE FINAL SIX

HARPER TEEN
An Imprint of HarperCollinsPublishers

HarperTeen is an imprint of HarperCollins Publishers.

The Final Six
 For information address HarperCollins Children's Books, a division of HarperCollins Publishers, 195 Broadway, New York, NY 10007.
www.epicreads.com

Library of Congress Control Number: 2017943575
ISBN 978-0-06-265895-1

Typography by Heather Daugherty
This book is set in 12-point Electra LH.

22 23 24 25 26 LBC 7 6 5 4 3

❖

First paperback edition, 2020

For the real Leo:

My son,

My heart,

My love.

ONE

LEO
Rome, Italy

A FUNNY THING HAPPENS WHEN YOU HAVE NOTHING LEFT TO live for. Your existence loses all its sharp edges. There are no more steep drops, no hills to climb. Colors blur and muddle together until your surroundings are a bunch of meaningless shapes and figures painted in the same shade of gray. There's nothing that could possibly surprise you or resurrect those old sensations of joy or fear. No human could be as unfeeling, as numb, as you are. And then, just when you're getting lulled into the monotonous routine, something snaps. *No more.*

I hope I won't be judged harshly for what I'm about to do. The truth is, I'm not sure I ever had a choice. This day has been beckoning me for a year—ever since the water rose up and swallowed our city. I'm supposed to be one of the "lucky ones" because I survived, but that couldn't be further from the truth. There's nothing lucky about hearing the screams of the dead every time you close your eyes, or waking up each morning alone, forced to remember all over again. The horror never loosens its grip. It follows everywhere you move, breathing down your neck, whispering in your ear.

I glance up at the clock, the numbers blinking 4:35 a.m. It's time to make my exit, before the neighbors wake up and spot me. But first, I let myself take one last look at home—or what remains of it.

The fourth floor of our *pensione*, once known as the Michelangelo Suite, is all that survived the flood. The high tide and storm swells pulled the first three floors under that day, sentencing everyone in those rooms to the worst kind of death. I should have gone down with them—I *would* have, if it hadn't been for the couple in the Michelangelo Suite requesting room service, sending me to the top floor with a breakfast tray at the moment the waves crashed through the windows below. You could say those hungry guests and this room saved me, but *why*? Why should I have survived with a couple of strangers when my family was drowning?

My eyes linger on the remnants of them that I salvaged from the sea floor. Papà's threadbare slippers sit on the ottoman beside Mamma's Elena Ferrante novel, the corner of page 152 turned down to mark her place. The ink is smeared, the words running together like tears, yet I can still see that the page ends in an incomplete sentence. One more thing Mamma never got to finish.

Angelica beams at me from her last school photo, and I pick up the cracked silver frame from its shelf. I study my little sister's bright eyes and dimpled smile one last time, memorizing her features. And then I take a breath and pull back the heavy sheet metal that covers the door, protecting against the tide.

This room once opened into a bright hallway lined with paintings, surrounding a stone staircase—but that was before *La Grande Inondazione*, the greatest flood Rome has ever known. Now the Tyrrhenian Sea laps at my doorstep, and when I venture outside, only a small wooden ledge separates me from the water.

In this new Rome, the only place to go is up. Each surviving structure has a ledge or makeshift dock like mine that connects to the *passerelle*: raised walkways far above the ground that lead us like a map to the places we need most. The upper stories of the basilica, hospital, and city hall; the Wi-Fi café; and even the public school's remaining classrooms are all accessible from here. Of course, most of us stopped going to school after the flood. The Wi-Fi café is the most common gathering place for the survivors and where I'd ordinarily be heading myself in a few hours, to watch the news with my neighbors and listen to accounts of similar catastrophes wreaking havoc in other parts of the world. It's our daily reminder that the Earth doesn't hate us alone.

We've all seen the jarring photos of New York's Times Square, its bright thoroughfares transformed into a deep river marked by the roofs of sagging Broadway theaters. We've followed the never-ending media reports about the curious case of our disappearing beaches, from America to Australia and beyond. The sea change is coming for everyone, rich and poor alike.

For those of us who want to travel across the Tyrrhenian, each of our docks houses a small wooden motorboat. It sounds like an easy out, right? Just hop in your boat and steer north toward Tuscany, leaving this sinking city behind. . . . Only it's not so simple. The rising tides and rough waves make the hours-long trip a risky one, and those who do arrive in the Tuscany region find it an overcrowded mess. It's not exactly an easy glide from there to the train station or airport, either. There's a months-long waiting list to escape, and only those flush with euros can afford it. Even if you do manage to get out, who's to say your new city or country of refuge won't be the next one hit by the climate's destructive sweep?

I wasn't always a quitter. In the first months following the flood, I was like any other survivor, scrambling to stay alive. Some of my neighbors had a safety net—relatives from dry regions who could take them in, or bank accounts filled with savings to help them rebuild. Not me. There was nothing to do but wait for the EU Disaster Relief funds to trickle their way toward me, if they came at all. So I found my own way.

I knew there were treasures at the bottom of the sea, mementos my neighbors would pay a mint for, but none of them would venture into the water where so many of us drowned. Only I was hungry enough, desperate enough—and could survive the deep dives. I'd done it before without any breathing equipment, back in my competitive swimming days, only then I was just showing off for my teammates. Now, my skill could actually keep me alive. So I became a scavenger.

My first week, I unearthed Raphael's *Madonna of Foligno* from the wreckage of the Vatican. It was so water-damaged that you could barely make out the Virgin Mary and child in the foreground, but I knew someone would see its value. I was right. The painting paid for a month of my meals. And in my second week I found a purse of commemorative coins from 2004, their emblem featuring the centenary of Puccini's *Madama Butterfly.* They were worth only five euros each, but being collector's items, I was able to fetch double. I kept going, scavenging and selling as each day bled into the next—until I found the true riches, curled up together in a bed of algae.

Papà's slippers, Mamma's book, and Angelica's photograph were all right there, waiting for me. It had to be more than a coincidence that these three small relics managed to stay entwined. It was a sign. And in that moment, with my sister's face staring up at me, I realized just what I'd been doing: ransacking and profiting from the dead. The guilt replaced the hunger in my stomach, and I promised myself

I would never do it again.

Since then, all I've wanted to do is join them.

I strap my heavy backpack over my shoulders and open the door, stepping out onto the ledge of the pensione. The cold water rushes at my feet, the dark sky closing in around me. And then I jump.

The murky water rises to my neck. I could just let myself go, right here . . . but I can't do it in front of my home. Instead I begin to swim, persisting against the weight of my backpack as I head for the deeper center, where the half-sunken Colosseum rests in the middle of the waves. The words of a Lord Byron poem I learned in school echo in my mind as I swim, making my way closer and closer to the ruins.

While stands the Coliseum, Rome shall stand;
When falls the Coliseum, Rome shall fall;
And when Rome falls—the World.

I grasp one of the arches of the Colosseum and rest my forehead against the stone in a silent good-bye. And then I let go—slipping my head underwater, relaxing my body like a limp rag. I let myself fall.

The disgusting taste of seawater fills my mouth, threatening to choke me if I don't drown first. I can hear the waves crashing overhead, feel the tide beginning to perform its job, pulling me down, down, down.

My adrenaline briefly spikes, and I could swear I hear

Angelica's voice snapping in my ear: "Swim, you idiot! *Swim!*" But I squeeze my eyes shut, ignoring every physical instinct that begs me to move, letting the water snatch me instead.

If you saw me now, you wouldn't believe the swimmer and athlete I used to be. The truth is, I could propel myself up to the surface in a matter of seconds if I wanted to. But that's the problem. I don't want to.

My thoughts are bleeding together now, playing a strange, jumbled movie just for me. Sleep is coming; I can feel it. And then—

An engine roars. Ripples form in the water overhead.

I know that sound. It's a—a *boat*.

I should just keep my eyes closed and let the fog of my drowsiness pull me further toward the brink. But my mind is still half-awake, warning me that the presence of a boat means something is amiss. No vehicles are allowed to cross the water outside of daylight hours, one of the many new rules enforced since *La Grande Inondazione*. Of course, the coast guard always has the option of sidestepping this rule—if they spot someone in danger.

And just like that, the haze before my eyes disappears. Consciousness returns, the death wish replaced by something else—shame. I know I can't let this innocent coast guard jump into the deep sea and do battle with the tide just to save me. That can't be my final act.

I spit the water out of my mouth and hold my breath, wriggling free of the backpack and pushing my body up, up.

My limp arms and legs are swinging back to life as I finally listen to my kid sister. *Swim*.

My head hits the surface. Air—sweet, beautiful air—fills my lungs, and I gasp, clinging to it.

The hum of the motor comes closer, and I rise up, waving my arms.

"I'm here!" I try to shout, though my voice has gone ragged and barely makes a sound. "Don't jump!"

But as the boat glides into view, my mouth falls open. It's not a coast guard boat. It's a sleek catamaran, with painted blue lettering on the side revealing a familiar logo: *European Space Agency*.

What is ESA doing *here*, of all places? Why now?

A man and woman stand at the bow of the vessel, wearing matching expressions of fierce concentration as they scan the surroundings. The woman is dressed in the dark blue uniform of the Italian military, the man in a business suit with an ESA shirt beneath the blazer. Thankfully, neither of them seems to notice me.

I didn't think anything could surprise me anymore, but it turns out I was wrong. Instead of sinking to the bottom of the sea, I am now swimming in the boat's wake. Whatever ESA is doing here in our wreckage of a city, it must be something big—and I don't want to miss it.

I keep pace with the boat, my breaststroke getting me through the last stretch of choppy water until we reach the makeshift docks. I can see my dilapidated home now, the Pensione Danieli sign still hanging hopefully from the roof.

And then, as the first rays of morning light filter through the sky, the boat turns toward Palazzo Senatorio, our city hall. Waiting on the front stoop that juts above the water is Prime Minister Vincenti with his wife, Francesca, and their daughter, Elena—my sister's best friend.

I duck back underwater, holding my breath as the boat docks. I can't let any of them see me. Lord knows how I would answer their questions.

After what feels like an eternity, I splash back up to the surface. The prime minister and his wife have disappeared inside, along with the two from ESA—but Elena is still there, angling a camera in front of the space agency boat. As I lift my head above the water, a flash of light sparks before my eyes. I blink rapidly, watching as Elena does a double take. *Shit*. I've been caught in the photo.

"Leo?" She rushes to the dock's edge. "What are you *doing*?"

I could make up a story—I could tell her I just felt like taking a crack-of-dawn swim. But no one would believe it in these treacherous waters, and I've never been a good liar anyway. My shame, the step I came this close to taking, will be written all over my face.

"*Ciao,* Elena," I call back, trying to make my voice as normal as possible. "It's . . . a long story. Nothing important."

She gives me a sideways look, and I know there's no getting away from her now. I might as well have this inevitable conversation on dry ground.

I swim forward, closing the distance between us, and then grip the bottom of the wooden dock, mustering my strength to pull myself up and over the edge. I land on shaky legs, my soaking clothes forming a puddle around me. Elena raises an eyebrow.

"At least you remembered to take off your shoes before you jumped in. Why not drop the clothes, too?" Two pink spots appear in her cheeks. "That came out wrong, I meant—um, let me get you something to dry off with. Wait here."

"Thanks." I avoid her eyes but not out of embarrassment. I can't look at Elena without seeing the empty space where my sister should be. And now I wish I'd never followed that stupid boat, that I'd never ended up here.

Suddenly, a thunder of footsteps descends on the elevated walkway, accompanied by raised voices. I crane my neck to look. My neighbors are awake far earlier than they should be—and they're heading straight for the top-floor entrance to Palazzo Senatorio.

This day just keeps getting stranger.

Elena returns with a large overcoat, and I drape it over my drenched clothes. I can hear the beginnings of a question forming on her lips, but I interrupt her.

"What's going on? Who were those people in the ESA boat, and what are they doing in Rome?"

Elena stares at me. "Do you really not know?"

"Apparently not."

"It's the calling of the draft. The Twenty-Four are being announced today!"

"The Twenty-Four?" I repeat. The words are familiar, like a long-forgotten taste on my tongue. My mind rushes back in time, before the sinking of Rome, before I lost everything. And then—

"Europa."

Elena nods, a slight smile lighting her features.

The memories feel like snippets from another life. I can remember sitting around the TV with Angelica and our parents, the four of us glued to the live United Nations press conference, where world leaders declared a state of war between humanity and our environment. I remember the government official showing up at our door with the Europa Mission & Draft pamphlets, outlining a plan to deploy young astronauts to build a new home on Jupiter's most promising moon, Europa. Then came the strangers, infiltrating our school the following week—"scouts," they were called—who studied us in their search for the perfect teenage candidates for the Europa Draft. Because, as the scientists said on TV, "Only the young can tolerate the radiation-resistant bacteria that will enable humans to thrive in the current conditions on Jupiter's moon. Only the young will still be fertile and able to procreate on Europa by the time it is terraformed and ready for a full human settlement."

Those heady days are a blur, like a dream washed away by the flood. I guess I never thought they would actually go through with the whole extravagant idea.

I turn back to Elena. "So you're saying they already

picked the finalists? But why wouldn't ESA and NASA just announce the names online? Why come all the way—"

I stop short, the realization practically knocking the wind out of me. "One of the finalists is from *Rome*?"

"Yes! Thrilling, isn't it? Unless it's me—then I'll have a heart attack." Elena shivers. "They're going to announce who it is in a live-streaming press conference at five thirty."

"Are you serious? We have to get inside!"

I break into a run, ignoring Elena's protests that I can't enter the Palazzo barefoot and dripping wet. There's no way I'm missing this, not when one of my friends or neighbors is about to be named a finalist to go to *Jupiter's moon*. I can just see my father pumping his fists in pride that a Roman was chosen, while my mother would clap her hand over her mouth in her usual dramatic way, torn between the excitement of it all and pain for the parents left behind.

The city hall's portico entrance sank in the Great Flood along with its lower floors, so I run straight from the dock up to the covered arcade that leads into the *piano nobile*, the new main floor. Inside, the old masters on the walls are caked in a coat of film from water damage, while the elaborate painted ceilings are marred with cracks. But the old hum of activity remains, and I follow the sound of voices into the Neo-Gothic Salon, a large foyer still standing with the support of its marble columns. A glass chandelier swings tenuously from the ceiling, a shaky vestige of the pre-flood days.

Filling nearly every square inch of the room are fellow

survivors: "the Last Romans," as they call us in the media. Everyone watches, rapt, as the Italian military officer and her companion from the ESA boat approach the podium at the front of the room, flanked by the prime minister and his wife. A trio of cameramen stand in position nearby, their equipment at the ready. My heartbeat quickens.

"I should go join my parents, but let's talk later, okay? You still need to tell me what you were doing when I found you." Elena's voice over my shoulder catches me off guard. I'd almost forgotten she was still here, eyeing me as water drips from my clothes onto the floor.

"Okay," I reply with a nod, though I'm banking on ESA's announcement detracting from any attention on me. "Thanks, Elena."

"*Buongiorno.*" Prime Minister Vincenti steps up to the microphone, his voice booming across the room. "Thank you for joining us this morning, on a day that is certain to bring pride back to Rome. I can see you are all as eager as I am to hear the news, so I won't keep you waiting. Please welcome Sergeant Clea Rossi of the Italian Armed Forces, and Dr. Hans Schroder, from the European Space Agency."

As the crowd applauds, I squeeze into a space in the very back of the room.

Dr. Schroder steps forward. "Thank you, Prime Minister, and all of you here today. It is a great pleasure for me to be in Rome. I thought I might never get to experience your city again in my lifetime."

The crowd quiets. We all know what he means. Our

homeland is growing extinct, following in the ancient footsteps of Baiae—the first Italian city to go underwater.

"As you know, the Europa Mission is the most pressing item on our planet's agenda," he begins. "Our chance to terraform and colonize Jupiter's moon can't come soon enough. So with that said, after more than a year of scouting and reviewing countless medical and academic records, I am delighted to announce that we have selected our Twenty-Four finalists. These teenagers will spend the next four months at International Space Training Camp in America, at the end of which a final team of six will be drafted and deployed to Europa." Dr. Schroder pauses. "And, yes. Our Twenty-Four includes one of you."

The room fills with a mix of whoops, cheers, and nervous laughter. I scan the neighbors to my left and right, wondering about each one of them: *Could it be you?*

"Sergeant Rossi, would you like to do the honors?"

Dr. Schroder steps back, giving Sergeant Rossi the podium.

She clears her throat, then looks out over her audience. "The finalist from Rome, who will depart on Monday for Space Training Camp, was chosen for their remarkable survival skills, as well as a singular ability that should prove crucial for the Europa Mission."

I hold my breath, trying to comprehend the idea of one of my own friends or neighbors leaving for America in just two days—and possibly leaving the *planet* altogether. I keep my eyes on the crowd, anxious to catch the first reaction of whoever is chosen.

"Your finalist from Rome is . . ."

The energy in the room thickens as we all lean forward, bracing for the name.

"Leonardo Danieli."

Wait.

No—that can't be right.

That's my name.

"He's right there!" a voice shouts.

More than a hundred heads swivel in my direction. The cameramen come running from the front of the room, their lenses trained on me. Standing between her parents, Elena lets out a sound somewhere between a moan and a shriek.

They chose . . . me.

One of the cameramen thrusts a microphone under my nose. "Leonardo Danieli, *what* is going through your mind right now? Shock, fear, excitement?"

I was supposed to die today. But I didn't. If I'd gone through with it, if I hadn't heard the boat and snapped out of it . . .

"I—I never imagined this was coming." My words tumble out, echoing across the silent room. "And I'm glad—so glad—I didn't miss it."

TWO

NAOMI
Los Angeles, California

"THIS IS A JOKE, RIGHT?"

I stare at each of the adults filling the principal's office, waiting for one of them to crack. *Whaddya get when you mix a high school junior, two bewildered parents, one* NASA *rocket scientist, a gun-toting US Army official, and the school principal?*

"Naomi," the woman from NASA begins, saying my name delicately, as though it might break. "It's not a joke. In fact, you should be very proud. Each member of the Twenty-Four was chosen for a particular skill set or trait that we need for the mission. You were chosen for your brilliant mind and scientific ability. If you make the Final Six, you'll have a vital part to play."

My parents clutch each other's hands. Mom lets out a sob, and a fist tightens around my heart. There's no way, no *way* this could be happening—but the grave faces across from me confirm the worst.

"You're telling me I've been drafted?" My voice is whisper thin.

The army officer, Major Lewis, nods. "Yes, though currently your only duty is to International Space Training Camp. The Europa draft won't be decided until the completion of training camp, at which point you will either be cut and sent back home, or—"

"Or I'll be deployed to Europa," I finish his sentence. "For good."

The room turns silent, except for the sound of my mother crying. I push out of my seat and to her side, wrapping my arms around her as I wonder how many more times I'll get to do this. How long will it be before I forget what it feels like to hug my mom and dad, before I forget the sound of my brother's voice?

"You can't do this." I raise my eyes pleadingly to the figures looming before us. "If you know as much about me as you say, then you know I have a little brother who needs me. You can't just split up our family and send me away!"

"Sweetie," my dad murmurs, his voice breaking. "It's a draft. That means they can do exactly that."

"The reality here is that we are at war," Major Lewis says, eyeing me with a frown. "We're at war with our own environment, and the fact that you are among the few with a chance to escape makes you one of the *lucky* ones."

O-kaaay. I didn't realize getting kicked off Earth was something to be *grateful* for.

But before I can retort, Mom speaks up, taking my hand in hers. "Please don't misunderstand my tears, Naomi. Yes, my heart is broken at the thought of separating from you, but I'm . . . I'm thankful that you're getting another chance." She looks into my eyes. "I honestly don't know how much longer we can go on like this. We've already been evacuated from three different homes in less than two years—who knows where we'll be tomorrow? And you know how worried I've been about you losing so much weight from the rationing. We're living in quicksand, and if anyone can be saved from this fate—well, I want it to be you."

She believes in it. My mouth falls open at the realization that my mother actually believes the hype, that the Final Six can possibly survive this pipe dream of a mission. And even if they—*we?*—managed to achieve the incredible, I'd choose dying with my family over living with five strangers on Jupiter's moon any day.

But as I look at the hope written across my parents' faces, I let my protests die on my lips. Instead, I turn to the NASA scientist, Dr. Anderson. "You say the trip includes a flyby to Mars to pick up the unused supplies from the *Athena* mission and get a gravity assist to Jupiter, right? Well, how do we know this mission won't result in the same outcome as the *Athena*? How do you know we all won't end up . . ."

I don't bother finishing my sentence. They know the word I'm looking for. *Dead*.

"It's simple: Mars was always a gamble—the crew of the *Athena* knew there was a good chance the planet would prove uninhabitable. But the tragedy caused us to take a closer look at Europa, which was revealed in our robotic missions to have the key ingredients needed to build a new Earth," Dr. Anderson explains. "Where Mars lacked a viable source of water and oxygen, Europa's wealth of oceans gives us access to both through water electrolysis. And unlike the *Athena* mission, the Final Six won't be spending any time on Martian surface. The spacecraft will manually retrieve the *Athena* crew's cache of supplies, and then use a booster to slingshot from Mars's orbit to Jupiter. None of you will be exposed to Mars's atmosphere."

I can tell by the way my parents are gaping at Dr. Anderson, they're trying to comprehend the idea of their daughter zipping from one planet to another. But I'm not done with my questions.

"And . . . what about the supposed intelligent life on Europa?"

Dr. Anderson and Major Lewis exchange a smirk. "That's just the Space Conspirator and other questionable websites drumming up tabloid fodder. We've found no evidence whatsoever of existing life on Europa. You have nothing to worry about."

I nod, though I'm hardly reassured. Something about her reply feels canned, the way an actress might sound after reciting the same lines twenty times in a row. But I know better than to push it.

Principal Hamilton has remained quiet ever since the announcement, but now she joins the conversation, gesturing to the window. "There's a crowd forming out there—it looks like the press. Is this why I was asked to call an assembly? Are we going public with the news about Naomi?"

No. Not yet. I shrink back against the couch, wishing I could blend into the upholstery and disappear. But at the principal's words, Major Lewis and Dr. Anderson spring into action.

"Let's get Naomi to the auditorium first before letting anyone in. The two of us will remain beside her throughout the press conference and—"

I break in, interrupting the major. "Why? Why do all these people have to know now?"

If there's any hope of me dodging this draft, it certainly won't happen with my name and face splashed across the media. The second I am revealed to the world as one of the Twenty-Four, I become *theirs*—theirs to experiment with, to make into a soldier, to send to another galaxy.

"We have no choice," Dr. Anderson replies. "As a government agency, NASA is required to report all news to the public within twenty-four hours, and the fact that the draft is a wartime mandate means an even stricter standard of transparency. We were able to hold your name back just long enough to give you this advance notice." She turns to the principal. "Do you know if the videoconference screens in the auditorium have been set up and connected to Houston yet?"

As Principal Hamilton darts behind her computer and begins clacking away at the keys, I'm tempted to shove everything off her desk, to send the computer crashing to the floor in my frustration. "Looks like we're a go," she says.

Terror bubbles in my chest. I look from the door to the window and back again, but there's no chance of escape. Even if I did manage to outrun all the adults in this room and get away, it's not like I could ever get my old life back—not as a draft dodger. I have no choice but to comply, and say good-bye . . . to everyone and everything I've ever known.

I rise to my feet, a prisoner resigned to walking the plank. "So what happens now?"

Major Lewis cracks a smile. "You're about to become one of the twenty-four most famous teenagers on Earth."

I wait behind the curtain of Burbank High School's dust-covered stage, flanked by the security guard sworn to "never leave my side" until I'm safely transferred to Space Training Camp. The pounding in my chest and the sweat dampening my brow reminds me of the last time I stood here in the wings, before the drama club's production of *Fiddler on the Roof* in my freshman year. I had only two solo lines ("Tradition, tradition!") but I was more terrified than the leads. That was my first clue that I belong in the classroom, in the science lab, behind a telescope—but never, ever on a stage.

That was the last time most of us set foot in this

auditorium. After another season of El Niño superstorms raged through LA, tearing the beach cities to shreds and forcing all surviving Angelenos to decamp to the Valley, the school pretty much dropped all extracurriculars. They had bigger things to worry about than drama club and sports—like our survival, and how to accommodate an influx of displaced students, known to us as the West Side Exiles.

I step forward, peering through a slit in the curtains. I can see my classmates and teachers filing into the rows of seats, while giant projection screens unfurl onto all four walls.

"I should warn you that I might throw up," I mutter to the guard beside me. "Why do they have to make such a spectacle out of this announcement, anyway?"

I don't expect an answer, but the guard, Thompson, speaks up. "I imagine it's because the Europa Mission is the one source of distraction and excitement for the public right now. And the greater the public interest, the more bargaining power the space agencies have to lobby Congress for extra funds to send you safely up there."

He gives me a wink that is meant to be reassuring but instead ties my stomach in knots. This is the problem with being a science nerd—I can't share in the public's hope for this mission. I know too much. I know the laundry list of things that can—and invariably *will*—go wrong.

Just then, through a break in the curtains, I spot the face I love most. My little brother, Sam, is sliding into a seat beside our parents in the front row. He glances from the stage to the surrounding screens, his expression agitated.

My heart seizes at the sight.

Even though he's two years younger, looking at Sam often feels like gazing into a mirror. We share the same dark hair, olive skin, and Persian eyes, the same high cheekbones and dimpled smiles. Of course, neither of us is smiling now. We've been attached at the hip since he was born, and now . . . now they're untethering us. Tears prick at my eyes, but before I can give in to them, I hear the sound of high heels clicking across the foot of the stage, and a hush comes over the room.

"You might have guessed the reason behind today's assembly," comes the sound of Dr. Anderson's voice. "Well, the rumors are true. We are thrilled to introduce you to Burbank High School's very own finalist in the Twenty-Four, one of just two Americans chosen: Miss Naomi Ardalan!"

The curtain rises, revealing me standing there in a daze, blinking under the glare of the spotlight. As the room explodes with flashing cameras, cries of shock, and smatterings of applause, I meet my brother's eyes, trying to convey a silent message to him. *I'm sorry, Sam. My brain was supposed to find a cure, to heal you—it wasn't supposed to get me taken away from you. I'm sorry things got so royally messed up. But it isn't over yet.*

"That's not all!" Dr. Anderson's voice rises an octave in her enthusiasm. "Today, twenty-three other teenagers around the world received the same extraordinary news as Naomi. Thanks to NASA's supercomputer, Pleidas, we are able to videoconference with *all* twenty-four finalists and introduce them to each other, and to you—right here and now."

My head snaps up. The sound of static echoes through the room, and then all noise fades away as the blank projection screens surrounding us fill with color—with faces.

I can hardly breathe as I gaze at the twenty-three strangers who will become my new, forced family. Dr. Anderson and Major Lewis take turns rattling off their names and countries one by one, as if this is the Olympics instead of a draft into space.

The finalists all look about my age, but that is the only feature we share. We are a mix of skin and eye colors, a blend of hair textures and body types. As I look from one face to another, I find that a few are fighting back tears or gulping in panic like me—but then there are the others, the majority, who smile broadly and wave with excitement. Which of us will prove to be right?

"Last but not least, from Rome, Italy, we have Leonardo Danieli."

I turn around, my eyes falling on the screen behind me. A boy with golden-brown hair and bright blue eyes is beaming in wonder. For some reason, the sight of his optimistic smile causes something to break inside me. *You don't know . . . you don't know what we're in for. We're not victors; we're goners.*

With my back to the crowd, I bury my face in my palms, letting the tears escape down my cheeks. I only need twenty seconds to cry—a trick I learned when Sam got sick.

I've always been his cheerleader, his strength, and I never wanted him to see my fear. But sometimes when I watched my brother hooked up to machines, when I heard the faint sound of his irregular heartbeat through the hospital room monitors—I couldn't help it. I had to turn away, to give in to the feeling of my insides being ripped apart. But only for twenty seconds. That was how long I could let down my guard without Sam noticing. It's a skill that comes in handy now, with so many eyes on me.

When I regain my composure and glance up, I get a shock. The Italian finalist, Leonardo, is watching me, his expression kind. He presses his hand up to the screen, his mouth forming a word. *"Hi."*

I take a step closer to the screen and raise my own palm, returning his greeting. His eyes lock with mine, and for a moment, I forget where I am, what this is—until Dr. Anderson resumes her speech.

"The twenty-four of you will get to spend this weekend with your families, in the privacy of your homes. Monday morning, your duties officially begin. You will be flown by private charter to the Johnson Space Center in Houston, Texas, for four months of training camp, after which time six of you will move forward. . . ."

I turn away from the Italian finalist, back to the audience—to my brother. His head is bent, his fist against his chest . . . as though someone has died.

But I'm not dead yet. And I can't leave my brother alone to grieve for real.

Something in me shakes loose. As Dr. Anderson continues speaking into the microphone, I back away slowly, until I am nearly backstage. And then I break into a run.

The guard has me in his clutches before I get more than a few steps from the stage, but I don't care. That millisecond of freedom reminded me of something.

I may not be able to dodge the draft, but if I play my hand correctly . . . I can get cut well before the Final Six is deployed to Europa. All I have to do is stay focused, and let nothing—no one—distract from my purpose.

The others can be the heroes, the space pioneers. I have something more important.

Home.

THREE

LEO

I SNAP OUT OF A DREAM AS THE VIDEO SCREENS MOUNTED TO the media room walls fade to black. Two dozen people I never knew existed, whose paths should never have crossed with mine, are about to become my entire world. And if I'm lucky, if I make the final draft . . . I will be tied to five of these strangers for life. The thought sends goose bumps prickling across my skin, and I'm hungry to learn everything there is to know about these twenty-three. I try to recall their faces, but even now, moments after the screens turned dark, I can only remember two: the girl with the deep brown eyes, who looked so sad in our moment of triumph—and the pale-haired boy who jumped in the air at the news, whooping with pride. It was the kind of unbridled reaction I might have had if I weren't still in a state of shock.

Prime Minister Vincenti opens the door, stepping into the room where I've been sequestered with Dr. Schroder since just after the news broke.

"Leo, security is still trying to contain the crowd, but the public is demanding another look at you. Would you be willing to go back out there and just . . . smile at the cameras for a few minutes?"

"What?" I stare at the prime minister, wondering if I heard him correctly. "But most of those people already know me. They've probably seen me cross the *passerelle* hundreds of times. Why—"

"That was before," he interrupts. "You may look the same and feel the same, but you're someone different now. After today, you're no longer just another neighbor or survivor—you're a legend in the making."

And as he speaks, I can hear their voices, growing louder as their chants carry toward our closed door.

"Leo, Leo, forza, Leo! L'italia é fiera di te!"

Emotion swells in my chest. It seems unthinkable that they're cheering for me, of all people—the same me who came so close to throwing my life away in the sea.

But I didn't, I remind myself. I'm still here, and somehow, I earned a place among the Twenty-Four. And I won't let this second chance go. I'll be worthy of it; I'll make my country proud.

"Okay," I tell the prime minister. "I want to see them."

A security guard posted at the door springs into action

as we step out of the media room. He leads the three of us into the marble hallway and toward the noise, his eyes darting over to me every few seconds, as though I'm the VIP to be protected instead of our prime minister.

We return to the Neo-Gothic Salon, and the crowd has nearly doubled. People are spilling out of the room, with barely an inch of breathing space between them. When they see us, their cheers escalate to a frenzied pitch.

"Leo, Leo, forza, Leo!"

They look at me as though I'm someone else entirely—like I've shed my old skin and revealed a superhero underneath. I want to laugh, to wave my hands in front of their faces and bring them back to earth, remind them that I'm just Leo from the crumbling Pensione Danieli. But then the realization hits me: if I make it to space, if I succeed in the mission . . . a hero is exactly what I'll be.

The thought sends a burst of adrenaline through my body, and I move with new purpose. I smile at the crowd of my neighbors, and I let myself soak in their roaring approval as the security guard steers the prime minister, Dr. Schroder, and me to the front of the packed room. Sergeant Rossi is still there, along with the prime minister's wife and Elena, the three of them attempting to calm the feverish crowd. But there's no restraining them now. A voice breaks into "L'Italiano," our unofficial anthem, and soon everyone is joining in—singing at the top of their lungs, clapping and swaying to the rhythm.

I can't stop grinning, even as a lump rises in my throat.

This is the first time I've seen any of my fellow survivors emerge from the shadow of our grief, celebrating life the way we used to. Looking at the faces in front of me, it's clear I wasn't the only one who had lost hope, who was searching for something to cling to. Somehow, today I changed that for us all. *Me*.

Sergeant Rossi hands me the microphone.

"Thank you." My voice comes out shaky, and I clear my throat. "Thank you for your love, your support. I won't let you down. I'm going to represent our country, not just in front of the world . . . but in front of the cosmos."

The room fills with whoops and whistles. Their voices drown me out, giving me a moment to say something to the one empty sliver of space I can find in the room—the place my parents and sister should be.

"This is for you."

My transformation continues with an offer to spend my last weekend in Italy at Palazzo Senatorio, as the Vincentis' guest of honor. I know the real reason for the invitation is so the prime minister's guards can keep their watchful eyes on me until I take off for International Space Training Camp, but it's a gift all the same. I can't imagine returning to the pensione now—its emptiness would suck me back in, would make today's news feel like it never happened. And so I jump at the chance to stay at the Palazzo, telling the prime minister I don't even need to go home to pack. The only possession I'm taking is safe on my finger—the Danieli family signet ring.

Instead of the deflated mattress and moldy comforter back at home, I'm now lying in a plush double bed under a soft duvet, my stomach full for the first time in months. I'm just drifting off to sleep when I hear a knock at the door. I pull the covers up over my head with a groan. Maybe if I ignore them, whoever is knocking will get the hint? But then I hear a voice.

"Leo, it's me, Elena. Can you let me in?"

Huh. That's not who I was expecting.

I drag myself out of bed and throw on the ESA shirt Dr. Schroder left for me. Is Elena here to hit on me or something? It almost makes me laugh to think about, until I remember that she is fifteen now, only two years younger than me. Still, I don't think I could ever go through with it. There's too much history. But Elena seems to have something else on her mind when I open the door.

"Sorry if I woke you," she says, shutting the door behind her. "I just . . . I needed to talk to you before I lost the nerve."

"Why? What's going on?" I take a seat at the foot of the bed, but she remains standing, her face creased with worry.

"It's—it's something I overheard my parents talking about in their room. I've spent the past hour going over it in my head, wondering whether or not I should tell you. My papà says that repeating state secrets is treason, and I don't want to go against him, but if something happened to you and I hadn't said anything . . ." Her voice trails off. Now she's got me nervous.

"What is it, Elena? Please, just say it."

"He . . . told my mom that there's a deeper reason you were chosen for the draft. He said the director of ESA—Dr. Schroder's boss—has been watching you for years."

It takes me a minute to digest her words, and then I grin with relief. That doesn't sound so bad. "Okay, so I was carefully vetted. Isn't that a good thing?"

"Except they were tracking you long before the Europa Mission was even approved," Elena says with a frown. "I heard Papà saying that it all started three years ago, after you got some attention from your first big swim championship. The ESA director reached out to him and asked for government permission to investigate you. He told my father that your speed, and ability to hold your breath underwater so much longer than normal, could make you some kind of . . . *weapon* for them."

I stare at Elena. "You sure you heard that right?"

"I know I did, because then Mamma asked what he meant, what kind of weapon? Papà said all he knows is that it has to do with Europa. He told her she couldn't say a word about any of this, and then he changed the subject. That's when I left."

I pause, letting this sink in. "So what you're saying is that ESA spied on me, and your dad helped them? Because they think I have some deadly underwater skills?" I try to make a joke out of it, but there's something chilling about the realization that these people have been watching me, invading my privacy, while I was in the dark.

Elena winces. "Yes. And that's why I'm convinced there's more to this mission than we've been told. These people obviously see you as something more than just a potential astronaut, and based on the secrecy . . . whatever they have in store for the Final Six has to be far more dangerous than they're letting on."

I take a moment to think. Elena's revelation might change the way I look at ESA and the prime minister, but it doesn't alter my feelings about the mission. Even if she is right and there is an untold danger on Europa, some unlikely reason that I'd be used as a weapon—what else do I have to live for? I can either help ensure humanity's survival, or I can remain a useless waste of space on Earth. There is no scenario where I don't choose the former.

"I'm glad you told me, but I wouldn't back out even if I could," I say. "If my skills are needed, and that's what gets me out of here and into space . . . then I consider that good news."

"But you can stay on guard while you're at training camp. Keep your eyes and ears open for anything amiss. If you get there and it turns out the mission is a whole lot riskier than we've all been told, promise you'll find a way to get word to me." Elena lowers her voice. "You're Angelica's brother. I don't want to see anything happen to you."

Angelica's brother. The words twist at my insides. It's been so long since anyone spoke of my sister like she still exists.

"Okay." My voice catches. "I promise."

FOUR

NAOMI

I DON'T GET TO SAY GOOD-BYE TO MY FRIENDS OR TEACHERS. I don't even get the honor of cleaning out my own locker. As soon as the press conference ends, the NASA-appointed guard whisks me and my family away from the auditorium and off school property, citing "crowd concerns." I glance over at my brother while the guard, Thompson, ushers us toward the elevated train. *What will we do without each other?* I can barely stomach the thought.

When we were little kids, I used to constantly refer to Sam as "mine," and I guess I never really shook the feeling. Maybe it's because I used some of my first words to beg our parents for a sibling, or because they let me pick out his name. Maybe it's the nights I sat up late at his bedside, studying charts that I swiped from our doctor's office as I tried to hack the code of his DNA—tried to understand how two kids of the same genetic makeup could be born with desperately different hearts. I promised him I wouldn't rest until he was better, that we would never be apart. But now I'm breaking my promise. I'm leaving him.

My body turns cold as I imagine what could happen while I'm away. Sam is stable now, but it's the unpredictability of his heart defect that makes it so terrifying. You never know when his body will reject the current medication, when he'll need to be rushed to the hospital and put through another invasive, short-term fix to stave off heart failure—

"Hey." Sam grabs my arm as we approach the train platform. "Remember what you always say: no problem has ever been solved by panicking."

I smile in spite of myself. My brother has once again read my thoughts.

"You're going to have enough to think about in the coming days," he continues. "You can't be worrying about me, too."

"I can't help it. It's what I do when it comes to you." My smile fades as I look at Sam, his sweatshirt practically hanging off of him. Even though I've been forcing him to take my extra meal portions, he still looks somehow thinner than yesterday. "There is just no way I can go—"

Sam stops me from finishing my sentence, elbowing me in the ribs and nodding at the guard. Thompson is to our right, his head cocked in our direction even as he answers a question of Dad's.

I know why my brother is being so careful. We've all been warned that resisting the draft is the surest way to land in prison. I can't afford to let anyone involved with NASA think of me as anything other than obedient—even when it's the last thing I feel.

The train comes rumbling across the tracks toward us, looking eerily empty without the after-school hordes. Sam and I climb in first, heading for our usual spot in the third car, but Thompson insists on us cramming into the front with the conductor, for "security purposes." It's a silent and stiff ride home, none of us able to say anything real with a guard listening in. I turn my face to the window, feeling a flash of longing for the days when we had the privacy of our own car. Most countries outlawed all motor vehicles after climate change was declared an international emergency, but by then it was too late. The gas emissions had already played their role, to devastating effect.

As the train rattles forward, I watch the sights go by, drinking in every dreary image—just in case today is the last chance I'll get to see my city. Then again, it's not really my city, not anymore. This place is just a sad imposter, only pretending to be Los Angeles.

From Burbank to Los Feliz, the number of families on the streets seems to swell. They huddle together on unpaved roads slick with mud, they cower under downed power lines, as they beg the passersby for something, *anything*. I want to close my eyes—but every day I force myself to look, to see them.

The train curves around a bend, and now we're traveling over the Hollywood Hills, where there's no longer any flashy Hollywood sign to serve as a beacon. Instead, there are houses and buildings covered with thick layers of ash, and deep crevices in the streets marking where the earthquakes hit.

"You're lucky to be leaving."

I turn sharply at the sound of Sam's voice. He is staring out the window alongside me, his expression unreadable. He forces a smile when our eyes meet, and I shake my head, wishing I could reassure him that I don't see it that way, that I'll find a way back home. How could I ever abandon him, especially now? But Thompson is listening. Instead, I loop my arm through my brother's and lean my head on his shoulder. We don't speak, but we stay close as the train hurtles toward home.

That night, while Thompson holds back the growing crowd of spectators outside our duplex, the four of us pile onto the couch in our combined living room/kitchen, planning to drown out the noise with TV. Dad flicks on the remote, and my stomach lurches at the face filling the screen. It's *me.*

"Ho-ly crap!" Sam exclaims.

"Our little girl," Mom murmurs to Dad, her voice quivering.

It's the footage from today's press conference. My skin

turns hot as I watch myself onstage beside Dr. Anderson, looking woefully unprepared for my primetime debut in a worn pair of jeans and turquoise hoodie, my dark hair pulled back in a messy ponytail. A close-up reveals the beads of perspiration on my forehead, the panicky expression in my eyes. I have the urge to crawl under the couch cushions and hide, but thankfully, the image on the screen quickly shifts from me to the *Newsline* desk as anchor Robin Richmond faces the camera.

"There she is, folks: one of our American finalists and a two-time World Science Fair champion, Naomi Ardalan." Robin's melodic voice dances across the syllables of my last name, and I shake my head in disbelief. "While she'll be representing the US, Naomi is actually a second-generation American. Her grandparents emigrated here from Iran, and sources tell me Naomi's interest in science and technology was spurred on by their stories from home, of the ancient Persians who invented algebra and hydrodynamics."

"Not to mention al-Sufi, who *only* discovered the Andromeda Galaxy," I say to the TV. Despite how weird this all is, I can't deny the warm glow in my chest at hearing my grandparents mentioned, their influence on my life recognized.

"If they could see you now . . . ," Mom says softly, and I squeeze her hand.

The graying anchorman Seymour Lewis takes the mic, his deep voice booming through the screen. "From the granddaughter of immigrants, we move on to a finalist whose family has been in the good ol' USA since just about the *Mayflower*: Beckett Wolfe, also known as the nephew of the president of the United States."

The footage flashes to the White House lawn, where a tall, muscular blond boy in a prep school uniform strolls beside President Wolfe. Dad and I exchange a glance. Back on the screen, Robin Richmond arches an eyebrow at her cohost.

"Smells a bit like nepotism, wouldn't you say?"

"Hold on a second." Seymour, the anchor known for flying to the president's defense, sits up straighter. "You know as well as I do that NASA and the Europa Mission leaders had final say in choosing the American finalists. Not POTUS."

"Right." Robin gives him a condescending nod. "And it's safe to say the president made his wishes abundantly clear: to have his own blood on the first Europan settlement. I wouldn't be surprised if he gave NASA some real incentives to pick Beckett."

"Oh, for crying out loud!" Seymour sputters, but Robin continues.

"I'll grant you that Beckett Wolfe had to have met the basic criteria, but let's be honest here: he is no Naomi Ardalan."

"Damn, Sis!" Sam yells, thumping my back proudly. "You just showed up the First Nephew on national TV!"

I can't help laughing, and for one brief moment, the mood among the four of us lightens. But then Robin turns back to the camera, a solemn expression on her face.

"When we return, two former astronauts who oppose the mission will join us to discuss the deadly risks these teenagers will face as they set out into space."

At those words, all our smiles vanish. Sam and I exchange a grim look. He follows the Space Conspirator just like I do . . . and we can both guess what the astronauts are about to say.

"They always have to interview the naysayers. It doesn't make them right," Dad says, aiming for a breezy tone even as the shakiness in his voice gives him away.

"Let's see what else is on," I tell him. The last thing we need is to sit here in fear, listening to all the dangers I'm about to encounter.

He changes the channel to *Breaking News Tonight* just in time for a segment titled "The Twenty-Four: Why They Were Chosen." Show anchor Sanford Pearce is settled in at his sleek glass desk, hands folded as he addresses the audience.

"From an Olympic medalist to the world's youngest tech titan, tonight we introduce you to the twenty-four teenagers who are setting out on a galaxy-spanning journey to change all of our lives."

A montage begins, set to a cinematic score. The strangers from today's press conference return, but instead of a collection of faces, I now get to see snippets of them in action. A boy with dark skin and black curls leads an interviewer through a garage-turned-office, proudly showing off the app he created to predict incoming earthquakes. A red-haired girl dressed in a white lab coat stands in the center of a formal room, while the man I recognize as King William V of England taps a sword against her left shoulder and then her right in some kind of ceremonial gesture. An Asian boy pilots a plane over the ocean, swerving past another incoming aircraft and calling out instructions to a copilot who looks a good decade his senior. And then someone familiar takes the screen, a tall, tanned boy stepping up to a diving board. It's the Italian finalist—the one who tried to comfort me.

Just as I'm peering closer, the footage fades, the montage ending on a split-screen image of me and Beckett Wolfe. My cheeks heat up in self-consciousness.

"Like most of you, we on the news team were especially curious about the American finalists, Beckett Wolfe and Naomi Ardalan," Sanford Pearce says into the camera. "Since their names were revealed this morning, we had a chance to do some research on these two exemplary teens. Take a look."

The images on the TV scroll back in time, back to the last Wagner World Science Fair. I'm caught off guard by the sight of my fifteen-year-old self. I look different . . . I look happy.

My idol, Dr. Greta Wagner, enters the frame and hands me a gilded trophy. It's the moment forever memorialized in the framed photo on my desk, reminding me every day to work harder, to think big, like Wagner.

"Last year, Naomi blew us away with her DNA editing solution, an experimental method of hacking into and correcting a patient's genomes. This year, she brings us another work of true ingenuity: the Ardalan radio telescope model, with its unique antenna and receiver design that would allow us to capture a clearer signal from other planets in our solar system."

As Dr. Wagner unveils my blueprints on the screen, my parents and Sam cheer in real time, right along with their younger selves in the footage. I smile with them, though my pride is dampened by the fact that the telescope was never built. Same with my DNA editing solution, which I dreamed up for Sam. Once Earth entered the state of climate destruction, there were no more grants or funds left for *anything* that didn't relate to our immediate survival.

"In fact," Dr. Wagner continues in the footage, "this is the kind of invention the folks at SETI would have jumped over themselves to use."

The great inventor and engineer purses her lips, her eyes darkening, and I know the reason for her soured expression. SETI—the Search for Extraterrestrial Intelligence Institute—was defunded three months before the Wagner Science Fair. The scientific community protested the loss, but there was no way around it: NASA and the government had deemed the search for extraterrestrial life "nonessential" in these desperate times. And that's precisely why the Final Six will be walking blindly into whatever is waiting on Europa—because unlike every previous space mission, there is no SETI to rule out the possibility of life.

My head snaps up.

I've just given myself an idea.

After saying goodnight to our parents, I grab my tablet and cross the hall from my pocket-size bedroom into Sam's. I find him staring at a screen of his own, his brow furrowed with worry.

"What's wrong? What are you looking at?"

I pull up a chair beside him at the desk, and he slides his laptop toward me. An article fills the screen, with the headline reading: "*Athena* Backup Crew Warns of Europa Risks." At the center of the page is a photo of the surviving astronauts, hugging through their tears at the memorial for the doomed *Athena* crew five years ago. A chill creeps up my spine, and I quickly close the page.

"I know. I tried asking the NASA rep about it today, and she fed me the company line about how this mission will be completely different . . . but we have even more important things to talk about. Have you been on Space Conspirator today?"

Sam shakes his head and I log on to the site, which has a brand-new landing page since this morning's announcement. Underneath the Conspirator logo is an artist's sketch of six shadowy puppets, staring at a faceless creature rising up from the ocean—while a caricature of a man and woman, meant to represent the Europa Mission leaders, pull the puppet strings. As Sam shudders, I click on the website's News tab and scroll, hunting for a certain article.

"That footage on TV gave me an idea—the part where Dr. Wagner mentioned SETI," I tell him. "If I could prove it, if I could show the world that the Space Conspirator's claims aren't just the ravings of some renegade scientists, but the truth . . . well, that would change everything. It would bring me home."

My cursor lands on the article I was looking for: "Scientific Probabilities of Life in Europa's Oceans." The *Conspirator* was right when it predicted the outcome of the *Athena* mission years ago. Why shouldn't it be right this time, too—especially when science supports the theory? As my brother starts to read, I jump out of my chair, too fired up to sit still.

"I'll go to Space Training Camp under the pretense of preparing for the Europa Mission—but in reality, I'll be on a whole other mission of my own. I can use the Johnson Space Center tools at my disposal to finish the job that SETI never got to do. I'll conduct my *own* search for extraterrestrial intelligence—focused solely on Europa."

Sam turns around in his seat, watching me with raised eyebrows.

"If I can prove the theory that there *is* a high probability of intelligent life waiting for us, that would completely turn public opinion of the mission on its head." I take a deep breath. "There is just no way world leaders would send us if they believed what I do. *Especially* when the president's own nephew is involved."

A slow smile spreads across my brother's face.

"So you're going to sabotage the mission from the inside?"

"I prefer the term 'enlighten the public.' But yeah." I grin. "Certain people might call it sabotage."

Sam reaches over to give me a fist bump.

"I like this plan. Go get 'em, Sis."

FIVE

LEO

"LEO, LEO, FORZA LEO!"

I pull back the curtains of the guest bedroom with a smile. It's just past eight in the morning on Departure Day, but my neighbors are already here, waiting on the docks to see me off. The sight fills me with warmth, and I can't resist cranking open the window.

"Vi amo tutti!" I call, waving at the faces below. And it's true—right now I love every last one of them standing there in the cold, cheering my name. My appearance at the window sends their cheers into overdrive, and I laugh to myself as I imagine what my sister would say. *They do know it's* you, *right?*

Just then, a knock sounds at my door.

"Leo, it's Dr. Schroder. Are you up?"

"Come in," I call, and he steps inside, carrying a small trunk.

"I have something you'll need for the trip. The Europa Mission leaders requested that all finalists arrive at International Space Training Camp already in uniform."

He hands me the trunk, and as I lift the lid, my pulse begins to race.

The first thing I see is a dark blue flight jacket lined with wool, warmer and softer than any of the threadbare clothes I've been wearing since the flood. The jacket is adorned with military-style patches: one bearing the ISTC logo, another with the logo of ESA, and a third patch emblazoned with my own name. The back of the jacket reads *Mission: Europa* in striking bold letters, and for a moment I can't speak. *This is really happening.*

Beneath the jacket is a pair of khakis, some high-tech sneakers, and a blue ISTC polo shirt glinting with a flash of gold. I take a second look—it's a golden pin of the Italian flag. My breath catches. I won't be leaving my country behind, after all. I'll be wearing our colors proudly against my chest.

I look up to meet Dr. Schroder's eyes.

"It's perfect. Thank you."

He grins.

"Glad you approve. See you downstairs in twenty minutes?"

I nod, adrenaline working its way through my body as the countdown begins. Stepping into the ISTC uniform and leaving Europe for the first time in my life seems almost like assuming a new identity. It's the second chance I never expected, even though a part of me still clings to who I used to be—when I was with my parents and with Angelica.

I pull the polo shirt over my head and step into the khakis and sneakers, which are as comfortable as they look. I drape the *Mission: Europa* jacket over my shoulders, and now I look the part. I am ready.

The guards escort the Vincentis, Dr. Schroder, and me to the Palazzo boat dock, where the crowd of onlookers breaks into a chorus of hurrahs at our arrival. I turn to Elena with a grin, and though she returns my smile, it doesn't quite reach her eyes. I can tell she's still preoccupied with last night's discovery, and I wish I could reassure her that it doesn't faze me. What matters isn't how I got picked—it's that I was chosen at all.

"There it is." The prime minister points straight ahead, where the boat's mast breaks the monotonous stretch of water. My heart lifts at the return of the vessel that saved—and changed—my life.

"Are you ready, Leo?" Dr. Schroder asks.

I take one last look around me, at the sunken new face of Rome. Even in its wrecked state, there is still something beautiful about my homeland. I know I'll never forget the way it looks right now, the morning sun gleaming against the waves.

"*Arrivederci, Roma*," I murmur. And then I glance at Dr. Schroder. "Let's go."

I've already said my good-byes to the Vincentis inside, but just before I step onto the boat, Elena grabs my wrist. She flings her arms around me in one last hug before whispering in my ear, "Remember everything I told you. Keep your eyes and ears open, and your guard up."

"I will. Don't worry, Elena."

But as I settle into my seat on the boat, watching my neighbors on the docks grow smaller, all I can think about is the adventure ahead.

Elena's warnings are already forgotten.

The sleek white Gulfstream lowers in the sky toward us, its engine emitting an earsplitting roar. Dr. Schroder pulls me back, and the two of us duck as the jet slides onto the Tuscan Airfield runway in a perfect landing.

"Did I tell you I've never been on an airplane before?" I shout above the noise.

Dr. Schroder's eyebrows shoot up.

"It's true," I say with a chuckle. "We never had the money for transcontinental travel, so all our family trips were by train, within Europe."

He places a hand on my shoulder. "And now you might be one of the few to travel farther than anyone else on this Earth."

The thought sends a flash of excitement through me. The farther I get from Rome, the more I want this—and the harder it is to imagine ever returning.

The jet parks on the concrete before us. Its automatic doors slide open, and a set of stairs unfurls from them. Our pilot, a captain from the Italian army, steps outside to greet Dr. Schroder and me, ushering us into the compact passenger cabin where we take our seats.

"It's so much more personal than it looks on TV," I comment to Dr. Schroder.

"Yeah, well, those big commercial airliners are a thing of the past," he says grimly. "Now that more than half of the world's tourist destinations are underwater, there's no need for them. This generation of kids growing up will likely never experience air travel, unless they work for the government or military."

"Speaking of, am I now considered part of the Italian army?" I ask. "Since I've technically been drafted?"

"You are representing Italy, but as part of a new World Army," Dr. Schroder explains. "It's all of us fighting together now . . . fighting to save the human race."

I nod, trying to appear calm, even as his words push my anticipation into overdrive.

"We're cleared for takeoff." The captain's voice echoes over the loudspeaker. "Please ensure your seat belts are fastened."

"Copy that," Dr. Schroder calls back.

I grip my armrest as the jet lurches forward. And then, like a thrill ride from the old amusement parks, we hurtle up into the sky at breakneck speed. The cabin shakes as the plane skims the clouds, my stomach flipping over with each pitch of the aircraft.

"Are flights usually this bumpy?"

Dr. Schroder shifts in his seat to face me, looking almost as queasy as I feel. "They didn't used to be. It's another one of climate change's side effects—the warming temperatures strengthened the jet stream winds and turned the skies hostile. But believe it or not, we're safer up here than we are down there."

"I believe it!"

I turn to the window, keeping my eyes locked on the glass to distract from the bumps and dips of the plane, and soon I've lost track of how much time has elapsed. It isn't until the anxiety presses against my chest that I realize I'm waiting for something that isn't coming—a break from the blue. The endless ocean dominates my view, overwhelming the dots of green and tiny slivers of land.

"You can see it clearly from up here: why this mission is so crucial," Dr. Schroder says, following my gaze. "Not long ago, when you were a child, the scenery below was vastly different. The scientists and climatologists tried to warn the public about the risks of carbon emissions and pollution, but . . ." He shakes his head. "Well, it's too late now. And we don't have much time left if we're going to escape the rising seas."

"No," I agree, staring at the foreboding stretch of blue. "We don't have much time at all."

NAOMI

It seems like all of Los Angeles is on the tarmac at Burbank Airport, watching as my heart breaks. I hold on to my family, trying to block out the noise and the pressure as the crowd shrieks my name, flashing their camera-phones and waving signs proclaiming the Twenty-Four "Our last chance for survival!" Only a few minutes remain until the NASA official and army major will come tear me away from my family. Dad pulls the three of us into a tight-knit group hug, and I bury my head in his shoulder, hiding my face.

"Naomi, *azizam,* we're going to miss you more than we can bear," he says in my ear, his voice choked with tears. "But . . . we know you weren't born for this planet. You were meant for something bigger."

"He's right." Mom cradles my chin in her hands. "As much as I want you beside me, you have too much to offer to stay in a world that's failing you. Go out there and—and change the universe."

"I—I would if I could, but . . ." My words falter as I watch my little brother wipe his eyes on his sleeve. Maybe in another life I would have leaped at this opportunity, but not now, not with my heart pulling me toward home. As if reading my thoughts, Mom adds, "Don't forget—if you make the Final Six and the mission succeeds, then the three of us are guaranteed a seat on the first human settlement spacecraft to Europa." She gives me a shaky smile. "So you see, we can all be together again . . . but in a better place."

I meet Sam's eyes, and I know we're both thinking the same thing. Mom is an eternal optimist, but whether the mission will succeed is a gigantic *if*—and even if it does, my brother's heart could never withstand a rocket launch into space. And there's no way anyone else is leaving him behind. So, no—there won't be a fairy-tale reunion for the four of us on Europa. Not a chance. Still, I force myself to nod along with her words, to let her hold on to hope. But then Sam is in front of me and I can't say good-bye to him, I *can't*; I choke on the words.

"I love you, Sis. It's—it's going to be okay." He lowers his voice. "You're going to go to Houston and show everyone what's possible . . . what's really *out there*. And then you'll come home." He looks at me hopefully. "Right?"

"Right," I whisper back.

I reach into the pocket of my *Mission: Europa* jacket and hand him a folded square of paper. "To read when you need me."

Sam smiles at me through his tears. "Our telepathy game remains strong."

My eyes well up all over again as he reaches into his coat pocket and hands me an envelope of his own. But instead of just a letter, I feel something small and bulky inside.

"Keep it safe." Sam gives me a warning look and I nod, stashing the envelope in the front pocket of my backpack.

"Naomi? Let's go."

I turn sharply at the sound of Dr. Anderson's voice. It's too soon; I'm not ready—but now the army officers are approaching, the jet doors are sliding open, the plane's engine is revving. I'm running out of time. I reach for my parents once more.

"Take care of my brother. Take care of each other. I love you all so much."

I get in one last hug with Sam before Dr. Anderson and Major Lewis's hands are on my shoulders, pulling me away from my family—and ushering me into a new life.

I peer through the jet window, watching as an island of concrete materializes below. This must be it: Space City, Houston. The land that gave us the *Apollo* missions and the International Space Station, that launched a million childhood daydreams—including mine.

When my mom showed a six-year-old me the historic video of Anousheh Ansari climbing inside the Soyuz rocket, becoming the first Iranian-American woman in space, I remember instantly picturing myself in her place. "That's what I want to do," I told Mom then, brimming with confidence. "Me and Sam can be the first brother-sister duo in orbit!" Even then, I never wanted to leave him. So once I learned the truth about Sam's condition, that it would preclude him from ever venturing beyond our Earth, I dropped the astronaut dream like a bad habit. And now the childhood wish is coming true . . . in spite of me.

"We'll be touching down any minute," Dr. Anderson says from her seat beside me. "Do you want to freshen up for the cameras?"

I shrug. "Not really."

At this point, looking attractive for strangers is the very last item on my priority list.

Dr. Anderson gives me a hint of a smile. "You might want to tighten your seat belt for this. The changing topography and climate in Texas have made landing extra turbulent here."

"How *did* you guys manage to keep Houston above sea level when the Gulf of Mexico swallowed other parts of Texas?" I ask as I tug my seat belt tighter. "Was it all because of the Houston Flood Barrier Project? And why didn't other cities do the same?"

My mind flashes back to the submerged Santa Monica Pier back home, and the old coastal communities of Venice Beach and Marina Del Rey—now nothing more than an endless blue graveyard. I wonder if they might have been saved, too.

"It took an eye-watering amount of money to build the Flood Barrier gates," Dr. Anderson acknowledges. "The only reason we were able to do it is because at the UN Climate Conference, back when the first indisputable signs of the change began, Houston was chosen as the site to protect and preserve at all costs. With the greatest minds from Stephen Hawking to Elon Musk insisting that the only way forward for humans was to colonize new planets, it was clear to the UN that all resources needed to go toward the best space training and launch program in the world. That would be here."

"That's why budgets were cut everywhere else," I realize aloud. "All the money is going toward getting us off Earth—instead of protecting the people on it."

Dr. Anderson gives me a sideways look. "NASA doesn't see it that way. The fact is, we have limited resources and we're facing a dying planet. We can either spread ourselves thin and make little impact—or we can focus all efforts on the Europa Mission and have a real shot at success."

It's obvious Dr. Anderson's been drinking the mission Kool-Aid. While I can somewhat follow her logic, I feel a wave of fury at the thought of all the people who told me no these past two years. No money for the genome surgery to fix Sam's heart, no grant for my radio telescope, no to *so many* things that could have improved the world for the living.

They'd better hope and pray Europa is the miracle they've built it up to be.

"Here we go," Dr. Anderson says over my shoulder as the jet shudders downward, giving us a clear view of the Houston cityscape, with still-standing skyscrapers connected by a network of skywalks. And then, my temporary new home appears in the near distance: the sprawling campus of Johnson Space Center.

"Something else we did to preserve the Space Center was elevate the buildings and move all facilities to the uppermost floors," Dr. Anderson comments, nodding at the window. "This way, even when the storms come, our staff and equipment remain safe."

The plane takes another swoop, and I grab the sides of my seat as the air sends us rocking and jerking toward a large runway spread out below us: the Ellington Field. But I've never seen a runway like this, teeming with people. While half the tarmac is like an airplane parking lot, with a row of small jets stationed side by side, the other half might as well be a stage. A dozen figures stand opposite the planes, dressed in the same uniform as me and surrounded by a cluster of photographers, cheering spectators, and an actual marching band. As our jet skids to the ground, I hear the faint strains of "You're a Grand Old Flag."

"That's for you," Dr. Anderson says with a smile.

My heartbeat picks up speed, my stage fright returning with a vengeance. Dr. Anderson unbuckles her seat belt and retrieves my carry-on luggage, but I stay put. I'm nowhere near ready.

"Go on," she says, touching my shoulder. "You can do this. I'll be right behind you—though you probably won't see me again after today."

I can hear the drumroll coming from the marching band, the shouts of my name from the crowd, and I swallow hard. *She's right. I can do this.* Besides . . . I have no choice.

I stand up, lift my chin, and make the shaky walk to the front of the plane. The door juts open, the stairs unfurl. And as I appear at the top of the steps, the band launches into "The Star-Spangled Banner."

Cameras flash in wild succession, and my fellow finalists assembled at the center of the tarmac all look up to stare at me. Standing in front of them are the mission leaders, the same pair the Space Conspirator depicted as holding the puppet strings: Dr. Takumi from NASA and General Sokolov of Roscosmos, the Russian Space Agency.

Beyond the barricades of the air base, hundreds of onlookers swarm, some even hopping to the top of the fence as they wave flags from the different represented countries, their faces almost manic as they scream a chant: "God bless the Twenty-Four, for they are our only hope!"

A knot forms in the pit of my stomach. If this collection of strangers pinning their hopes on us is representative of the world, then that means millions are depending on the success of the Twenty-Four. But don't they *realize* all the risks involved with the mission? Don't they know that we're just glorified guinea pigs, forced to perform under Murphy's Law, which practically guarantees something going horribly wrong in space or on Europa?

No, of course they don't. Without doing the research, there's no way to know the risks. Maybe they don't even want to know.

Dr. Anderson gives me a slight push, and I make my way down the airplane steps. When we reach the foot of the stairs, she takes my arm, steering me to the mission leaders. Dr. Takumi, Solar System Ambassador and the president of International Space Training Camp, moves forward first. Something about his presence causes me to take an involuntary step back.

Maybe it's his stature, which requires me to crane my

neck to meet his eyes. Or maybe it's his eyes themselves, which have a fierce glint to them, even as his lips form a thin smile. His head is shaved, highlighting his sharp features and the lines creasing his face. As he looks at me and extends a hand, I think of the puppet master on the Space Conspirator home page, and a shiver runs through me.

"Welcome, Naomi, to International Space Training Camp," he says, his voice deep and authoritative. "I am Dr. Ren Takumi, and this is General Irina Sokolov, the commanding general of the Europa Mission."

"Nice to meet you," I reply, my throat feeling like sandpaper.

While Dr. Takumi wears a black variation of our uniform, his second in command is dressed in red, the color of the Russian space program. General Sokolov's auburn hair is cropped in a pixie cut, and her brown eyes are intent as she studies me.

"Congratulations on making the Twenty-Four, Naomi," she greets me. "I hope you're prepared to work hard."

"I—yes. Thank you." I glance up at the sound of another jet overhead, and Dr. Takumi points me to the line of arrivals.

"Please join your fellow finalists, and once everyone is here, we will proceed to the Space Center."

I can feel my heart thumping loudly in my chest as I approach the others. *What are they like? Will I get along with them? Is this going to be at all bearable?* I recognize a couple of their faces from the news segments, particularly my fellow American, Beckett Wolfe, who stands at the end of the line. I fill the empty space beside him, just as a jet nearly identical to mine swoops down.

"Hi, I'm Naomi," I half yell over the sound of the plane. "You're Beckett, right?"

Beckett turns and peers down his nose at me. He points to the name sewn across the pocket of his jacket uniform. "Obviously."

Ew. Let's hope the other finalists aren't anything like the First Nephew, who rolls his eyes as he turns away from me. I can see it written clearly on his face—his disdain for the too-ethnic noncelebrity he's forced to share the American spotlight with. *Sorry, dude. I didn't ask to be here.*

As the next jet hits the ground, the marching band transitions into a pulsating new song, swapping their snare drums for a pair of tablas. The music is electric, the melody beautiful. And as an Indian boy with a mile-wide grin steps off the plane, I'm surprised to feel myself getting caught up in the spectacle, joining in the crowd's applause. There is something powerful in the seamless transition from one country's music to another, in the sight of so many different flags waving together in the wind, and my chest swells with unexpected emotion.

The Indian finalist, Dev Khanna, joins me in line, and I can tell right away that he's much friendlier than Beckett. He returns my smile and we share a quick handshake before the band segues into its next song. Another plane touches down, its wings painted in the colors of the Italian flag.

Italy . . . that means it's the boy from the videoconference. The one who tried to comfort me.

I stand up a little straighter as Leonardo Danieli emerges from the jet. His face lights up at the sight of all of us, at the sound of the music from his country, and he half dances down the steps of the plane. I can't help but grin as I watch him.

Our eyes meet for a split second—I can tell he recognizes me, too. And in that moment, his smile seems to grow.

LEO

It feels like I'm living someone else's life as I take in the scene on the tarmac. It's too thrilling, too awe-inspiring, to actually be happening to *me*. Adrenaline surges through my veins as I stand with the rest of the Twenty-Four, listening to Dr. Takumi deliver a speech for the cameras broadcasting us live to the world.

"Today marks the start of mankind's most important step—the very step that will secure our future." His voice rings out across the airfield. "On behalf of the six space agencies and our staff at ISTC, we are delighted to welcome the most extraordinary teenagers from around the world to our campus at Johnson Space Center. We combed the globe to find these unique individuals standing before you, all of whom possess the strength, smarts, and youth necessary to achieve our highest aim."

And I'm one of them. It still seems unthinkable that I made it this far, especially compared to the geniuses all around me.

"From the get-go, the Europa Mission's stringent prerequisites kept the draft pool relatively low. Our finalists were required to be between the ages of sixteen and nineteen, with clean bills of health and near-perfect vision. Their bodies needed to meet the anthropometric requirements for long-duration space suits, while their minds had to test above the eighty-fifth percentile for IQ. They were also required to speak fluent English, the home language of Space Training Camp, in addition to their native tongue. Yet even with all these boxes to tick, we were still able to select finalists who brought something else—something *unique*—to the table."

It must be my imagination, but I could swear Dr. Takumi is looking straight at me as he says those last words.

"In the coming weeks, we will train, challenge, and test the Twenty-Four, both physically and mentally, to prepare them for a life in space. This training period will help us carefully evaluate each finalist and ensure that we choose the *right* team of six," he continues. "One day, years from now, this mission will be taught in schools; it will be known as the defining moment for the continuation of the human race. But those future students won't be learning about it here on Earth." Dr. Takumi pauses, a ghost of a smile on his face. "They will study the mission from their new schools, their new homes, on *Europa*!"

The crowd roars, the onlookers whooping and rattling the fence surrounding the airfield in their exhilaration, as Dr. Takumi gives credence to our deepest, wildest hopes.

"It all starts now!"

He lets out a piercing whistle, and suddenly two open-air trolleys come rolling toward us, driven by men in US Army camouflage. Dr. Takumi and General Sokolov jump onto separate vehicles, as Takumi calls out his first official command. "Finalists, come aboard!"

I make a beeline for Dr. Takumi's trolley, and I sprint past the other competitors to land a seat up front. Maybe it's silly of me to take the ride so seriously, but I'm determined to seize any face time I can get with the key figure deciding my fate.

The trolley rumbles forward, leaving Ellington Field behind and heading onto a main street. It's my first time seeing sidewalks and stoplights again, and I glance around in shock, feeling like I've traveled back to the past—to when the world was normal. Of course, there's nothing normal about riding in a motorcade, with a marching band in the trolley behind us playing a medley of national anthems from our represented countries. When the Chinese national anthem transitions into my own, it's like hearing from an old friend. I smile up at the sky.

Our motorcade turns onto NASA Parkway, and I draw in a sharp breath. If I thought I'd seen crowds in Rome, or even just minutes ago on the tarmac, that was nothing compared to the hordes lining these blocks in the sweltering heat.

They brandish flags and posters; they jump up and down in hysterics as our procession passes, some in tears, others shouting out "good luck" in multiple languages. I can feel what each stranger on the sidewalk is thinking: *Please let this work. Let them save us.*

The trolley pulls through an open gate, and our group cheers as the Johnson Space Center sign looms before us. The campus is vast as a city and protected like a fortress, with barricades on all sides to hold back the rising tides. We pass dozens of numbered buildings and bunkers before the trolley stops at the largest one, Building 9. Twin flags soar above it, one featuring the American Stars and Stripes for NASA, the other bearing the international logo of the ISTC.

Dr. Takumi jumps off the trolley first, and we follow him to the front steps as the photographers and reporters on our tail clamor for one last good shot.

"Wave good-bye," Dr. Takumi instructs as the twenty-four of us gather before him and General Sokolov. "This is the last time anyone outside of training camp will get to see you until the first round of eliminations."

First round? My palms begin to sweat.

I glance at my fellow finalists, gauging their reactions. Some of them are beaming for the cameras and waving, while others can't hide their nerves. But as I scan the group, I realize I'm looking for someone in particular—the American from the videoconference. The girl whose sadness struck me that day.

When I finally spot her, I notice she is mouthing

something to the cameras, her dark eyes urgent. *What is she trying to say?* I take a step closer to her, just as the doors to Building 9 fly open and Dr. Takumi beckons us inside.

This is it. My pulse quickens as we follow Dr. Takumi, leaving the old world behind.

SIX

NAOMI

I TURN AROUND FOR ONE LAST LOOK BEFORE THE DOORS CLOSE behind us, cutting me off from any semblance of normal life. I can feel the gravity of this place pulling me farther away from Sam and my parents, and for a moment my feet refuse to move. And then a girl with chin-length dark hair and a nose ring elbows me in the ribs, muttering, "Hurry up," and I force myself into motion, following the pack of finalists down a long hallway.

Dr. Takumi and General Sokolov bring us to a halt in front of the elevator bay, where framed, autographed photos of astronauts from the past adorn the walls. I move closer, my heartbeat picking up speed at the image of Sally Ride upside down in zero gravity, at Scott Kelly and Mikhail

Kornienko stepping into the Soyuz. It's surreal to think we're standing within the same walls where, ages ago, these legends were made. I wonder what they would think of the Europa Mission—if they, too, would balk at the risks.

"Armstrong shouldn't have to share a wall with that guy," Beckett Wolfe comments to no one in particular, making a face at the portrait of Yuri Gagarin hanging beside Neil Armstrong's. "There was just no one at his level in those days."

I cringe, dying to correct him but not quite in the mood to draw attention to myself. Thankfully, there are other finalists here eager to school him.

"You do know Yuri Gagarin was the first human in space, right?" interjects a boy I recognize from the TV segment on the Twenty-Four. *Jian from China,* I remember. *The pilot.*

"Sure, but the goal of the space race was to get to the *moon,*" Beckett says, drawing out the word to prove his point. "Not to just chill out in orbit. That's why we won."

"Yuri Gagarin was a hero." General Sokolov steps in, narrowing her eyes at Beckett. "I'd hardly refer to his landmark achievement as 'chilling out.'"

That shuts Beckett right up. I meet Jian's eyes, and we exchange a grin. I have a feeling this will be the *perfect* place for the First Nephew to overcome his superiority complex.

The general leads half of us into one of the oversize elevators and up to the third floor, where we reconvene with Dr. Takumi and the rest of the finalists in a stark white corridor, with signs pointing the way to the Space Center

Auditorium. I recognize the gray-carpeted theater as soon as we walk inside, with its array of flags framing a curved stage. This is the setting of every historic NASA press conference I've seen on-screen—only this time the audience seats are empty, waiting for us to fill them. A group of adults in ISTC uniforms mills about onstage, a hush falling over them as we enter with Dr. Takumi.

"Take your seats in the first two rows," he instructs us, before sweeping up the steps and onto the stage.

I sit between a boy with wavy brown hair and a lopsided grin, who introduces himself as Callum Turner from Australia, and the girl with the nose ring and lilting accent, Ana Martinez from Spain.

"Nice to meet you," I whisper to the two of them before Dr. Takumi steps up to the podium, harnessing everyone's attention with his direct gaze.

"Finalists, welcome to your new home and training grounds. Joining me onstage are the ISTC faculty, made up of the top minds in aerospace and science, who will be preparing you for the mission ahead," he announces. "We'll begin by dividing you into four teams of six. Each team will be overseen by one of our faculty: experienced, retired astronauts known as team leaders, who will serve as your chaperone and guide throughout this process. Meanwhile, your teammates are the finalists you'll be training and spending most of your time with here—and you *will* be evaluated on how well you work together and get along. We've put careful thought and consideration into each team, to encourage a spirit of both competition and cooperation."

It's like the first day of school, but with fatal consequences. I shift uncomfortably in my seat, wondering which of these strangers I'll be stuck with.

As Dr. Takumi launches into staff introductions, my uneasiness gives way to interest. These are no ordinary teachers—they are a mix of scientists, engineers, and former astronauts from around the world, combined with sergeants and lieutenants from the United States Army. Looking at the faculty in front of us, it's clear that we're in for the space-travel equivalent of boot camp.

"Of course I saved the best for last," he continues, looking down the line of his staff with a secretive smile. "Not long ago, the world watched as we sent two humanoid robots on a flyby probe of Europa, to gather data and confirm the habitability of Jupiter's moon. The success of that first mission is the reason you are all sitting here today." Dr. Takumi pauses for effect. "Since the robots have already proven themselves indispensable and have a firsthand knowledge of Europa . . . they will be accompanying the Final Six on the mission."

My mouth falls open.

"No. Way," I whisper to Ana beside me as the room buzzes with excited murmurs. We all know which robots he's talking about—we followed their progress religiously, the same way our parents geeked out over the Mars *Curiosity* rover before us—and the thought of traveling through space *with them* is like a fantasy beyond anything my childhood self could have dreamed up.

"Without further ado, I'm proud to introduce you to the most advanced artificial intelligence currently in existence: Cyb and Dot!"

The curtain drops to reveal two majestic machines. They are the size and shape of humans, with terrestrial legs and dexterous fingers, but their bodies are encased in shells of machinery, like powered suits of armor. Dot's body is bronze and Cyb's is platinum, denoting their difference in status, while their faces are masks of metal, with a pair of round blue camera lenses for eyes. Sliding plates on each of their torsos reveal a digital tablet—the wand that activates the magic of AIOS, the Artificial Intelligence Operating System. I'm practically salivating at the sight of it. And as the robots march to the front of the stage, I can't help rising to my feet, leading the room in a spontaneous standing ovation.

I know all the work that went into creating such exceptional AIs—the complex algorithms and encoders that gave Dot and Cyb their brains, the hundreds of sensors and dozens of PowerPC processors that make up their guts—and I feel a twinge of longing. To get to learn from these robots and one day develop artificial intelligence of my own . . . *that's* a dream that gets my blood flowing.

I just don't want to have to leave the planet in order to achieve it.

The robots turn to give Dr. Takumi and General Sokolov a formal salute, and the general crosses the stage to join them.

"Cyb has been programmed to autopilot the spacecraft to Europa, and will therefore serve as my proxy commander," she reveals. "Dot will provide backup support. Because of their importance on this mission, and their ability to form unbiased opinions based on logic, the robots will join Dr. Takumi and myself in deciding the first eliminations. Which brings us to our next piece of news." She glances at Dr. Takumi, and he nods for her to continue.

"Right now, the abandoned *Athena* supply ship is still orbiting Mars and carrying with her two decades' worth of preserved food and resources. By including a Mars rendezvous on your trajectory to Europa, we're able to not only salvage some of the billions invested in the *Athena* mission, but more importantly, provide for all of your needs on Jupiter's moon. There's just one problem." She lets out a long exhale. "Based on this week's images and data from SatCon, we have reason to suspect a fuel leak."

My eyebrows shoot up. *That would mean—*

"Without a human crew to patch the leak, the supply ship will eventually run out of fuel—and tidal forces will pull her out of orbit." The general's voice echoes my grim thoughts. "Luckily, that process takes time . . . but not long enough for us to have the luxury of four months of training."

"That's why we're moving up the Europa launch to one month from now," Dr. Takumi announces, to the sound of our gasps. "Likewise, your training will be compressed into a more rigorous four-week course. It may sound daunting, but with Cyb and Dot joining you on the mission, that amount of training should be sufficient. You won't be entirely alone up there."

I feel my throat closing up in panic, as the shock of his words reverberates through the room. *One month?* How can anyone be ready that quickly? To have to leave Earth so *soon*—

"Meanwhile," he adds, "half of you will be eliminated from the draft in two weeks' time."

Judging by the aghast expressions I see all around me, most of my fellow finalists have zero desire to go home so early—but the thought sends hope flooding through my chest. While the others are busy trying to impress the robots, I can make a point of falling *below* their radar, presenting myself as a perfectly average, elimination-worthy candidate. And then I'd be safe from Europa. In just two weeks I could be on my way home.

Except . . . there's the not-so-small matter of the promise I made to my brother, and to myself. I have a theory to prove first, and succeeding would mean that I can ensure *all* of us get to return safely to our families. Pulling this off before the first elimination will be a major stretch—but I have to at least try.

"Now, let me address the elephant in the room." Dr. Takumi's voice takes on a warning tone, pulling me out of my thoughts and back into the present. "We are well aware that some of you might be tempted to sabotage or diminish your cofinalists, in order to advance your own standing in the draft. The ISTC has a zero-tolerance policy where this is concerned, and anyone who attempts it will face severe punishment."

I stifle a laugh. They certainly don't need to worry about that with me.

"Others among you may have the opposite aim. Some of you might try to play down your abilities, to sabotage your *own* chances." Dr. Takumi's eyes move across the room, studying each one of us, and my face turns hot.

"You should know that we can see right through any of these attempts," he continues. "The twenty-four of you will be closely monitored, both during training and in regular psychological evaluations. If we find you guilty of self-sabotage *or* attempting to thwart one of your teammates, you will be punished accordingly. Lesser infractions will require you and your family to pay a steep fine, while larger crimes carry the same sentence as resisting the draft: long-term imprisonment."

The room is dead silent now. Fear churns in my stomach as I realize the risks I'll be taking with my plan. *But it's not impossible,* a voice in my head whispers. I can still investigate and expose the mission from the inside—I'll just have to outsmart a bunch of brilliant adults and two AIs in order to do it. *Great.*

"And now, without further ado, let's assign your teams!" Dr. Takumi smiles broadly, a jarring transition from his talk of crimes and jail time. "First up is Team Lark."

A young woman bounds to the front of the stage, tall and willowy, with dark skin and braided black hair. She must be in her twenties, unusually young for a retired astronaut, and I find myself wondering what her story is.

"When I call your name, please come up to the stage and form a line behind Lark," Dr. Takumi instructs. "First on the team is . . . Asher Levin from Israel."

A boy in the row before me jolts out of his seat. I watch as he makes his way up to the stage, raking a hand through his auburn hair, the expression behind his glasses a mixture of pride and nerves.

"From Singapore, Suki Chuan."

There's a shuffling a few seats down from me as Suki slides out of our row. She walks up the steps with her head held high, a look of steely determination in her eyes—the picture of poise. I have a feeling I'll look like a bumbling deer in headlights in comparison when my own name is called.

"Next, from the United States, Beckett Wolfe."

Beckett strides up to the stage with a smirk, barely mustering eye contact with Asher and Suki while shaking their hands. I don't envy those two getting lumped into his team.

"And, also from the United States, Naomi Ardalan."

What? My head jerks up in surprise. Why would they put both American finalists on the same team? I can tell my counterpart is thinking the same thing, as his smile twists into something sour. The First Nephew clearly doesn't appreciate having another American here to steal his thunder.

"Go on," Callum whispers beside me, and I push out of my seat, forcing a deep breath as all eyes in the room momentarily focus on me. I climb up to the stage, even as I'm itching to run in the opposite direction, and take my place beside Beckett.

"Hey." Asher leans over and offers me a handshake, while Suki gives me a tentative smile. I smile back at them, relieved to have a couple of friendlier faces on my team.

"Just two more to go for Team Lark," Dr. Takumi continues, and I brace myself, wondering who will be joining us next.

"From Italy, Leonardo Danieli."

Him. My spirits lift as the boy from the videoconference grins and makes his way toward us. Something tells me this team will be a little more bearable with him on it.

"Ciao," he says, a charming dimple appearing in his cheek as he shakes my hand. "You can call me Leo."

"Hi, Leo."

I hold his gaze a second longer than I should, almost missing the announcement of our last team member: Katerina Fedorin from Russia, a former Olympic figure skater. As she joins us, Dr. Takumi nods in satisfaction at the sight of our completed team.

"The six of you may be excused. Lark, please show your finalists to their rooms and common areas."

"All right, team." Lark turns to face us. "Let's get this show on the road."

The grand tour begins on the fifth floor, which Lark refers to as "the Hab"—the place where we will sleep, eat, and spend all of our downtime between training. The elevator doors open onto a blue-carpeted corridor, and we follow Lark as she leads the way to the first stop, the cafeteria.

"We'll meet here every morning for breakfast at seven a.m.," she says as we step through the automatic glass doors. "Lunch is a quicker, on-the-go meal provided for you in between your training sessions, and then we'll return here for dinner in the evenings at six thirty. You'll find there's one thing in particular you don't have to worry about at Space Training Camp." She winks. "Rationing."

"What do you mean?" I blurt out. I don't dare get my hopes up, but if she's saying what I think she is—

"The government agreed to waive all ration restrictions for the Twenty-Four," she replies. "Since, after all, anyone making the journey into space needs to be in peak condition. So you may get homesick, but you'll never go hungry."

I meet the eyes of my fellow finalists, nearly all of them looking as gleeful as I feel at the prospect of eating until our bellies are full. I know I can't get used to this, that I'll be back to living on canned soup and bread when my prayer is answered and I make it back home—but I can have my fill while I'm here. The thought has me practically light-headed with anticipation.

"We'll eat meals as a team, right here," Lark continues, tapping her knuckles on one of the long folding tables filling the center of the cafeteria. She points to the now-empty buffet counter, which snakes around the back of the room. "Each day's menu alternates between the different cuisines of our represented countries. Tonight, you have a choice of both American and Chinese food."

A choice? That's almost as unbelievable as no rations. I catch Leo peering around the cafeteria wide-eyed, and my stomach growls in solidarity.

Lark leads us to the library next, and I feel my body begin to relax at the comforting sight of the stacks, at the nostalgic scent of leather-bound books. Libraries have always been my happy place, and as long as I have one I can escape to here . . . well, I just might survive whatever is thrown at me.

"What's the deal with the Wi-Fi?" Beckett asks, eyeing the row of desktop computers.

"Internet access is only available to finalists here in the library," Lark answers. "We have a list of preapproved websites you can access, and online video-chatting will also be made available to you once a week, to contact your families—"

"Wait, what?" I interrupt. Lark shoots me a look of disapproval, clearly not a fan of being cut off midsentence, but I can't help myself. "What are preapproved websites? Does that include email?"

"Considering that you are all training and competing for a spot on the most important mission in history, Dr. Takumi and General Sokolov can't allow for any unnecessary distractions," she says tersely. "So that means email, texting, and all social media are off-limits at ISTC. However, those of you who are chosen for the Final Six will have full internet access at all times aboard the spacecraft."

I stare at Lark in disbelief. I was *counting* on emailing my family every day, on having round-the-clock messages from Sam and my parents to hold on to whenever I missed them too much to breathe. That was supposed to be my one solace while we were apart. I should have guessed it wouldn't be that simple. We might as well be prisoners here.

"And I thought leaving my phone behind was tough," Asher says with a woeful shrug. But I'm not as able to let it go.

"So basically we're restricted from contact with the rest of the world, until the point at which we literally have to *leave* the world?" I give Lark a desperate look, hoping she'll recognize how unfair this. Maybe she can go to bat for us—

"Don't worry," Beckett says, his voice dripping with condescension. "As soon as you get cut, you can go running back to posting selfies."

I flash him a withering glare and am just about to make a snappy comeback when Lark holds up her hands.

"*Enough*. Trust me when I say that you'll be so busy here, you won't even have the time or energy to go online. And now, if you'll follow me, there's more to see in this room."

Lark leads the way past the stacks and into a lounge opening off the library, complete with leather armchairs, a projection screen, and a cabinet lined with DVDs.

"This is where most astronauts-in-training like to relax in the hour break between dinner and curfew," she says. "And if you still haven't gotten your fill of space by the end of the day, we have all the movies you could want, even the old classics like *Interstellar* and *Hidden Figures*."

"What about *Apollo 13*?" Katerina asks with a sly grin.

Lark pauses. "Yeah. Believe it or not, we do have that one." She clears her throat. "Okay, one last stop before I show you to your dorms."

I follow Lark and my teammates out the door, still stewing over the ironhanded internet restrictions. Why was I the only one to object? Maybe my cofinalists are afraid to rock the boat, but how could they not *care* that we're being effectively shut off from the outside world? Plus, "preapproved websites" sounds like just a fancy term for censorship. I'm willing to bet my life that Space Conspirator won't be on it, or any other site that doesn't further the Europa Mission's agenda. This isn't the NASA I know, that I grew up worshipping.

Then again, no one here is even pretending that it is. The ISTC has taken over . . . and that means a whole new set of rules.

Once the seven of us are piled into the elevator, Lark presses the button for the top floor. "Most of your time will be spent indoors, so Dr. Takumi has generously made the Telescope Tower available to the finalists during your downtime. It may be small, but it's my favorite spot on campus."

The lift doors open to the outside heat. We follow Lark down a concrete pathway to a spiral staircase, which leads to the circular balcony above us. A tall sheet of plexiglass serves as a railing, making it impossible for anyone to fall . . . or jump. And at the center of the tower is its namesake, a long and lean equatorial mount telescope, pointed skyward.

"Cool," Leo murmurs, stepping up for a closer look.

In the past, I would have been the first to run and peer into the lens. Ever since my grandparents bought me my first kid-size telescope, showing me how I could see the same stars from my Los Angeles backyard that they once gazed up at in Iran, I've been entranced by them. But now, knowing how dangerously close I am to being sent up there . . . for the first time in my life, the sight of a telescope feels more like a warning.

"You can see some of the most distant planets and stars in our solar system from here," Lark says. "Including Europa."

A shiver runs through me. There is something more than a little eerie about seeing the place where six of us will be forced to live and die—looming above as just a speck in the sky.

Lark glances at her watch, and then turns toward the stairs.

"All right, let's show you to your dorms."

We make our way back to the Hab, and this time Lark turns in the opposite direction from the cafeteria and library. This new corridor is softer, with plush carpeting and rounded windows, colorful mission patches and photographs decorating the walls, and even the occasional accent table adorned with books on display. It's like crossing from an industrial space into a residential one.

"The girls' dorm is to the left, boys' to the right," Lark says as we reach a fork in the corridor. "There will be two of you to a room, and you'll find your rooming assignments posted on the door."

My stomach nose-dives at her words. It's not that I expected we'd each get our own room . . . but I certainly hoped.

Lark leads us through the girls' dorm hallway, passing doors with plaques bearing the names of finalists from other teams, until we reach one belonging to us. *Naomi Ardalan & Suki Chuan*. I give Suki a small smile, wondering if she feels the way I do about rooming with a stranger.

"You have a couple hours to unpack and settle in before we meet back at the cafeteria for dinner." Lark reaches into her jacket pocket and hands us each a laminated pass. "This serves as the key both to your room and the approved common areas. Make sure to keep it safe, and remember—this pass won't open any doors beyond your own room and the spaces I just showed you. All other rooms, corridors, and buildings here at ISTC are off-limits unless you are with me or another member of staff. That means absolutely *no* venturing to the Mission Floor, the labs, or anywhere else on your own. All that'll get you is the wrath of Dr. Takumi, which, trust me, you don't want to see." She looks intently at each of us. "Do you understand?"

I join the others and nod obediently, but I can feel my

heartbeat quickening. Why all the secrecy? Why are we confined to just four spaces on this massive campus?

What are they hiding?

The door closes behind us, plunging me and Suki into silence. For a few moments we just stand there, both of us frozen in the awkwardness of the situation. But then I clear my throat, force myself to get a grip. I may not be much of a social butterfly, but I need a friend here. Maybe having a roommate will turn out for the best.

"So, um, what do you think? About all this?" I ask, realizing as the words come out of my mouth that I really do suck at making small talk.

"I think . . ." She takes a shaky breath, and for a second I wonder if she's going to tell me something real—but then her expression closes up. "I think we should try to get some rest while we can. We're going to be on an exhausting schedule."

She strides forward and flicks on the lights. Our luggage is already here waiting for us, and Suki drags her bag to the bed farthest from the door, effectively claiming the quieter side of the room without asking me. But I have bigger things to worry about than a potentially inconsiderate roomie.

I sink onto the bed on my side and glance around at our surroundings. The room is about what I expected—small and stark, with two twin beds, a pair of matching white desks and swivel chairs, and a closet and chest of drawers to share. The walls are bare, save for a large, sleek mirror near the door. At first I'm surprised that the ISTC even bothered with such fancy mirrors in each room, until an LED screen lights up within it. A message on the screen displays our names and today's schedule, with a clock reminding us that we have T-minus two hours until dinner.

"I would have preferred a window to that," I tell Suki, nodding at the Mirror Screen of Stress.

"Hmm" is all she says in response, before opening her duffel bag and folding her clothes into our chest of drawers. I'm in no hurry to unpack, but Suki is making it clear that we're not about to break the ice and bond. I might as well fix up my side of the room with some reminders of home.

I hop off the bed and grab my carry-on, unzipping the compartment that holds my photos and posters. I pull out the framed photo of me with Dr. Greta Wagner from the science fair two years ago and set it in a place of honor on my desk, then use a couple thumbtacks from the desk to pin up my favorite poster, of Albert Einstein sticking out his tongue. And then I unearth my most precious photo of all—from Persian New Year, back when I was fourteen. My father is leaping over a blazing fire per New Year tradition, a childlike grin on his face, while me, Sam, and Mom watch with our arms around each other, practically crying with laughter. It's an image that's always made me smile—until today.

Nothing can make this place feel like home, not when my family is a thousand miles away. And if I thought I had a solid plan up my sleeve to get back to them, Dr. Takumi's litany of rules and restrictions is forcing me to reconsider everything.

"I—I think I'm going to take a nap," I fib to Suki. Of course there's no chance I'll fall asleep, but I need an excuse to turn away from her—to hide my face and let the inevitable tears fall.

SEVEN

LEO

"HOW GREAT IS THIS?"

I circle the dorm room I share with Asher, surveying all the luxuries that I once took for granted. A comfortable bed, our own heating and AC unit, furniture that looks sturdy enough to withstand the storms . . . who needs anything more? But someone has gone to extra lengths to make up for my sad lack of clothes—planting T-shirts and socks, boxers and swim trunks, khakis and sweaters into the chest of drawers, all in my size.

I'd almost forgotten what it felt like to be taken care of until now. The thought of no longer having to fight for every scrap of food, every piece of cloth on my back, makes me feel ten pounds lighter. I flop onto the bed, gratitude flooding through me.

"It's pretty cool," Asher agrees, rifling through his luggage. He starts unloading books and photos onto his desk, and I wonder if he'll notice that I don't have a single belonging to unpack. But if he does, he's polite enough not to comment.

"Were you as shocked as I was to get drafted?" I ask.

Asher gives a modest shrug. "I mean, I definitely hoped to get picked, and once I became a fighter pilot in the Tzahal—that's the Israel Defense Forces—I figured I had a shot. That was my plan even before the Europa Mission: to become an astronaut by starting out as a pilot." His eyes cloud over. "But now that we know they're having a *robot* fly this mission, I'm not so sure what I'm doing here."

"They can't leave it all up to an AI, though," I point out. "What if there was a systems failure or a technical issue? I bet Dr. Takumi and the general still need at least one human onboard with piloting experience."

Asher nods, looking slightly more hopeful. "Thanks. I just . . . I need this." He glances down at the floor. "You know how it is—not having a home to go back to."

"I know." I don't elaborate on how much I've lost—I'm sure my lack of belongings says it all. But I feel a pang of sympathy as I remember that the rising of the Mediterranean Sea pulled millions of homes underwater, giving Israelis no choice but to flee.

"I hope you make the Final Six," I tell him suddenly.

"I hope we both get to go."

Asher smiles. "Me, too."

Asher and I step through the doors of the cafeteria into a hum of conversation and a cloud of tempting smells. Three faceless utility robots are stationed behind the buffet counter, their plastic-coated synthetic bodies moving in unison as they prepare our dinner. I elbow Asher in amazement, and he lets out a low whistle.

"Yeah, this is different from home, all right."

We join Lark, Beckett, and Katerina at our table, seconds before Naomi and Suki slide in. Naomi's eyes are red-rimmed, her expression wary, and I have the unexpected urge to reach across the table, to make her smile. But her head is turned to the front of the room, where Dr. Takumi, General Sokolov, and the rest of the faculty are surveying the scene from an elevated platform. Dr. Takumi rises to his feet, and silence falls over the cafeteria.

"Good evening, finalists," he greets us. "I imagine right now your families are all in front of their TVs, watching the media coverage from today and feeling immeasurably proud of you."

If only.

"However, our real work begins tomorrow," he continues. "During training, you will be expected to push your bodies and minds beyond your limits, beyond fatigue. This is what distinguishes astronauts from amateurs."

I sit up straighter, hoping Dr. Takumi can see the

determination in my face. I *won't* be one of the amateurs. Whatever it takes, I won't let myself slip.

"Throughout this process, you will alternate between learning the skills needed for the arduous journey into deep space and those needed to survive and build a permanent home on Europa. Your focus is critical." He pauses. "The tools you learn down here could be precisely what saves your life up there."

The silence in the room seems to thicken at his words. He holds our gaze for one more moment, and then nods approvingly.

"And now, dinner is served. When I call your team name, take a tray and line up at the counter."

As soon as it's our turn, I practically shoot out of my chair. One of the utility robots swivels forward as I approach the counter. "Would you like the American meal, the Chinese meal, or both?" it asks in a genderless, mechanical voice.

"Um, both, please?"

I watch in awe as the robot piles fried chicken with collard greens and corn bread onto my plate, before handing me a second dish of mapo tofu and a bowl of shrimp dumpling soup. I can barely remember the last time I ate like this. For a while the only sounds around me are the clatter of silverware scraping against plates as the six of us dig in, until Katerina leans forward.

"Did any of you see the new BBC documentary about Europa?"

"Yeah, my uncle showed it at the White House," Beckett says through a mouthful of food. I catch Naomi give a slight eye roll at that, and I stifle a laugh.

"Wasn't it amazing?" Katerina raves. "The coolest part was when they showed how Jupiter appears twenty-four times bigger in Europa's sky than our own sun looks to us. Can you *imagine* the view we'd get every day? I think that's what I'm most looking forward to: sitting out on the ice surface and seeing Jupiter right in front of me, looming large."

"It'll definitely put all of Earth's sights to shame," Lark agrees, an inscrutable expression crossing her face.

"What I keep thinking about is the landing," I say, leaning back in my chair as I imagine it. "That moment when we're the very first to set foot on a whole other part of the universe . . . it's like we get to be Marco Polo, but on an infinitely bigger scale."

"Yeah, and the rocket launch," Asher joins in, his face lighting up. "I've watched so many online and always wanted to be up there myself, strapped inside the flight capsule, ready for liftoff. But I never pictured getting to go somewhere so far off the map. That's the most surreal part about all of this." He glances at Suki sitting across from him. "What about you?"

There's a brief pause before Suki answers, her voice quiet but firm. "Getting away from Earth—that's what I can't wait for."

I raise my glass to hers.

"I'm sure we can all toast to that."

But Naomi shakes her head, stabbing at a piece of corn bread with her fork.

"I don't get it. You guys are acting like this is a vacation instead of a draft. If we get picked, we could *literally* explode into flames before we even reach Europa, or wind up starving to death if the *Athena* fuel leak costs us our supplies. Or we could make it to Europa with no problem, only to get killed by the environment or . . . something else." She takes a deep breath. "I just think we need to be a little more realistic."

"What, are you scared?" Beckett jeers.

"We should all be scared," Naomi says under her breath. I can tell there's more to her words than she's letting on, but before I can ask, Lark jumps in.

"Look, risk is an inherent part of space travel, but that doesn't mean those worst-case scenarios will actually happen. I know the fuel leak sounds alarming, but SatCon is keeping a sharp eye on it twenty-four hours a day—and moving up the launch date ensures the Final Six should make it to Mars in time so salvage the supply ship." She looks at us intently. "If there was ever a mission destined for success, it's this one. Europa is the first time we've had the collective brainpower of all the international space agencies together on one project. You can trust that they're making this mission as safe as it can possibly be."

"No matter *what* happens, it's still got to be better than staying on Earth and waiting to die," I remark. Suki and Asher both nod in agreement, but Naomi gives me an incredulous look.

"You can't be serious."

"I am. And if you don't know what I mean"—I smile sadly—"consider yourself lucky."

She furrows her brow, about to say something more when Lark clears her throat.

"How about we end our first night on a lighter note? I want to see us become a real team, which means we need to start getting to know each other fast. Why don't we go around the table and share a little something about ourselves?"

When no one volunteers, Lark says, "Okay, I'll go first. I was born and raised in Huntsville, Alabama, home of the US Space and Rocket Center. That's what got me interested in space from an early age, and I studied engineering at MIT before joining NASA straight out of college. My first spaceflight was actually the final trip to the International Space Station, but when Dr. Takumi offered me the chance to help him develop the ISTC, I retired from space travel to join him here."

"You were on the last ISS mission?" Naomi stares at Lark. "So then you were here training when the news broke about the *Athena* crew. Did you know—"

"And that's enough about me," Lark cuts her off, with a short laugh. She turns to our teammate sitting to her right. "Katerina?"

"Um, some of you might have seen me on the final

Olympics," Katerina says with a fleeting smile. "But what most people don't know about me is that I'm really good at math. That's part of what made me so strong on the ice—instead of being nervous, I would focus on the number of rotations and the geometrical angles I needed to hit to land the perfect jumps."

As we continue around the table, I learn that Suki was the youngest-ever engineering student in her university's history, after skipping multiple grades in pre-tsunami Singapore, while Naomi tells us about her prizewinning radio telescope invention. The more my teammates list their accomplishments, the more beads of sweat I can feel forming on my brow. *How* am I supposed to compete with this group?

By showing Dr. Takumi and General Sokolov that I'm just the swimmer and diver they need to survive Europa, I remind myself, recalling Elena's words. If what she overheard was true, then I'm just as integral to this mission as the academics . . . maybe even more.

Beckett is the last of our teammates to speak, and when it's his turn, he glances around the table at each of us, like he knows something we don't. "Interesting, isn't it, that each of us has the exact same strength as someone else on this team? Suki and Naomi have the same engineering and science background, Asher and Katerina are both math prodigies—and me and Leo are the swimmers." He cocks his head. "You would almost think we're all being pitted against each other."

Lark tries to laugh off his theory, but it's too late. The six of us are already looking at each other differently. And at the thought of another swimmer here, all the food I just ate threatens to come rising to the surface. That was supposed to be my ace in the hole. *What if he's as good as me?* It's been over a year since my last swim meet or training session with my coach; I am far from competition-ready.

"What was your best race?" I ask Beckett, trying to sound nonchalant.

"The four-hundred-meter freestyle."

"Oh." I swallow hard. "Me, too."

I should have known they would have more than one swimmer in contention here, with all the underwater elements involved in terraforming Europa. But in my excitement, I never even considered it.

I just assumed it would be me.

Training Day One kicks off with a crack-of-dawn wake-up call from our dorm room's interactive mirror, followed by a jittery team breakfast where, unlike last night, no one seems to have much of an appetite. And then, before I know it, we're following Lark to the elevator bay—and to our first training session.

The elevator dings as we land on the sixth floor. Lark sweeps through the lift doors first, leading us to a concrete wall straight ahead.

"Each team is running on a different schedule, so you can receive as close to individualized attention as possible during training," she says, glancing behind her to make sure we're all within earshot. "Your first session today takes place on a life-size mock-up of the *Pontus*: the spaceship that will fly the Final Six to Europa."

Lark presses the badge hanging around her neck to a quarter-size symbol on the wall, and I hear a gasp behind me as the concrete splits apart. The wall juts open, revealing the gleaming white facades of space capsules and the outstretched arm of a robotic crane, beckoning us forward.

"Here we go."

Lark steps through the opening, and we follow her onto the Mission Floor. It's a vast expanse the size of an American football field, with a series of hulking, interconnected cylindrical structures running the length of the floor. The walls and ceiling are painted to resemble the pitch-black sky you'd see from the windows of deep space, while a futuristic blue light offsets the darkness. General Sokolov steps out of one of the capsules, dressed in a red flight suit adorned with mission patches and insignia.

"Good morning, and welcome to the *Pontus*," she announces. "What you see before you are the capsules, modules, and nodes that make up the most cutting-edge spaceship ever built—the Final Six's home base for the duration of the journey to Europa."

I turn to Asher standing beside me, and we exchange an excited glance. *This is getting real*.

"Not only does the spacecraft transport you from Point A to a very far-off Point B, it also serves as a life preserver, shielding you from the deadly elements and punishing conditions of deep space. However, this very shield can easily become a weapon if you fail to understand how it works and what makes the *Pontus* tick. All it takes is one innocuous mistake—for example, failing to close the airlock doors securely—and you could be killed within seconds."

She lets those words hang in the air, the image of an explosive death lingering above us, before she leads the way to the first space capsule.

"In the coming days, you will face emergency drills to test both your understanding of the spacecraft and your ability to survive a crisis onboard—so pay close attention as I walk you through the *Pontus*."

The general climbs into a giant cylinder in the shape of a spinning top, with four thrusters protruding from the bottom. We follow her inside, emerging into a glowing, blue-lit flight deck. Two massive tablet screens hang from the ceiling, angled downward to face the five leather seats at the center of the cabin, all in the reclined position for liftoff. Another pair of seats rests in front of a glass cockpit, with an array of flight instruments between them, and an 8K electronic navigation display unfurling across the glass. As the six of us look around in wonder, General Sokolov strides up to the cockpit.

"While Cyb will be piloting the spacecraft under my command, one of the Final Six gets to take this seat beside the AI and serve as copilot. Upcoming flight simulations will test your abilities and determine who is best suited for this role, as well as help us fill the other key posts for the mission: lieutenant commander, communications and tech specialist, science officer, medical officer, and Europa underwater specialist."

Asher elbows me in the ribs, a grin lighting his face. He's sure to snag the copilot seat, and I know he must be thinking I'm a lock for underwater specialist. And I should be—it's the job I was born to do. But as Beckett flashes the general a confident smile, I feel a pang of worry.

"Most of the journey will be flown in cruise control, thanks to the new algorithm technology implemented in our flight computers and avionics," General Sokolov continues. "However, three key stages in the spaceflight must be executed manually, due to their complexity and the higher degree of risk involved. That would be the escape trajectory from Earth, the rendezvous with the Mars supply ship, and the landing on Europa. While Cyb and the copilot keep us on course, we'll need two members of the Final Six to complete an Extravehicular Activity, or EVA—otherwise known as a spacewalk—and oversee the docking of the *Pontus* to the Mars supply ship. If anything goes wrong there . . ."

"We die?" Naomi guesses.

"You die," the general confirms. "But the remaining four will still be expected to fulfill the mission."

I hear Katerina gulp beside me, and I can feel the ripple of tension running through the six of us, but the general is already moving on, opening a round hatch at the back of the capsule and crouching onto her hands and knees.

"Follow me."

We crawl through the tunnel behind her, making our way from one equipment-filled module to the next, as she points out the functional cargo block that provides our power and propulsion, the utility hub that stores our payload racks and emergency supplies, and the crew quarters, where we'll spend most of our time onboard—complete with private sleep stations, a galley kitchen, gym, a communications bay with a pair of large-screen desktop computers, and two bathrooms with "space toilets." My pulse quickens as I take in our surroundings.

I can picture myself here so clearly. I can see the shadow of my future self sitting in the communications bay chair; I can *feel* the pride and elation of delivering progress reports to Houston and the watching world. I know the choice isn't up to me, but in my mind, I'm already there.

"There's something about the geometric design in here." Naomi speaks up, turning around slowly. "The whole spacecraft reminds me of someone, actually—of Dr. Greta Wagner's work."

General Sokolov pauses, looking at Naomi in surprise. "That's an astute observation. The *Pontus* was, in fact, a collaboration between SpaceInc and Dr. Wagner."

Naomi's face lights up, and she breaks into the first real smile I've seen from her yet.

"So Dr. Wagner's involved in the mission? Is she coming here? Do we get to work with her during our training?"

The general purses her lips. "I'm afraid not. While we

are grateful for her contributions to the *Pontus*, we chose to end our contract with Dr. Wagner."

"What?" Naomi stares at her. "Why?"

"She had some differences with the rest of the team," Sokolov says cryptically. Before any of us can ask what *that* means, the general turns on her heel, moving toward a tube-like tunnel at the back of the crew quarters. "Now, through the passage straight ahead, we'll reach one of the most critical structures in the entire spacecraft: the airlock." She pulls a lever, and the passage door shudders open. "You all go in first. I'm right behind you."

Beckett climbs inside, followed by Katerina and me, all of us forced to shimmy forward on our stomachs through the tight confines. I hear the sound of a steel plate shifting into place as the general closes the hatch, and then her voice echoes through the tunnel.

"The airlock is the last thing you'll see before exiting into open space, and your first stop upon returning to the ship from your EVA. As you move between the *Pontus*'s controlled, breathable environment and the toxic realm outside, the airlock's pressure prevents the outside poisonous gases from entering our spacecraft. And as soon as you hang up your suit, the airlock mechanism automatically filters out those same gases." She pauses. "I'm sure now it's clear why a simple failure to immediately secure the door would get you killed."

"Yes," the six of us respond in unison.

We reach a heavy round hatch with six interconnected

latches covering its surface. General Sokolov crawls past us and demonstrates how to work the rods to unfasten each latch, until the airlock door swings open and we tumble inside.

"Don't worry. This will be a lot more graceful when you're floating in zero g," the general says as Katerina and Naomi smack into each other and Beckett hits the floor with a thud. The general looks up sharply as the last of our team, Suki, topples inside. Sokolov's eyes flit between the open hatch door and my teammate.

"Didn't you hear what I said about closing the hatch, Suki?"

Suki's face drains of color. "Y-yes. I did."

"And yet you were the last one into the airlock and failed to follow my express command." The general's voice is ice cold. I have a sinking feeling in my stomach as I watch her stare Suki down.

"But I—it's only because I thought you were going to—"

The general grabs Suki by the shoulders and pushes her toward the hatch. "Go back in the tunnel."

Suki eyes the general nervously but does as she's told, crawling through the hatch. Once in the tunnel, she presses her hands against the open door, her mouth forming a question—just as the general slams the door shut from the inside, barely missing Suki's fingers. The airlock chamber turns dead silent.

"What's going on?" Suki's muffled voice calls from outside the steel-plated door. "How do I get out of here?"

"You don't," the general says. "Not until your next training period in thirty minutes."

"What?" Suki's voice rises in panic. "But there's hardly any air in here. I won't be able to breathe!"

"Imagine that feeling magnified to the hundredth power," General Sokolov says coolly. "*That* is what will happen if you or any of your teammates use the airlock improperly in the vacuum of space." She turns to face the rest of us. "You're all receiving a crucial lesson, one that will save your lives if it sticks with you."

And then, proceeding as if Suki weren't trapped in a confined space behind the hatch door, the general moves deeper into the chamber, motioning for us to follow. But I can't concentrate, my mind back in the tunnel with my teammate. I can tell Naomi feels the same way, and as General Sokolov shows us the equipment lock where we'll purify our space suits, I catch her sidling away from the group, edging her way toward the hatch door. *What is she about to do?*

Instinctively, I take a few steps closer to her, while staying within the general's line of sight. Naomi presses her face to the hatch and begins to speak.

"Can you hear me, Suki? It's Naomi. We need to keep you relaxed, and your pulse even. As long as you don't panic and deplete your oxygen levels, you have enough air in there to survive for more than double the time. Close your eyes—let's see if we can trick your consciousness into falling asleep . . ."

Something tugs at my chest as I watch her, risking a

punishment of her own to help a girl she only just met. I glance behind me at General Sokolov, in the middle of demonstrating the space suit purification mechanism, and I catch her gaze flickering in Naomi's direction too. But the general doesn't react. She simply watches Naomi out of the corner of her eye while continuing with the lecture, an unreadable expression on her face.

Lark is waiting on the Mission Floor when we emerge from the space capsule, and she zips us from the *Pontus* mock-up to our second training session on Level 4. I can smell the chlorine even before the elevator doors open, and my muscles clench on cue. *Time to compete.*

"For years, this floor was home to the Neutral Buoyancy Lab," Lark says, taking us through a long white hallway. "NASA engineers built an underwater mock-up of the International Space Station, and astronauts-in-training, like myself, would wear neutral-buoyancy suits to simulate the microgravity of space while we practiced for our EVAs. But when the Europa Mission was approved, Dr. Takumi had this place redesigned and repurposed for something else: preparing the Final Six for the underwater operations necessary to terraform Europa for human settlement."

She pushes open a set of double doors, and my mouth falls open. From the colossal pool and elevated diving boards to the dozens of countries' flags dotting the walls, it's like we're inside one of my old Olympic dreams. But when we step closer, I spot the differences. I've never seen a swimming pool this deep—it appears almost fathomless—and sitting about fifty or sixty feet underwater is a massive block of *ice*. The ice is covered in crisscrossing red ridges . . . just like the surface of Europa.

A man in a diving wet suit crosses the floor toward us, and Lark gives him a salute before taking a seat in the stands.

"Welcome, finalists. I'm Lieutenant Barnes, United States Navy SEAL and PADI master scuba diver."

This is my moment. I straighten my shoulders, my adrenaline kicking into gear as he speaks.

"As you know, the Final Six's first and most crucial task upon landing entails drilling through Europa's ice crust to reach the ocean and rocky surface beneath—the most Earth-like segment of Jupiter's moon, where we will build our human colony," he says. "We need one exceptional leader and athlete to serve as underwater specialist and spearhead this effort, but the other five must become scuba-certified divers as well."

It has to be me. What are the chances that anyone else here can come close to executing the kind of deep dives I performed as a scavenger in Rome? I was tailor-made for this, my body built for it.

"On that note, today we'll begin with a diving tutorial," Lieutenant Barnes continues. "You all have bathing suits on under your uniforms, correct?"

We nod, as Lark's instructions from last night suddenly make sense.

"Good. Once I hand out your diving equipment and

wetsuits, change out of your uniforms and meet me at the edge of the pool."

I'm about to tell him that I actually don't need any equipment when it occurs to me that I might want to keep that particular trick under wraps until the right moment. I stay quiet as Lieutenant Barnes passes out backpacks filled with scuba tanks and rebreather sets, diving helmets and masks. And then out of nowhere comes a whirring sound, followed by a series of beeps punctuating the air. We all turn in the direction of the sound—and find the lead robot, Cyb, advancing through the double doors toward us. The sight makes the hairs on the back of my neck stand on end.

"It must be here to evaluate us," Katerina says, watching Lieutenant Barnes jog over to the AI. And as the six of us exchange glances, I can feel an instant shift in the mood, an undercurrent of competition crackling between us now that Cyb is here. I already knew I had to be at the top of my game today, but this is starting to feel as high stakes as the Olympic moment I once visualized.

I'm so preoccupied staring at Cyb, straining to hear what it's saying to Lieutenant Barnes, that I fail to notice my competitor moving past me and tossing his uniform on the floor. It isn't until I hear Asher murmur "*What* is he doing?" that I glance up—and see Beckett climbing up to the three-meter diving board.

"Oh, boy." Naomi cringes.

I hold my breath, watching as Beckett stretches his body in a pencil-straight shape, assuming a dive pose. His form looks good so far. . . . And then he leans his head forward and lifts his legs, leaping off the springboard in a swan dive.

His entry is flawless. My heart sinks at the realization that my edge is no longer mine alone.

"You don't need to teach me that one, Lieutenant," Beckett boasts from the water. And though he's speaking to Barnes, his eyes are locked on Cyb, making sure the robot saw.

Lieutenant Barnes arches an eyebrow.

"Noted. Does anyone else consider themselves exempt from this lesson, or should I continue?"

The thumping in my chest tells me what I have to do. I may not be a pompous jerk like Beckett, but right now, I need to take a page out of his playbook. I have something to prove.

I strip off my uniform and walk right past the three-meter diving board Beckett chose—climbing up to the ten-meter instead. I hear someone say "Oh, God." And it's the last thing I hear before my body tenses, my muscle memory taking over as I perform a twist dive from thirty feet high, somersaulting through the air before entering the water with a clean splash.

Nailed it. If this were a meet, I would outscore Beckett in both difficulty and execution. *And* this *is what happens when you try to show the rest of us up, Beckett* Wolfe.

He climbs out of the pool with a scowl on his face while our teammates gape at me. I glance up at Naomi, who watches me with raised eyebrows and a half smile. The thought that I might have impressed someone as accomplished as her makes my shoulders puff up with pride.

"Well done," Lieutenant Barnes says at last, striding toward me with Cyb at his side. "You must be Leonardo Danieli."

"That's me."

I hoist myself out of the pool with a grin. I'd almost forgotten how good it feels to do what I love, what I'm best at. For a second I can almost imagine that I'm home, that Angelica and my parents are there in the stands, whistling and cheering my name just like they used to at all my swim meets. But then I feel the heat of Beckett's glare and am returned to the present moment.

Something tells me he won't take this embarrassment lightly.

EIGHT

NAOMI

WITH THE MORNING WE'VE HAD, I'M EXPECTING OUR AFTER-noon training to be a little more sedate—maybe even in an actual classroom, so we can sit and catch our breath after the past few hours of crawling through space capsules and diving into freezing water. But of course, my wishful thinking is way off base. It turns out that our most action-packed hour is still ahead of us.

Our first clue is when Lark escorts us down to the first floor and through the main entrance doors, leaving the ISTC campus behind. A tram shuttle is waiting outside, and that's when she reveals what's in store.

"Today wasn't just about diving underwater. Get ready,

because you guys are about to experience an in-air, *parabolic* dive!"

Lark's voice is brimming with enthusiasm, but her words fill me with dread.

"The Vomit Comet," I murmur.

"That's right!" Lark grins at me, clearly missing the trepidation in my voice. "We're going to take a parabolic flight around Houston on a special A500 Zero-G plane. Once the plane reaches an altitude of twenty-four thousand feet and an angle of forty-five degrees, it will free-fall in the air—which simulates the effect of being in orbit. So today, each of you will discover just what it feels like to be weightless in space."

"Awesome!" Asher exclaims, fist-bumping Leo and Katerina. Suki gives a rare smile, and even the First Nephew looks cheered out of his dark mood from the past hour. Are my teammates all adrenaline junkies or something? How am I the only one here freaked out by the thought of nose-diving in a plane? My hands are already sweating, my pulse accelerating. I never could stand the feeling of my stomach dropping out from underneath me—it's the reason why I've sworn off thrill rides since I was a little girl, after a particularly hairy experience on the Pirate Ship at the Santa Monica Pier. Exhibit A for why I'm not cut out to be an astronaut.

I keep my clammy hands pressed to my knees during the tram ride to the Space Center heliport, blocking out the snippets of conversation around me as I try to pretend I'm back with Sam and my parents, that I'm relating the story of "this crazy thing we did at space camp!" from the safety of home.

A gleaming plane with the *Zero-G* logo painted in blue lettering waits for us on the heliport, its cabin door open and air stairs unfurled. My breath turns shallow as the tram skids to a stop and Lark directs us to the aircraft.

"Let's go!"

My teammates race up the steps and into the plane, free of the panic that holds me in its grip. *I don't want to do this, I don't want to do this, I don't—*

"Come on." Lark nudges me forward. "I'll be in there with you."

I swallow hard and force one foot in front of the other until I'm inside the cabin. There are only a few rows of seats in the back while an empty, white-painted chamber takes up the rest of the space. I slide into an empty seat next to Suki as Lark starts passing out barf bags to store in our pockets.

"This *is* known as the Vomit Comet for a reason, so don't be too embarrassed if you throw up. One of NASA's medical officers is standing by in case any of you need extra attention, but most likely you'll experience only mild airsickness. And don't worry—the more you practice, the more your body will adjust. That's why in the days leading up to launch, astronauts will often complete up to forty parabolas at a time."

I squeeze my eyes shut, my stomach already roiling at the thought of the rapid ascent and plummeting drop ahead of us. It's nerve-racking enough that we have to do this once—I can't even contemplate the idea of "practicing" forty times in a row, as if free-falling in a plane is some kind of sport.

"We're about ready for takeoff, so sit tight and wait for the signal. Once we reach altitude, remove your shoes and follow me to the Float Zone," Lark says, gesturing to the empty white space stretching ahead of us.

The wheels below us push forward, scraping off the pavement. *Inhale, exhale,* I instruct myself, though I can barely manage to take a full breath. The plane soars into the sky, the pilot steering us up a treacherously steep incline, and I grab Suki's arm involuntarily, desperate for something, anything to hold on to. She squeezes my hand, her first friendly gesture since we became roommates.

"You'll be okay," she says, as our roles from this morning are reversed.

I try to smile. "Thanks. I just—I'm meant to be a scientist on the ground. You know? I hate heights, I hate drops . . . this daredevil stuff is not exactly my strong suit."

"Well, someone must have thought you can do it," Suki replies. "That's why you're here."

A light flickers above our heads, followed by the sound of a chime echoing through the cabin.

"That's our cue!" Lark shouts over the din of the aircraft. "We're ready for our first parabola! Follow me to the Float Zone."

The others spring out of their seats, all too eager for the real-life roller coaster ride ahead. Suki and I follow, my heart in my throat as we step into the Float Zone and Lark instructs us to lie on our backs. I lie down next to Suki with Leo on the other side of me. As my body touches the floor, I realize how close he is, his skin just inches from mine. I turn my head in the opposite direction, a flush burning my cheeks.

"When the plane curves to the forty-five-degree angle, you'll feel a g-force of 1.8 times the Earth's gravity on your body," Lark calls across the floor. "The best thing you can do at this point is stay still. Don't make any quick movements until the free fall."

Oh, God. She wasn't kidding about the force. I bite back a scream as the weight of gravity presses against my chest. The blood rushes from my head to my feet, and it feels as though someone is yanking my insides with a rope, dragging every part of me down to the ground.

The plane's engine turns quiet.

"This is it!" Lark shouts. "Get ready for zero g's!"

I grip the floor with my hands, bracing myself. The plane dips, and I gasp as the excess-gravity weight melts off my body. Then, in one breathlessly quick motion, the plane plummets into free fall. My screams are all I hear, my terror is all I know as our seven bodies rise up off the floor like the dead resurrected. We flail our arms and legs, grasping at air while the plane shifts yet again—and then we are floating. We are *flying*.

A giddy sensation bubbles in my stomach. Something is happening to me up here, something I didn't expect. I am floating upside down, my feet touching the ceiling—and I *don't* feel like I'm going to die, or even throw up. It's just the opposite. I feel as though all the weight in my life has been lifted, and I am free.

The chamber echoes with our intermingled whoops, shrieks, and laughter as the seven of us somersault through the air and float backward over the passenger seats. Leo drifts toward me as the plane dives yet again, and the two of us smack into each other on the ceiling. I burst out laughing, and he grins, impulsively taking my hand and twirling me through the air.

"I *have* always wondered what it's like to dance on the ceiling," he says with a wink.

My stomach flips, and this time I'm not so sure it's from the zero gravity. I watch as Leo floats over to Asher, and then I lift my arms like a bird, skimming across the air to the main cabin and back again.

After each parabolic dive, one or two of my teammates turns a shade of green and reaches for the barf bag—but strangely enough, it doesn't happen to me. My body is stronger than I thought. And as we plunge into our last parabola, I find that I can't stop smiling. It's hard to believe something so extraordinary, so magical, came from this experience I was dreading.

Until the plane touches down, I am light as air. I am weightless.

Our team returns to ISTC campus disheveled and delirious from the adventures of the day, all of us craving the same three things: shower, food, bed. But as soon as we step off the elevator and onto the Hab floor, those simple plans slip from view. A commotion is coming from the boys' dorm—a guttural cry that pierces at my chest. Lark breaks into a run and we race after her, stopping in our tracks when we see a group of five finalists clustered outside a closed door, their faces grave.

"What's going on?" Lark demands.

Dianna, the British finalist I recognize from the TV segment on the Twenty-Four, is the first to speak. "There was a typhoon in Tianjin last night—where Jian Soo's family lives. The reports are saying it's one of the most violent storm lashings China has ever seen." Her voice drops. "The majority of the city is under the Hai River now, and . . . they haven't found any survivors."

I sink back against the wall, my heart breaking for the boy behind the door—for everyone in China. And all too quickly, my mind is picturing myself in Jian's shoes, hearing the same shattering news about my own family. *What if LA is the next city hit by disaster . . . and I'm not there?* The thought seizes me with fear, renewing my desperation to get away from here—to get *home*.

"Dr. Takumi and our team leader are in there with him now," the Australian finalist, Callum, says. "We just—we felt weird leaving without knowing if Jian's okay."

"He won't be okay." Leo speaks up, staring at the closed door. "Not anytime soon. You don't ever get over something like this. The best you can hope for is to survive it."

I look at him and it dawns on me—he must be speaking from experience. "Leo is right," Lark says. "We should give Jian some privacy. Why don't you guys go to the lounge and try to relax a bit? I'll wait here and see if they need anything."

I doubt any of us will manage to relax after what we've just heard, but we trudge toward the lounge anyway. What else can we do? Only Beckett splits from the group, and I wonder briefly what he's up to before turning to Suki, who's walking alongside me.

"Another city down." I shudder. "I can't even imagine what Jian is going through."

But Suki doesn't respond. She just gives me a sideways look before quickening her pace—as if she wants to get away from me. I watch her in confusion, wondering how her warmth from this afternoon could so quickly turn cool.

"Here's a thought," Katerina says once the ten of us are huddled up in the lounge. "Is there anyone in this room who *hasn't* lost a family member to climate change? Does anyone here even have a safe home to go back to—one where you don't have to worry about waking up underwater, or under rubble? When you think about it . . . we're all like Jian Soo."

I glance around and am struck by the sight of everyone nodding or murmuring in agreement. Everyone but me. I thought being forced to move three times in the past two years was bad, but I'm beginning to realize just how fortunate my situation is in comparison to that of the others here. The fact that my family is still intact is even rarer than

I knew—and the realization makes me all the more anxious to hold on to them.

"I don't even have a country to go back to if I get cut," Asher says, studying the floor. "The flooding demolished most of the land." He looks up, his expression determined. "Europa is my only shot."

"It's the only shot for most of us," Dianna points out. She shuts her eyes. "We just have to pray the right six are chosen, and that the rest of us can handle the outcome."

Someone stirs behind me, and I turn to see Leo push out of his seat, backing away from the lounge—away from this conversation. On impulse, I get up too, following him into the library.

"Are you okay?"

He keeps moving through the stacks, ignoring my voice until I reach for his arm, stopping him in the History of Spaceflight section.

"Leo. What's wrong?"

"I can't think about it," he blurts out. His eyes are haunted as he stares straight ahead, like he is somewhere else entirely and I'm not there. "Can't think about what would happen if I had to go home."

"Why?" I whisper.

"It's . . . like being trapped inside my grief." He swallows hard. "Always waiting for them to walk through the door, listening for voices that will never come. I couldn't do it anymore."

A lump forms in my throat. "I'm so sorry, Leo. You—you

don't have to tell me anything else, if you don't want to."

I reach up to squeeze his shoulder, and his eyes refocus on me.

"I had a sister." The words come tumbling out, as if they've been bottled up for too long. "Angelica. You would have liked her. She was smart, funny, the light of our family. A real firecracker, too. She could stand up to anyone, and no one could match her wit." He smiles to himself, but then his expression falters. "I wasn't supposed to ever see her like that—my baby sister underwater, her *face*—"

He breaks off, unable to speak, and I close the space between us, wrapping my arms around him as my own eyes well with tears. I can hear his heart pounding through his shirt, can feel his chest rising with each hollow breath.

"I'm sorry . . . I'm *so* sorry. And I—I know how you feel, in a different way." We break apart, and I lean heavily against the stacks. "My little brother, Sam, is everything to me. When he was diagnosed with his heart condition, and the doctors told us he was living on borrowed time—it nearly broke me. Especially when we discovered it's from a genetic mutation, something I could have gotten too, but I didn't." I shake my head, the years of pain returning anew. "I'm the big sister. It should have been me instead."

Leo looks at me with understanding.

"We're supposed to be their protectors. Not the survivors."

"Yeah," I whisper. "Exactly."

A clatter of footsteps echoes through the library as

another group of finalists enters, jarring us from the moment. Leo and I step out of the stacks, a slight shyness between us now that we've both just revealed something so personal. But there's something else too, and I can see it in his eyes before we go our separate ways.

It's the feeling of solidarity—of finding a friend in the dark.

I can't sleep that night, my mind spinning between thoughts of Europa and fears about home. It doesn't help that I've now gone my longest stretch yet without talking to Sam or my parents. I can feel the hole of their absence like a physical pain, a wound made sharper by worry. I never had to wonder before how they were doing, how Sam was feeling—I was always right there, close enough to know everything with just a glance. But now all I can do is guess, and the uncertainty has me wide awake. If I could just *talk* to them, if I didn't have to wait till the stupid scheduled video-chat, then maybe I'd be okay. . . .

And that's when I remember—the envelope from Sam. I didn't want to open it in front of Suki, but now that she's fast asleep, I have my chance.

I throw off the covers and reach under my bed, grabbing the flashlight stowed there in case of storms. I tiptoe over to my backpack, the light's thin glow hovering above it as I unzip the hidden compartment and pull out the white envelope. I tear it open . . . but there's no letter to be found. Instead, I'm holding a metal flash drive. One that I recognize.

My heartbeat quickening, I shuffle through my backpack until I find my handheld tablet—the only personal electronic device we were allowed to bring to Space Training Camp, since it works without a cellular or WiFi connection. I power it on and plug in the drive, climbing back under the covers as it loads.

A spinning alien head pops up on the screen, and I stifle a gasp. It's just what I suspected. *Sam, you are one crafty little bro*.

The drive contains my own hacking software—the prototype I coded two years ago, when I was desperate to access the Burbank Hospital computers. Sam was struggling to stay alive then, his heart fighting against the old medication, and I couldn't just sit and wait. I needed the internal data, the files and DNA sequencing that hospitals never release—just in case I could see something that the overwhelmed, scattered doctors might have missed. So I put my computer skills to their best use. I was already adept at Python, so it was just a matter of coding the server scripts, and then I was in.

My software is how I hacked Sam's DNA records and figured out that he needed a biotech drug instead of a pharmaceutical, and it's what ultimately led me to come up with my DNA editing solution. But after that, I thought my hacking days were behind me. I haven't touched this flash drive since then—but my brother had the foresight to make sure I didn't leave it behind.

The thought gives me a burst of excitement even as a

chill of fear runs down my spine. I know why Sam did this. He's counting on me to get the inside intel that could stop this mission and bring the Twenty-Four home . . . but would I actually dare to infiltrate NASA computers?

On one hand, if my suspicions about the dangers and extraterrestrials are right, I would be protecting my fellow finalists—but after tonight, I'm not so sure they *want* to be protected. Is it at all possible that what's out there on Europa is the lesser of two evils?

I drop the drive back into its envelope. I can't make any hasty decisions—not when the possibility of getting caught hacking NASA would land me in jail, maybe even for life. For now, until I decide what to do . . . the most important thing is to make sure the drive stays hidden.

NINE

LEO

THE SECOND DAY OF TRAINING DAWNS, AND WE ARE THRUST back into the ISTC's breakneck pace, with no more word from Dr. Takumi about the China tragedy. It's as though we've grown so conditioned to natural disaster that we can only spare one night to reflect before it's on to the next. Still, I can feel the shadow of last night's news hanging over all of us at breakfast, underscoring the urgency of our mission, as Lark talks us through the training day to come. My stomach clenches at the sight of Jian Soo, showing up to the cafeteria with puffy, red-rimmed eyes and a stricken expression. Both of us will have to harness our grief while we are here—to let it propel us forward instead of backward.

After breakfast, Lark leads us through a series of

corridors into the virtual reality lab: a vast space centered around a 360-degree video screen, its walls climbing with electronics and wires, the ceilings blinking with LED sensors and tracking cameras. Three swivel chairs sit in front of the screen, each with a joystick attached to an armrest. Stacked on each seat are a headset, boxy chest rig, and sensor-laden gloves. My fingers twitch in anticipation. It looks like we're preparing to infiltrate a video game.

"Good morning, finalists." General Sokolov steps into the room through a rear door, an ISTC tablet glimmering in her hands. The six of us stand at attention, giving her the military salute Lark taught us to return her greeting.

"Today, you're going to experience the most high-tech training system astronauts have ever received on Earth," she begins. "Once you're hooked up to the equipment and sensors, the software known as DOUG—Dynamic Onboard Ubiquitous Graphics—will start modeling on the screen the very sights and scenes you'll find in space from your vantage point on the *Pontus*. At the same time, your headsets provide a 3D virtual representation, plunging you straight into the action, while your seats move in sync with the simulation. So, sitting in this chair and donning the gear will take you as close as anyone on Earth can get to deep space—without ever leaving this room. You'll find yourselves surprised by how lifelike it feels."

Awesome. Asher and I exchange a grin.

"Today's simulation places you near Jupiter orbit at the tail end of your journey to Europa, spacewalking during a pre-landing equipment check," the general continues. "Three of you will be outside the *Pontus* performing your EVAs, connected to the ship by a tether. You'll initially hear instructions from me through your headsets, but the purpose of the sim is to see how each of you reacts during an emergency scenario—one that just might require you to use your backup jetpacks." The corners of her mouth turn up in a conspiratorial half smile. "Your goal is to make it back to the airlock in one piece, with your teammates, by the end of the sim. The three of you will be able to communicate with each other via your headset radios, just as you will in a real-life EVA. Got it?"

We all nod, though I can tell from the faces around me that I'm not the only one wondering exactly how this is going to play out. I watch as General Sokolov peers down at her tablet, giving it a series of swipes—and then the door behind us blows open, followed by the whirring and beeping sounds I recognize from yesterday.

I turn around to the sight of both robots, Cyb and Dot, marching toward the general at an eerily identical stride. The six of us step back, clearing the way for them, as their presence once again sends a jolt through the room. I can see my teammates standing up a little straighter, their jaws tightening, eyes locked on the AIs. They are the wild cards in all of this—the machines with the power to sway our destinies.

The general nods at the robots in greeting, then refocuses on us.

"Dot, Cyb, and I will plug into the simulation as

observers, each of us reviewing your actions on the screen, as well as your heart rate, brain waves, and other physical reactions tracked by the wearable equipment. First up . . ." She glances down at her screen. "Beckett, Leo, and Naomi."

My competitive instincts return at the sound of my name, and I remember the mantra that used to run through my mind before every international swim meet: *Go make my country proud*. I plan to do just that while I'm here.

The three of us approach the chairs in front of the screen, and General Sokolov fits the VR equipment onto our bodies, attaching the bulky white rigs to our chests and strapping the elastic LED markers to our shoes. I slide my hands into the haptic gloves, watching the palm sensors light up as I stretch my fingers. Last is the headset, a wireless black-and-white mask of machinery that promises to immerse us in virtual space as soon as the general gives us the go-ahead to lower it over our eyes.

She points to the joysticks found on our armrests. "When the simulation calls for you to use your jetpack, you'll trigger the thrust with your joystick. As you know, jetpacks are self-rescue devices filled with propulsive gases. Wearing one of these manned maneuvering units on your back is like having a power you can access whenever you're in need—the power to, essentially, fly. But it takes skill to control the thrusters." She reaches for the stick, demonstrating its commands. "These are the motions you'll use to ignite the thrusters, with a long thrust for speed and smaller thrust to steady your direction."

Dot and Cyb cross to the console rig behind us, and I can hear the low hum of their machinery as they stand near me—like an AI form of breathing.

"Dot and Cyb, plug into the sim," General Sokolov commands.

"Copy that," the robots answer in unison, and my skin prickles at the surreal sound of their voices. It's the first time I've heard them speak, and I never realized until now that Cyb is programmed masculine, Dot feminine.

"Finalists, lower your headsets to your eyes in three . . . two . . . one. Remember, we aren't expecting you to know exactly what to do. We're looking to test your instincts."

I catch one last glimpse of Asher, Katerina, and Suki, watching us with rapt attention. And then I slip the mask over my eyes.

A cry of amazement escapes me as I look up to find myself floating in an inky black sky. A majestic, colorful spinning sphere looms far in the distance above me, casting its bright shadow over the darkness. *Jupiter.* Even at hundreds of miles away, the gas giant dominates the sky. It's a few moments before I can tear my eyes away and take in the rest of my surroundings.

I am hovering on the edge of one of the *Pontus*'s outer modules, my feet skimming a platform between the side of the ship and the glowing wing of a solar panel. When I glance down, it appears my clothing has transformed from the ISTC uniform to a heavyweight space suit, with a thick tether cord running from my suit's harness to a handlebar on the module. I spot a flicker of movement across from me, and then Beckett appears, crouching on the opposite solar panel. A crackling sound comes over my headset.

"Houston is reporting a damaged solar array interfering with our power supply." General Sokolov's voice echoes over the radio. "Leo and Beckett, we need you to find and cut the snagged wire and install the stabilizers—you'll find the tools in your equipment belts, with step-by-step instructions downloaded to your wrist monitors. Do you copy?"

"Copy," Beckett answers, and I'm quick to echo him. But inside my suit, I'm sweating at the realization that I have no idea what I'm doing—and he is the last teammate I'd ever choose to depend on for help.

"Naomi, with your computer skills, we've put you on the robotic Canadarm, positioned in front of our External Multiplexer-Demultiplexer. Please run diagnostics on the computer and confirm all systems a go for approach to Europa."

"Copy that." Naomi's voice crinkles over the radio, and I glance up, my eyes widening at the sight of her balancing on the edge of a moving crane, swinging above the *Pontus*.

"Approaching the first solar array," Beckett says, and I refocus on the golden panel in front of me, crossing toward it in the short, bouncy steps my tether allows as I fight against the change in gravity. I am first to spot the torn layer of solar cells, and I reach into the tool belt attached to my suit, pulling out a long wire that matches the image blinking on my wrist monitor screen. And then I feel something smack against my shoulder.

Beckett has caught up to me, the force of his motion knocking the tool out of my hands. The wire spins, floating away from me into the vacuum of space. I curse under my breath as Beckett sidles up to the torn array, ready to make this task his triumph alone.

"General Sokolov, I'm getting warning signals from the external computer. They're coming through in Morse code and binary." Naomi's voice returns, muffled by a piercing, arrhythmic beeping in the background. "The message is, *Incoming meteorites at direction nine o'cl—*"

But before she can even finish her sentence, the stillness of space is broken by a flood of shards as meteorites come flying through the air toward us. I scramble backward, away from the solar panel and toward the module, but I'm too late—the rocks slice at my tether, and I shout into the void as my body is flung adrift from the *Pontus*.

"My tether's gone!" I yell into the radio, before remembering the general's instructions from the VR lab. *Use the jetpacks.*

I press down on my joystick, pointing myself back in the direction of the spacecraft and triggering the thrust. But I didn't realize how powerful the jetpack's force would be; it knocks the breath from my lungs. I weave and duck past the flying shrapnel, but I can't get the hang of the pressure controls. Each push of my trigger blasts me too far, and now I'm spiraling through the air like an orbiter, moving too fast to feel my own limbs.

"Leo, slow down!" I hear Naomi shout through my headset. "You have to ignite a shorter thrust and redirect your position to three o'clock—" She breaks off with a scream, and I look around wildly, following her directions and maneuvering the thrusters with shaky hands, until I finally see the Canadarm through the shower of meteorites—cracked in two from the blast. Naomi dangles off the edge, reaching toward one of the handlebars on the *Pontus* module as the crane starts to whip around like a spinning top, but her gloves only grasp at air.

"Beckett, a little help, please!" I snap through my headset, before radioing the general again. "Naomi and I are both detached from the spacecraft. I'm using my propellers to launch toward her." But Sokolov remains unresponsive, and I think I know why.

"I'm caught under the battery module," Beckett groans, and I turn to see a figure in the distance hanging upside down from the spacecraft, his foot stuck in wire netting while his hand fumbles for his tool belt.

"Hang on!" Naomi calls out. "Looks like I can operate the Canadarm through my wrist monitor. Even with the arm broken, if I can just direct this piece of the crane to swing in the right direction, I can grab you both and we can make a jump for the airlock. Leo, can you close the distance with your jetpack? Aim for six o'clock."

"On it!" I yell back, determination setting in as I push down on my joystick. *This time had better work*. I lunge forward through the void, using every spare ounce of my strength and coordination to direct my hurtling body toward the spinning robotic arm as it shifts direction, flailing toward the *Pontus*. Naomi reaches out, and my glove grasps hers.

"Almost there," she says with a smile, and for a moment I'm mesmerized by her composure under pressure. But then the crane swings again, and I clamber on top of it in the nick of time, Naomi grabbing hold of my waist as the Canadarm whirls closer and closer to the *Pontus*.

"We're about to drop down to the battery module, Beckett!" Naomi shouts. "Get your tether ready for us, and we'll cut you loose and make it to the airlock together."

But Beckett is one step ahead of us. As we circle closer to the module, I can see he's managed to unearth a steel cutter from his tool belt with his free hand, and is slicing through the netting. Once extricated, he starts pulling his way across the spacecraft from handle to handle—heading for the airlock without us.

"Beckett, she said to wait!" I yell through the radio.

"This way makes more sense," he argues. "I can get to the airlock faster and prep it for opening, so we don't waste time there."

Naomi and I exchange a glance. We know what he's really up to—angling to be first, to win the challenge.

"If we don't jump now, we'll miss it," she says, gripping my glove in hers. "Engage the thrusters one last time."

I can feel my heart clanging as we let go of the crane, our two bodies propelling through open space with a gust of fuel. My free hand claws in front of me for one of the handles or knobs to break our fall, and then *smack*. My glove grips something solid, my feet scratch against metal—

"And that's a wrap. Welcome back to Earth."

A voice cuts through the scene. I shake my head to rid myself of the sound, still trying to get to the airlock . . . until it disappears from view. Someone lifts the mask from my eyes, but I'm not fully in the real world yet. My hand is still in Naomi's, my feet kicking the legs of my chair as I try to make our way to safety. When I finally open my eyes, the sight of the room and its equipment is a relief and yet, somehow, seems all wrong. Naomi and I drop each other's hands, and I notice a flush creeping up her cheeks.

"That was—that felt so real." I blink up at General Sokolov standing before us. "I almost forgot it was just a sim."

She nods approvingly. "That's the idea. Our technology works with your consciousness to make the simulation as immersive and authentic as possible."

"But why did it stop before we got to the airlock?" Beckett asks with a frown. "I was so close."

Yeah, you were. I shoot him a glare. *Traitor.*

"I saw what I needed to see," the general says, a cryptic expression on her face. "Now, all three of you did well and displayed strong instincts, but one of you in particular stood out. Cyb, I take it we're on the same page?"

I hold my breath as the robot unplugs from the VR grid and wires, turning to face us. "For the ability to read and decipher machine code, the understanding of velocity and propulsion mechanisms, and ability to think on her feet, the winner of this round is the American: Naomi Ardalan."

I watch as Beckett's face turns to stone, and Naomi's flush deepens. And to my surprise, as much as I wanted to win . . . hearing her name feels almost as good.

That night in the cafeteria, something is different. The buffet counters are dark, with none of the usual savory smells wafting through the room.

"What do you think is going on?" I ask Asher as we head to our table.

"No idea, but let's hope nothing's wrong. I've been dreaming about this meal all day." He rubs his stomach hopefully.

We slide into our seats as Dr. Takumi enters the room, stepping up to the raised faculty platform and looming above us all with his rodlike posture and fixed gaze.

"From now on, dinner will be pushed back half an hour—however, you are all still required to meet here at the usual time so we can incorporate something vital into our schedule. It has to do with the RRB." His voice takes on an almost reverent tone as he says the name.

"Radiation-resistant bacteria is the foremost reason the twenty-four of you are sitting here. Not only does the advent of the RRB make it possible for us to finally explore Jupiter orbit without risking deadly radiation exposure, but the vaccine's age limit caused us to seek out a new pool of astronauts . . . and find you." His eyes rove over the crowd, and my senses heighten as his glance lands on me.

"Those of you who make the Final Six will be required to self-administer daily injections of the RRB as soon as you enter the solar system's radiation belt," Dr. Takumi continues. "Not only will the RRB protect you during spaceflight, but it shields your body from Europa's extremely hazardous rays—so missing a single dose could be catastrophic. That's why we must use this time, the last days on Earth for six of you, to gauge your reactions to the experimental serum. If any of your bodies are going to react adversely . . . now is the time to find out."

He clears his throat. "That said, each of you will receive nightly preemptive shots of the RRB, starting now. We've set up a small outpost for the NASA medical officer here on the Hab floor, just down the hall. That's where you'll line up every night before dinner to get your shots. Team leaders, please escort your finalists there now."

"Well, this is interesting," Asher says as we rise to our feet. He looks almost as uneasy as I feel. It never even occurred to me that some of us might not be able to tolerate the RRB. *Please don't let me be one of them.*

We follow Lark and the rest of our fellow finalists out of the cafeteria and down a carpeted corridor, until we reach a pocket-size, sterile white room. A petite woman in a lab coat stands by the door, clipboard in hand.

"All right, who's ready to go first?" she calls out in greeting.

No one answers, not even the most competitive among us. Instead, most of the Twenty-Four jostle for a spot at the end of the line. It seems I'm not the only one here who's creeped out by needles. Still, it occurs to me now that volunteering to go first could be a mark in my favor—and I'll take any slight edge I can get. I raise my hand, and the medic beckons me through the open door.

She motions for me to have a seat before slipping on a pair of latex gloves and filtering a glowing blue liquid into a hypodermic needle. As she preps my arm for the puncture, I look out at the crowd of finalists, watching us warily as they wait their turn. My eyes meet Naomi's.

It might be that I feel closer to her because of what we experienced together in today's training sim, or because she's the only person here who knows my sister's name. Either way, finding her face in the crowd is like a breath of relief. She smiles at me, and as the nurse plunges the needle into my arm, I hardly feel the sting.

But then Naomi's gaze shifts, something pulling her attention behind me. It's the row of blue vials, lining the office wall. I can almost see her mind at work as she studies them, her eyes narrowing, and my curiosity stirs.

What does she know that the rest of us don't?

TEN

NAOMI

THE SCREAM SLICES THE AIR OF OUR DORM ROOM. I WAKE WITH a jolt as my roommate lets out a second earsplitting shriek, thrashing and kicking against her mattress. My fingers shake as I fumble for the light switch.

"Suki! Wake up!"

But she won't stir. I jump out of my bed and run to hers. Suki's face is pale and glassy, her forehead slicked with sweat. I'm startled to find her eyes open, with only the whites showing, and I shrink back, suddenly afraid . . . of what, I don't know.

"*No*—don't go, *don't go!*" she wails, tears streaking down her cheeks.

I can't let her continue like this. I reach for her arm, but she automatically slaps my hand away. She must be fighting something in her dream, and right now I am the stand-in. I'm bound to get hit again if I stay this close, but I have no choice. Her screams are agonizing, like sharp fingernails scratching at a bloody scab, and I use all my strength to shake her back into consciousness.

"Wake up!" I shout in her ear, gripping her shoulders. "Suki, wake *up*!"

It does the trick. She blinks, dazed and panting as she takes in her surroundings. And then, meeting my eyes, she starts to cry—the kind of unrestrained, racking sobs I never would have expected from someone as calm and collected as Suki.

"It's okay," I whisper, placing my hand over hers. "You're okay. It was just a dream."

She shakes her head violently.

"It wasn't," she chokes out through her tears. "It was the same nightmare I'm forced to remember every day. Only . . . only I've never dreamed it like that, so vivid and full of every horrific detail—" She breaks off, crying too hard to speak.

"What do you mean?" I ask, fearing her response. What if I'm the wrong person to help her? I don't know what to do—

"I watched my mom and siblings die. I saw the whole thing, and I couldn't stop it."

My hand flies to my mouth.

"One minute I was in the kitchen cleaning my drunk of a stepfather's mess, watching my mom and brother and sister play bocce ball through the window, and the next . . ." Fresh tears spill from her eyes. "You wouldn't believe what I was thinking then. I was worried about what would happen when I went back to school, when I'd have to leave the three of them at his mercy. I was so distracted worrying about a future they would never have—that I missed my split-second chance to save them. I heard the sound of the roar, and I wasn't quick enough to recognize it as a warning."

I squeeze her hand, my heart in my throat as she speaks. I wonder if I should interrupt and tell her she doesn't have to say any more, not if it's too painful to remember. But something in her voice lets me know that she needs this, and I stay silent.

"The wave looked like a hundred-foot cobra, arched and ready to strike." Suki's voice drops to a whisper. "By the time I saw it, it was too late. The tsunami had already seized my family and everyone else on the beachfront, sweeping them all out to sea. The water came pouring in, crushing the front door and chasing my stepfather upstairs, but I let it carry me outside. I swam against the current, searching for my family—but there was no hope. All I saw were piles of bodies and upturned boats slicing the faces of the drowned. I've tried to wipe that image from my mind, but I can't, I *can't.*"

"I'm sorry—I'm so sorry." I throw my arms around her, realizing that I am crying too. My stomach churns and my chest aches as I imagine what she went through. Her words trigger my memories of seeing the tsunami all over the news, the horror my family and I felt at the photos of the carnage. But by the next day, there was a new disaster to report, and the world quickly moved on from mourning Singapore. You become numb to the daily tragedies, until the next one happens to you.

As I look at Suki, and think of Leo and Jian, I can't help seeing the Europa Mission in a different light. If it worked, what an *escape* it would be . . . But I am too scientific for blind faith. I wish I could believe in the mission, I wish I could forget what my hypothesis and my gut are telling me about Jupiter's moon. But I can't.

"Where did you go after?" I ask, wiping my eyes. "What did you do?"

Suki shakes her head bitterly.

"I didn't have a choice. I had to stay with the drunk, because I was still a minor and had no money of my own. I thought it would be just a few more months stuck with him in that house, and then I'd go back to university and be gone for good." Her eyes drop. "But I soon found out the university went under, too."

"So this is the first time you've left since . . ." My voice trails off, and she nods.

"Yes. And now that I've gotten away, I'm *never* going back. I'm going to make the Final Six, or I'll die trying."

"I understand," I murmur, wrapping my arm around her. She leans her limp head on my shoulder, exhausted from the conversation. But her forehead is burning, and I sit up in alarm.

"Suki . . . are you feeling sick?"

She shrugs slightly, and I press my palm to her forehead. "You're burning up. I should call the medic—"

"I just need sleep." Suki bats my hand away and sinks under the covers. "Don't call anyone, okay?"

"Okay," I sigh. "I'm going to get you a cold compress though."

I throw on a sweatshirt over my pj's, and I'm almost out the door when Suki sleepily calls my name.

"Thank you. For being a friend, even though I haven't exactly been the warmest." She takes a breath. "I guess I was afraid to get close to anyone I'm competing against."

I turn around, my insides constricting at her tearstained face. "It's okay. I understand—and you can count on me."

Morning dawns and Suki is still pale and feverish, with a fiery red rash running down her arm. I bite my nails with worry as I stare at her.

"This looks serious, Suki. Please, just let me take you to the medical office."

"No. I can't let the judges find out and decide I'm too weak for the draft," she argues. "Especially now that we only have a couple weeks to prove ourselves before the first eliminations. I just have to get through today without it being obvious there's anything wrong with me, and then hopefully this—this flu will go away."

So she hasn't suspected that it's more than just the flu. Either that, or she's in denial. I wonder if I should tell her my opinion, if maybe that will convince her to see the nurse, but I keep my mouth shut, afraid to stress her further. Instead I help Suki apply concealer to her puffy eyes and lend her a long-sleeved tee to wear under her ISTC shirt, before giving her my arm to lean on as we walk to the cafeteria. She stumbles on our way down the hall, and I stop to steady her.

"Are you feeling dizzy?" I ask.

She hesitates before nodding.

"Suki, *please* let me—"

"No way." She cuts me off. "You know why I can't risk getting cut. I can't go home."

I rub my face with my hands, torn. "Okay, fine. Just stay close to me all day."

She squeezes my arm. "Thank you."

I link my arm with hers as we step into the cafeteria, and when it's time to hit the buffet line, I order for her, grabbing every high-protein item on offer. Back at the table, our teammates are busy quizzing Lark about her astronaut years, and I think Suki and I are doing a reasonably good job of pulling off our act—until Leo leans in across from me.

"What's wrong with her?" he whispers.

"Um . . ." I glance around me. Leo and I are at the far end of the table, and the others are still absorbed in their conversation, paying little attention to us. I could tell him without them overhearing, and it would be a relief . . . but am I certain I can trust him?

I turn to Suki, who's now dragging her spoon through a bowl of oatmeal as if it requires colossal effort. She's right beside me, and at the same time, she seems to be somewhere else.

"Naomi." Leo looks at me knowingly. "I know something's up. You don't have to tell me, but just let me know if I can help."

I close my eyes. God, I would love some help. I lean across the table until our faces are so close I can feel his breath against my cheek. And I whisper, "I think she's having a reaction to the RRB. But you can't tell anyone." I pull back in time to see the alarm register on Leo's face.

"But if she's sick, shouldn't we get her some help?"

"Believe me, I said the same thing. But for now at least, we have to do as she asked and not say a word. I don't want to be the one to blow her chances of making the Final Six."

It hits me how ironic my words are. If my brother were here, he would tell me I'd be doing Suki a *favor* by risking her spot in the draft and keeping her here on Earth. But now, knowing what she's been through, what so many of my fellow finalists have suffered on our planet . . . I feel my conviction starting to waver.

Today's first training period takes us to the third-floor Altitude Chamber: a cavernous space made almost entirely out of ice. It looks like an empty indoor igloo, with nothing but scattered orange cones and piled blocks of ice filling the space. Lark passes out thick puffer jackets before dropping us off, and I feel a sprig of hope that maybe this cold is just what Suki needs—maybe it can break her fever.

"What's up with her?" Beckett asks loudly, watching as Suki holds on to my arm, leaning most of her body weight against me. I feel my shoulders stiffen in defense.

"She didn't sleep well last night. That's all."

Lieutenant Barnes, our instructor from the diving tank, is waiting for us inside, this time dressed in snow-weather gear. And he's not alone. Dot is with him, the robot's artificial eyes roving over each one of us.

"Welcome to the Altitude Chamber," the lieutenant greets us, with a sweep of his hands. "The space we're standing in is a NASA-engineered replica of Thera Macula, the ice-surface terrain where the Final Six will land when they reach Europa."

A ripple of excitement runs through my teammates. Katerina does a little spin on the ice, managing to make it look elegant even in tennis shoes. "It feels like home," I hear her murmur to Asher before Lieutenant Barnes continues.

"In preparing for any mission, astronauts-in-training will generally spend two hours a day exercising, three times a week, to prepare their bodies for the physical changes that occur in space. We often put them through military-grade obstacle courses, in addition to the standard gym routines. At the same time, our scientists develop altitude chambers like this one to help astronauts' bodies adjust to the environment they'll be entering. However, in your case, with so much training we need to pack into so little time, we've decided to kill two birds with one stone: by combining the physical challenge of a military obstacle course with the

Europa Altitude Chamber."

I exchange a nervous glance with Suki. Could there *be* worse timing for a training session like this?

"Europa has no atmosphere, which means no wind or weather—so you'll be safe from all the climate-related crises that plague us on Earth." Lieutenant Barnes pauses, smiling at my teammates' reaction to that. "There are only two environmental issues on Europa that we're aware of. The first is the occurence of icequakes, which should feel similar to a low-grade earthquake. The second are known as water eruptions: when shifting tectonic plates cause enormous plumes of water to shoot out of the ice. While these events might sound unsettling, both are fairly mild compared to what we've been through here on Earth."

I eye the lieutenant suspiciously. How can he say that with any authority, when he's never experienced either of those things for himself? Besides, even if these are the only environmental issues they're "aware of," how soon will it be before the hands of humans wreak havoc on this new world, just as we did on Earth? I'm beginning to wonder who should be more afraid: us of Europa's unknowns and its potential intelligent life . . . or them of humans and our tendency to destroy.

"To complete the course, you'll run sprints around the path of orange cones and jump over the ice-block hurdles, dodging any simulated icequakes or water plume eruptions that may occur," Lieutenant Barnes instructs us. "Your challenge is to make it through the obstacles without falling, and without touching the water or the cones. You'll complete the course in pairs, and whoever has the fastest time and fewest deductions at the end wins. Got it?"

I cringe. This is an athletic feat beyond my comfort zone—and way beyond what Suki is capable of right now.

She turns to me in panic. "I—I can't mess up," she gasps. "I need to win."

I resist the urge to tell her *that's* not about to happen in her state. "Let's be partners," I suggest instead. "I'll go at your speed, so you don't seem off compared to the others."

"Thank you," she says, her face flooding with relief. "I can't thank you enough."

"No problem," I tell her, though a small voice in my mind reminds me of Dr. Takumi's warning. What if I'm not a good enough actress to pull this off—what if they figure out that I'm throwing the game on purpose? Then again . . . my paltry athletic skills could come in handy here. It won't take that much effort to make Suki look decent.

"All right, line up in pairs!"

Leo and Asher stand at the head of the line, with Katerina and Beckett right behind them, and me and Suki going last. I watch, nerves mounting, as Leo and Asher take off the second Lieutenant Barnes blows the whistle. The two of them weave around the cones at a breakneck speed, occasionally slipping on the ice but catching themselves before they touch the ground. And then the first icequake hits. I'm not even *in* the obstacle course and my body sways, hands gripping my knees to keep from falling over and dragging

Suki down with me. Asher hits the ground, but Leo keeps running, leaping over one of the ice blocks with such confidence that I can't look away. Asher gets to his feet, and I hear Katerina cheering him on as he catches up, running to the hurdles. Just as Leo soars over the second-to-last hurdle, a four-foot-high gust of water bursts from the floor. I gasp, but he doesn't stop moving, his face a mask of determination. Another blast of water hits right before his final jump, and in one of the most stunning sights I've ever seen, Leo takes a flying leap, soaring above the water plume and hitting the finish line.

"Wow," I whisper.

Asher finishes not far behind, and then the whistle blows for Katerina and Beckett. Knowing we're next has me too jittery to watch, and instead I attempt to give Suki a pep talk.

"Once we get out there, for these next few minutes, just try to block out whatever you're feeling, okay? Pretend you're as good as on your healthiest day, and just . . . just go kick ass."

She nods, but her eyes are distant, her face sweaty even in this cold. My heart sinks.

"And . . . next!"

"That's us," I say with a gulp. "Let's get in position."

Suki and I assume the runner's stance at the starting line, my muscles tensing in anticipation. When the whistle blows, I hang back a split second to let her go first, and then I follow. Running on ice is harder than it looks, and when the ground below me rattles from the first icequake, I fall smack on my butt. Hoisting myself back up, I spot Suki making a valiant effort, her hands gripping her shins to keep from falling in the quake. I resist the urge to cheer her on and I keep running until the water plume hits. My feet slide out from under me, and I tumble back down onto the ice.

"Come *on,* ladies!" Beckett shouts from the sidelines. "Way to represent America, Naomi."

I grit my teeth. That obnoxious sonofa—

A sickening crash sounds, echoing through the chamber like shattered glass. My heart nearly stops at the sight of Suki crumpled at the side of the ice block, having failed to clear the hurdle. I scramble upright and run at full speed for the first time today, until I reach her. Her face is contorted in pain.

"Are you okay? I'm so sorry, I should never have let you—"

Lieutenant Barnes swoops down, interrupting my babbling. "Let's take a look at that ankle," he says as Suki manages to sit up.

"I'm okay," she wheezes. "It's just a light sprain. I'm fine, really."

I close my eyes briefly. Is she seriously going to refuse help *again*? I feel a gentle pressure on my shoulder, and I turn around. It's Leo, his blue eyes full of concern. The rest of our teammates crowd around Lieutenant Barnes and Suki, but Leo is here for me. I step off to the side so we can talk alone.

"I don't know what to do," I tell him under my breath. "I told her I'd help her, but . . ."

"But something is clearly wrong." He finishes my sentence. "And not because she missed the jump. That could happen to anyone. It's the way she . . . *is* today."

I know just what he means. Our poised, laser-focused teammate is like a different person ever since last night—since the RRB. I turn to look back at Suki, who is hobbling to her feet with the help of Lieutenant Barnes.

"She's done," someone says behind me, and I whip around to find Beckett, watching the scene with a patronizing look on his face. "Her head's clearly not in the game."

"Will you just shut up?" Leo snaps at him, and I feel a rush of gratitude.

Beckett raises his eyebrows at Leo. "I would have thought you would be glad for a little less competition."

"Then you weren't paying attention, because I just beat your time out there," Leo shoots back. "If anyone needs lighter competition, it's not me."

"You only 'beat' me by two seconds," Beckett scoffs. "I'd call it more of a coin toss. Besides, you've already shown all you've got. I'm just getting warmed up."

"*Right*. That's what all second-place finishers say."

As much as I love watching Leo take the jerk down, I don't want to leave Suki alone with the others for much longer. I grab his arm. "Let's go find out how she's doing."

We turn our backs on Beckett and return to Suki, who forces a smile when she sees us.

"Sorry about all that. I was just—just telling Lieutenant Barnes that my ankle really doesn't hurt badly enough to bother with the medic. I'll try to rest it today, and I'm sure I'll be better by tomorrow."

"I appreciate the spirit," Lieutenant Barnes says with a nod. "That's what we like to see here at ISTC. I'll tell Lark to keep you off your feet today, but I'll expect you back in fighting form tomorrow."

"Absolutely." Suki beams, and I have to admire her performance. Maybe that fall knocked the zombie-like symptoms out of her—she certainly seems more alert and eager now. Or . . . maybe that's just how desperate she is to stay. The need trumps everything, even agonizing pain.

"Back to work!" Lieutenant Barnes calls out, gathering everyone toward him. "I have the final scores based on your times. Coming in last, with an incomplete, is Suki, preceded by Naomi in fifth, also with an incomplete."

The two of us exchange a miserable glance, even though the results aren't exactly a surprise. I hear Beckett stifle a snort, and I have a sudden urge to kick something.

"In fourth place, with a time of four minutes and thirty seconds, is Asher. Katerina takes third with four minutes even."

The question is, *why* am I so frustrated? I wanted Suki to do well, not me. I've already gotten more attention here than I intended, considering my ultimate goal is to go home. But the defeat leaves a sour taste in my mouth. Is it possible . . . am I actually getting swept up in the competition of it all?

"And in second place, we have Beckett with a time of three minutes, forty seconds. That makes Leo our winner, coming in at just three minutes, thirty-eight seconds!"

Everyone applauds—except Beckett, of course. Leo smiles broadly. I smile back.

Suki seems to inch closer to normal as the day wears on—still a little too pale, and sweating even under the blast of the AC, but I can see the life coming back into her eyes. Still, when six thirty rolls around and it's time to line up for our second shot of the RRB, I urge her yet again to tell the nurse about her symptoms. "I mean, doesn't it seem a little . . . unwise to get another dose without telling them how you've been feeling since last night?"

Suki remains stubborn as ever.

"I told you—I *have* to make the Final Six. I can't go back. And if I give them any reason to think I'm not as strong as the others here, then it's over for me."

And so I watch, holding my breath, as she gets another dose of the serum. Leo gives me a questioning look, but he doesn't say anything either, both of us guarding her secret . . . for better or worse.

We proceed from the medical office to the cafeteria for dinner, and it's as odd a segue as you could imagine, going from injections to the British menu of bangers and mash. Once we're seated in front of full plates, Dr. Takumi makes a surprise announcement—the kind I've been waiting for since the moment I arrived.

“After the meal, team leaders will escort you to the library for your first weekly video-chat with your families. All of your next of kin have been notified and will be waiting by their computers at the designated time—”

The whoops and cheers from all four cafeteria tables nearly drown him out. The thought of *finally* getting to see and speak to Sam and my parents has me giddy, too overcome to eat another bite. Katerina and Asher beam as they launch into an animated conversation about who from their hometowns they expect to see in their video-chats, while Beckett joins in half-heartedly. I’m amazed he’s not taking the opportunity to gloat about webcamming with the White House, and I’m about to whisper as much to Leo when I notice his crushed expression. Suki pushes her full plate away, her eyes trained on the floor, and my heart twists for them both. There can’t be anything worse than knowing that the only people who matter won’t be there on the other side of the screen.

“I don’t have to go, do I?” Leo asks Lark under his breath.

“You want to stand up your date?” Lark raises an eyebrow at him, and Leo stares at her in confusion.

“I don’t have a next of kin,” he says. “So I figured . . .”

“That you wouldn’t have a video-chat? Not a chance,” Lark says with a grin. “We received a *very* impassioned letter from a certain Elena Vincenti asking for communication privileges with you. I couldn’t say no to a letter like that.” She lowers her voice to a conspiratorial tone. “And her being the prime minister's daughter certainly helped me get a yes from Dr. Takumi!"

My face turns strangely hot as I listen, though I don't know why I care. So what if he has a girlfriend back home?

"The PM's daughter?" Beckett cocks an eyebrow. "You're a dark horse."

"It's not like—" Leo starts, his cheeks reddening, but Asher interrupts.

"Own it, man." He fist-bumps Leo, and I feel my insides go twitchy with irritation. And for the first time since we met, the sight of Leo's smile makes me feel worse instead of better.

By the time we make it to the library for our turn at the computers, I'm practically bursting out of my skin. I can't stop fidgeting as Lark sets up the video-chat monitors and logs each of us in; I wait impatiently for her to finish getting Katerina set up before coming around to my seat. Finally I'm logged in, my eager face staring back at me from the left-hand corner of the screen. And then—

"Naomi!!"

"*Azizam!*"

Sam and my parents' faces fill the screen, and as I gaze at them, it's like taking my first real breath after days underwater. My eyes fill with tears as I forget everyone else in this room, forget everything but them.

"It's so good to see you," I manage to choke out. "I miss you so much."

"Not as much as we miss you," Mom says, placing her hand up to the screen.

"How are you, sweetie?" Dad asks, and I notice he's wearing the fuzzy green sweater I got him for Father's Day. I'd give anything to be able to reach through the computer and hug him.

"I—I'm okay. I can't stand being away from you guys—it's just as hard as I thought it would be. But luckily I made a couple of friends here, and that helps a little."

"Of course you did," Sam says with a wistful smile.

"That reminds me. We have something to show you," Dad says, his voice rising in excitement. I hear him fumbling offscreen, and then he holds up a copy of *Time* magazine. "Incredible, right?"

I suck in my breath. It's *us,* the Twenty-Four, on the cover of the magazine—under a bold headline that reads, "The Teenagers Saving the Human Race."

"Wow," I murmur. It's surreal to see me and my teammates on the cover of a magazine—but more than pride, the sight fills me with fear. Fear that we're leading on the public, lifting their hopes too high, when there's no guarantee our story won't end differently from the *Athena* disaster—or that Europa won't turn out to be every bit as perilous as Earth.

"They devoted the most space to you and Beckett Wolfe," Sam adds, taking the magazine from Dad and flipping through the pages until he finds what he's looking for. He holds an article up to the screen, a feature titled "The

First Nephew and the Iranian-American Prodigy," with a glossy photo of me and Beckett standing stiffly next to each other on arrival day.

"Knowing how President Wolfe feels about immigrants, he must *love* all the attention on our heritage." Dad laughs.

"That's true," I say with a smile. Beckett is probably just as thrilled to have to share all his press with me. I know it's petty, but I can't help feeling a flicker of satisfaction at the annoyance this headline will cause him.

"Enough about me, though. I've been dying to know how you guys are doing." I peer closer at the three of them. "Sam, how are you feeling?"

"I'm okay. Going to all my appointments and taking my meds. You don't need to worry, Sis," he says with a wry grin.

But as I study him through the screen, I feel a wave of anxiety. He looks even thinner than when I left, and there's no hiding the weariness in his eyes.

"Are you resting enough? Eating enough? I thought families of the Twenty-Four were supposed to get extra food—"

"Yes to all three," Sam says, chuckling. "*I'm* fine—but I can see space camp hasn't changed you a bit."

I try to smile, to shake the feeling that his reassurance is just a put-on for my benefit.

"We're taking great care of him, sweetie. Don't worry," Mom says, wrapping her arm around Sam. I feel a pang in my chest at the sight of them, so close while I'm an impenetrable distance away.

"What's it like over there? Are you enjoying yourself at all?" Dad asks, looking at me hopefully.

"Actually . . . yeah, sometimes. The training we've done so far is pretty incredible. It's like we're in Hogwarts for space, but instead of teaching us magic, they're preparing us to get kicked off the planet." I laugh. "I'll have a ton of stories for you when I come home."

In the silence that falls, I can almost hear them all tweaking my sentence in their minds: "If *you come home*."

"So, did you open my letter?" Sam asks, trying to sound casual.

I know the real question he's asking: Do I plan to use the flash drive with the hacking software, and am I making progress on my true mission—to return to them, to stay on Earth? I have to assure him that I'm keeping my promise to come home, without giving myself away if Lark or anyone else overhears.

"I did, and in answer to your question . . . I'm still figuring it out," I reply. "But I will."

My parents are clearly confused, but before they can ask what we're talking about, Lark signals for our attention.

"Time to log off. It's the next team's turn at the computers."

My stomach plummets. We *can't* be done so soon—and I can't fathom the thought of only ever seeing my family like this, in painfully short bursts through a computer monitor.

"I love you guys," I say, swallowing the lump in my throat. "I don't want to say good-bye."

"We love you more, *azizam*," Dad says gruffly, and I can tell he's getting choked up. Mom's eyes are watery as she blows kisses through the screen, and Sam gives me the goofy secret hand signal we made up in elementary school. I thought he'd forgotten it, and I laugh through my tears.

"Love you, Sis. I really miss you."

And then the screen turns black, its emptiness leaving me with renewed resolve.

I have to set a plan in motion.

ELEVEN

LEO

THERE'S A BANGING AT MY DOOR, A SHOUTING THAT PIERCES through my dreams. I wake with a start, blinking at the clock beside me as it flashes 3:30. Did I imagine the noise? What could be going on at this hour?

But then I hear a familiar voice cry out for help, and I throw the covers off me. I step into the first pair of pants I can find and open the door.

It's Naomi. As soon as she sees me, her face crumples.

"Suki's in trouble," she gasps. "Everything was fine, I thought she was getting better, and then—then—"

Asher joins us in the doorway, rubbing his eyes.

"What's going on?"

"Something's happened to Suki," I tell him. "Let's go."

The three of us run down the dark corridor to the girls' wing, a few bleary-eyed finalists peeking their heads out of their rooms at the sound of the commotion, until we're standing at the door to Naomi and Suki's room. I can hear a strangled sound coming from inside, and Naomi hesitates before opening the door.

"I—I should prepare you. It's really bad—"

"It's okay," Asher tells her. "I was in the military, and Leo . . ." His voice trails off, but I know where his sentence leads. *Leo's whole family died. He can handle a sick teammate.*

"Come on," I tell Naomi. She gulps and opens the door—and my whole body tenses in panic.

A wild animal is convulsing on the bed, shaking and foaming at the mouth. Her head snaps in our direction as we enter, and she opens her mouth to speak, to yell—but all that comes out are garbled sounds. The effort seems to agitate her more, and now she's rattling the bedframe with her shaking, her skin turning a bluish-gray hue. This isn't Suki—it can't be.

"I've never seen anything like this." Naomi stares at the bed in terror. "At first I thought it was a seizure, but it's only getting worse. I wanted to take her to the medic, but I can't lift her by myself, and you're not supposed to move someone when they're having a seizure—if that's even what this is." She breaks off, shaking her head helplessly, and I turn to Asher.

"Go get help, okay? Try and make it back as fast as you

can." I sound far stronger than I feel, and Asher nods, looking relieved to have something to do. As he races out of the room, I take a few tentative steps toward Suki.

"It's—it's going to be okay," I stammer, though I know she's not listening. She's too far gone. "Help is coming, and—"

In the space of a breath, Suki reaches up and seizes both my wrists. Her force catches me off guard, and I shout out as she presses her fingernails into my skin.

"What's she doing?" Naomi cries.

"I—don't know—how did she—get—so strong?" I choke out.

"*Tā hái huózhe*." Suki stares at me with frantic eyes and repeats the phrase in a distorted voice. "*Tā hái huózhe*."

"It's Mandarin," Naomi pants. "Please tell me you understand Mandarin."

I shake my head.

"*Tā hái huózhe*," Suki says again, this time in a whisper. And then she drops my wrists—and her body turns limp.

"No!" Naomi screams, running to her side. I drop my head in my hands, dreading the moment that I know is coming. I can't see another dead body, not another person—

"She's breathing!" Naomi holds two fingers against her pulse, and relief floods through me. There's still a chance.

Footsteps come pounding toward us, and the door flies open. As Asher returns with Lark and Dr. Takumi in tow, Suki's body jerks forward, her convulsing recurring more violently than before. She pounds her head against the wall as she thrashes, still crying out the unfamiliar phrase, "*Tā hái huózhe.*" I can see tears in her eyes, and I turn to Dr. Takumi and Lark in desperation.

"What's happening to her?"

"And what's she saying?" Naomi demands from behind me. "Can you understand her?"

Lark's face drains of color as she takes in the scene. She turns to Dr. Takumi, who doesn't say a word either. He simply steps forward, his presence in the middle of the dorm room only adding to the heightened sense of fear—and he reaches for Suki. I hold my breath as he lifts her off the bed and she shrieks, her head whipping back and forth, her hands clawing at the air. Still managing to maintain his composure, Dr. Takumi reaches into his jacket pocket and pulls out a syringe.

"What are you do—" But before Naomi can get out her question, Dr. Takumi plunges the needle into Suki's skin. And everything turns quiet.

"This light sedative should do the trick," he says, tightening his grip around Suki. He moves toward the door, and Naomi jumps in front of him.

"Where you taking her? What's happening?"

"I'm afraid she's had an adverse reaction to the RRB," he says coolly. "I'm taking her to the larger medical facility at Johnson Space Center. We'll keep you updated as necessary."

The four of us watch as Dr. Takumi carries her away, until all that's left of Suki is the stench of fear. Lark sighs heavily.

"I'm sorry you all had to see that. When the body rejects

a vaccine, it can on occasion cause catatonic symptoms that are frightening to witness. But you can trust that Dr. Takumi is getting Suki the best care possible."

"If the RRB is so risky—" Naomi starts, but Lark cuts her off.

"For the vast majority of you, it isn't. Suki is the only one of the Twenty-Four to exhibit any symptoms."

So far, my mind adds. Could one of us be next?

"I know it'll be hard to sleep after this," she acknowledges. "But we have another busy day tomorrow, and you'll want to be well rested."

"Wait." Naomi looks at her in disbelief. "So no matter what happens to Suki, tomorrow is business as usual?"

"That's how it works in our field," Lark says. "At NASA, I trained with the crew of the *Athena*, and I saw some of my closest friends die. I was devastated, but I still had to show up to work. Our goals at NASA remained the same: to push the boundaries of space and find a new home for human life. That doesn't change when something bad happens." She moves toward the door. "And there's no reason to believe that anything irreparable happened tonight. If I know Dr. Takumi, he won't spare any expense to make sure Suki returns to her old self."

"Let's hope," Naomi murmurs under her breath.

"On that note," Lark continues, "I suggest we go back to our rooms and at least try to get some sleep."

"You guys go ahead," I tell them. "I'll be just a few more minutes."

Lark gives me a sideways look, but she doesn't try to stop me.

"Just don't make it much longer."

"Goodnight, Naomi. I—I hope you'll be okay," Asher says, his eyes flicking back to Suki's empty bed before following Lark out of the room. And then it's just the two of us.

I watch as Naomi crosses to her side of the room, decorated with photos and posters where Suki's is bare. She sinks to the floor, leaning against her bedframe with her head pressed to her knees.

"This is all my fault," she says dully. "I suspected something was wrong twenty-four hours ago. I shouldn't have listened to her. I could have *prevented* this."

"You don't know that," I say, clearing a space next to her on the floor. "Plus, it seemed like she was getting better. I thought she was over the worst of it when I saw her at dinner. How were you to know something like this would happen?"

"I shouldn't have let her get another injection," she continues, through gritted teeth. "Maybe she *was* getting better, but the second shot is what did it."

"This isn't your fault." I rest my hand on her arm. "You didn't create the RRB, and you didn't force her to take it. You tried to get her help and she refused. As someone who knows a thing or two about guilt . . ." I take a deep breath. "You have to let it go."

She is quiet for a moment. "Yeah. I guess you're right."

Her eyes roam back to Suki's empty bed. "There's no way I'm going to sleep tonight."

"I can . . . stay here with you. For as long as you want."

She smiles slightly. "Thank you. I really don't want to be alone right now."

I smile back, something stirring in my chest as I look at her.

"I need a distraction." Naomi sighs, leaning her head back against the bed. She glances at me out of the corner of her eye. "You know where I always wanted to go, before the floods?"

"Where?"

"Italy," she says. "I had this dream folder at home, where I'd store photos and articles of places I wanted to go, things I wanted to do. I pictured taking this victory trip with my brother one day, when he was all better. The plan was to spend three weeks going between Venice, Florence, Rome, and the Amalfi Coast, seeing all the landmarks and tasting all the regional dishes along the way." Her smile fades. "It would have been amazing."

"I wish you could have seen it too," I say quietly. "Maybe, if things had been different . . . we would have met there instead."

"Yeah." She is silent for a moment, and then she asks, "Will you tell me about it? Rome?"

A fist closes around my heart. It's been so long since I've let myself remember what it was really like—when the Colosseum and the Spanish Steps stood on dry land. When my family was alive. But the images are already rushing to my mind, and I hear myself start to speak.

"Maybe everyone thinks their city is the center of the world, but Rome really was. We had history right in our backyard—the Gladiators' stadium, Vatican City. We had Michelangelo, Fellini. But even with all the history, somehow it never felt old. The city was filled with loud, pulsing *life*. Everywhere you went, there were people of all ages in cafés and restaurants, out in the nightclubs, cheering in the streets for the football teams on game day. I loved the noise."

"Sounds awesome," Naomi says, closing her eyes. I can tell her body is relaxing, her tight shoulders loosening, and I continue.

"Even though it was technically a big city, there was a closeness among the locals. My neighbors were all involved in each other's lives. If I went out with a girl once, Mrs. Conti next door would ask about her for weeks afterward." I laugh. "My family's pensione hosted a regular Sunday lunch for the locals and hotel guests. We stuffed ourselves with six courses of food, and then my mother would sit at the piano and everyone would sing the classic Italian songs—the songs we all knew by heart. Sometimes we'd be there for hours. Angelica had an amazing voice. The rest of us were just loud, but she could really sing."

Naomi shifts a little closer to me, as I feel some part of myself leaving this room—returning home, bringing my family back to life. I look down at the Danieli signet ring on my finger, tracing the cursive letter *D* with my thumb.

"It was paradise. And . . . I guess I'm lucky I got to experience it, before it was all gone."

"It sounds like heaven." Naomi rests her head on my shoulder. We stay like that for minutes or hours—time seems to disappear—until the sound of her soft breathing lets me know she's managed to fall asleep.

As gently as I can, I lift her into my arms and onto the bed. She stirs but doesn't wake, and I pull the covers up around her.

"Goodnight, Naomi," I whisper.

I look at her onc last time. Her expression is so peaceful as she sleeps, as though the trauma we witnessed with Suki never happened.

I step out of the room, feeling my way through the dark back to the boys' dorm. All the while, her face remains imprinted in my mind.

I wake up a zombie the next morning, half delirious from barely any sleep. Asher and I get ready in a hurry, both of us anxious to sec if, by some miracle, Suki will be waiting for us at our team table for breakfast. But when we walk into the cafeteria, we find her seat empty. Lark and Dr. Takumi are missing, too.

"I guess she's still getting treatment," I tell Asher. "God, I hope she's okay."

I lock eyes with Naomi across the room, and I am suddenly wide awake. Asher and I slide into our seats, with me beside her.

"Hey," I say, giving her a small smile. "How are you doing?"

"Hi. I'm . . ." She shakes her head. "I don't know. I just want to find out what happened to my roommate."

As if on cue, Lark dashes into the cafeteria, followed by Dr. Takumi at a slower pace. Before Lark even makes it to her seat, Naomi, Asher, and I pounce on her with questions, while Katerina and Beckett listen curiously, the two of them still in the dark about Suki.

"Dr. Takumi will explain everything" is all Lark says. But from the look on her face, I have the sinking feeling that it's not good news.

Dr. Takumi strides to his perch at the front of the room and holds up his hands for silence. "I have an unfortunate announcement to make. As you may have noticed, one of our Twenty-Four is absent today. Regrettably, Suki Chuan had to be cut early, due to her suffering an adverse reaction to the RRB. She is no longer a finalist for the Europa Mission."

The news hits me like a blow. I turn to Naomi just as her expression crumbles. Gasps and exclamations of shock ripple through the cafeteria, and my stomach lurches at the realization that Suki is gone, her chance at a future ruined in one night.

"Where is she?" Naomi whispers to Lark, her lower lip quivering.

"Still at the medical center. It'll be some time before

she's back to her old self, but don't worry," Lark says. "She's getting the best care."

"To anyone concerned this might happen to you: the good news is that the odds of an allergic reaction to the RRB are still very slim. If you haven't experienced symptoms yet, chances are that your body is accepting the serum. However, what happened to Suki is the precise reason we monitor your reactions before you leave Earth." Dr. Takumi pauses, intensifying his gaze on all of us. "If you feel *anything* out of the ordinary, I expect you to come directly to me, or to your team leader. The last thing you want is a medical complication to arise on Europa—when you're largely on your own." He clears his throat. "And now, let's try to move beyond this unfortunate circumstance and start today on the right foot."

He gives the signal for us to line up at the buffet counter, but no one at our table moves. Even Beckett looks uncertain.

"Damn. One down already," he says, breaking the silence.

"She didn't deserve this." Naomi's voice breaks as she turns back to Lark. "When can we see her? We should at least go visit."

"Um, I'm not sure about that," Lark says, glancing away. "The medical center doesn't allow visitors at this acute stage, outside of immediate family."

"She told me she doesn't have any living family, though, except a stepdad she doesn't get along with," Katerina objects. "Naomi's right. We have to go visit her."

Asher and I nod, and Lark leans forward, lowering her voice.

"I know it's hard, but you need to let this go. Trust me—nothing good can come from pressing the issue. You can't do anything for Suki now, but the five of you *are* still in the running to make the Final Six. That has to be your focus. *Nothing* else."

She's right, I know. None of us can afford to get distracted and lose our grasp on this opportunity, least of all me. And yet . . . why do I get the feeling that her words contain a veiled threat?

A pall hangs over the five of us as we move through our training day a diminished team. The only one among us who seems in any way cheery is, of course, Beckett. As Lark escorts us to the diving pool for another session with Lieutenant Barnes, I glance behind me and notice Beckett walking alongside Naomi and Katerina, saying something to Naomi that makes her flinch. I slow my pace until I'm in step with them.

"I mean, when you think about it, she was probably your biggest competition," I hear him say. "I did my research on the Twenty-Four before I got here, and it's obvious you were both up for one of the academic spots on the mission. Your chances just got a lot better now that she's gone."

"My friend is in the *hospital,*" Naomi snaps. "You think I care about who beats who in the draft?"

Beckett shrugs, unfazed.

"She wasn't that much of a friend, though, was she? You knew her for, like, a week."

Naomi shoots him a withering look.

"She was my roommate. Maybe it's hard for *you* to care about someone you're spending nearly twenty-four/seven with, but some of us don't have the same trouble."

"I'm just saying." He gives her an appraising look. "I think you latched on to her because you missed having your sick brother to take care of."

Fury rises within me, and I jump between the two of them.

"Hey, man, why don't you shut the hell up?"

I want to grab him by the collar and toss him against the wall; I want to make him pay for talking to Naomi that way. But before I can, she sidesteps me and seizes the back of his shirt, shoving him so roughly that he stumbles into Katerina.

"Never talk about my brother again," she hisses.

"Enough!" Lark swoops down on us, yanking Naomi away from Beckett. "This team has been through plenty without you two adding to the drama. Unless you *want* to see what Dr. Takumi is like when he gets angry, you'll drop this fight and start behaving like supportive teammates. Got it?"

They both grumble their assent while refusing to look at each other. As soon as Lark's back is turned, Naomi elbows past Beckett, and Katerina catches up with us.

"I know he might have acted like a jerk, but Beckett's not all bad," she says in a hushed voice. "I've talked to him a few times, and, well . . . let's just say people wouldn't envy him if they knew the whole story with his family."

"I don't care what his story is," Naomi says flatly. "He didn't just act like a jerk, he *is* one."

"Besides, we all came here with a past and you don't see the rest of us making enemies," I point out.

"Yeah," Katerina concedes. "I don't know . . ."

Our conversation cuts off as we enter the room surrounding the diving pool, with Lieutenant Barnes waiting for us at the water's edge. As we get closer, through the water I can see what looks like a one-seater submarine, parked on the ice that blankets the bottom of the pool. A glass dome surrounds the driver's seat of the vehicle, while the pressure hull is a bulky steel sphere attached to battery pods and thrusters. A set of dividers lines the pool, reminding me of my racing days—and despite the morning we've had, I feel the faint stirrings of excitement.

"Let's go, team!" Lieutenant Barnes beckons us toward him.

We gather around, and I'm expecting him to start by saying something about Suki, to reassure us in some way—but he doesn't. Instead, he delves straight into the task at hand, as though there is nothing unusual about our team of five.

"Today's focus is water survival," he begins. "What you see before you at the bottom of the pool is a submersible: the same model of underwater vehicle that members of the

Final Six will drive in Europa's ocean after drilling through the ice."

"Amazing," Asher murmurs, and I nod in agreement.

"When you touch down on Europa, you will initially live in an inflatable home on the ice's surface," Lieutenant Barnes continues. "However, to create a habitable environment for a mass settlement of humans, we need you to drill down into the ice crust to enter the postulated subsurface ocean. With Cyb and Dot's navigational guidance, you will locate the massive pocket between the icy surface and the ocean interior. That pocket is where you will uncover an endless stretch of rocky land, be able to produce oxygen from the nearby ocean using water electrolysis—and where you will be safe from the radiation and drastic temperatures, thanks to the ice shield overhead. And *that* is where you will plant your flag and establish our new human colony." He pauses. "That's our holy grail."

As I picture it in my mind, I feel a rush of certainty that this will be my legacy. This has to be the reason I survived the flood—to lead us to the next world.

"Now, finding and building up this section of land will involve many back-and-forth trips in the submersibles, particularly for whoever is the designated underwater specialist. That's why today you'll be getting a crash course in how to drive these vehicles—and how to escape in an emergency."

We watch as the lieutenant demonstrates the challenge before us, diving into the water and swimming down to the submersible. He unlatches the glass dome and climbs into the driver's seat before deploying the thrusters and using the foot pedals to fly across the pool floor, hands-free. As he reaches the opposite end of the pool, through the transparent window of the glass dome we can see him fiddling with a gear box—and then the submersible shoots up through the water like a miniature rocket, breaking the surface of the pool. He climbs out of the vehicle to the sound of our applause.

"You'll perform the challenge one at a time, starting with a dive down to the submersible at the blow of my whistle," he directs us. "Entering the vehicle, you'll find a touch screen that controls the power, thrust, speed, and emergency functions. I've programmed the submersible so that after you complete a set of driving laps around the pool, an alarm will go off, requiring you to use the emergency thrust-booster technology to propel up to the surface. I'll be timing each of you to see who can complete this drill in under five minutes.

"To cap off the challenge, once you emerge from the submersible, you will swim just below the surface and attempt to hold your breath underwater for a full two minutes. It may seem counterintuitive to all the equipment you're learning to use, but astronauts must be prepared for anything—including the unlikely event of a systems failure in Europa's waters. In a rare case like that, the ability to hold your breath until you can reach the surface would mean the difference between life and death."

Lieutenant Barnes passes out wet suits, and the five of us peel off our uniforms down to the bathing suits we're wearing underneath. At the sight of Naomi in her one-piece, my skin turns hot. I look away quickly.

"When I call your name, line up at the diving board. This will be the order you'll complete the challenge in."

My name comes last, and I watch from the end of the line as my teammates dive into the pool one by one. Naomi struggles with the submersible, but Asher and Katerina get the hang of it after a couple minutes of fumbling. To my chagrin, only Beckett achieves the one-two punch of successfully working the submersible on his first try and holding his breath the full two minutes. And then it's my turn.

I step up to the tallest springboard, conscious of all eyes on me as I dive off the edge. And as soon as my skin touches the water, it's like a key clicking into place. I gasp as an electric current courses through my veins, turning my arms and legs into vibrating, tingling energy—a sensation I've never felt before. All I know is that my body is clamoring to move, and I follow its order, tearing into a freestyle stroke. My body zooms through the pool like a cartoon in fast-forward, and I know without seeing a stopwatch that I'm crushing all my previous times. *How am I doing this?* I've always been fast, but this is speed on another level. It's as though my limbs are made of jets.

In a matter of seconds, I'm in front of the submersible, lifting the lid on the glass dome and climbing inside the compact driver's seat. A touch screen blinks from the inside of my glass window, and I reach for the Power button, pushing the foot pedal. And then the vehicle hurtles forward, zipping through the water like a thrill ride, and I laugh out loud from the sheer joy of it.

A high-pitched alarm blares inside my driver's seat compartment, while the touch screen lights up with urgent red letters: *WARNING!* O_2 *AT 5%*. I grin, knowing this means I get to use the thrust-booster.

My fingers fly over the touch screen, jabbing different buttons until I find ENGAGE EMERGENCY THRUST. A rumbling echoes from the engine below me, the pool water ripples around the submersible—and the vehicle shoots straight up, breaking the surface with a loud splash.

I open the pilot's seat hatch and climb out of the glass dome, still thrumming with adrenaline.

"That was awesome!" I yell from the pool. No one responds, and as I glance at my teammates, I notice they are all looking at me strangely.

"Your time is three minutes even," Lieutenant Barnes reads from his stopwatch, raising his eyebrows.

"Holy . . ." I trail off, taken aback by my own speed.

"All right, when I blow the whistle, finish the drill by holding your breath underwater for two minutes. Ready?"

I nod. This will be a cinch, after my days diving in Rome without any breathing equipment. I hear the shriek of the whistle, and I plunge back underwater, sucking in my breath. The two minutes pass effortlessly—I could always manage that—but then I hear the Lieutenant's muffled voice shouting out, "Five minutes!" and, what feels like only seconds later, *"Ten!"*

The weird thing is, I'm not even struggling. Normally by this point I'd be hungry for air, but right now, I feel like I could stay down here another ten minutes or more. Still, a nagging voice in my head tells me I've shown off plenty for one day. I don't need to make this whole training period the Leo Show. So when I hear Lieutenant Barnes cheer, "*Fifteen* minutes!" I finally rise out of the water.

A tall shadow looms at the edge of the pool, and as the water clears from my eyes, I see who it is. Someone must have sent for Dr. Takumi while I was underwater, because there he is, standing in front of my thunderstruck teammates.

Dr. Takumi extends his hand as I hoist myself out of the pool, and our eyes meet. He gives me a rare smile—and I know I've done it.

I've impressed the most important figure here.

TWELVE

NAOMI

WHAT I JUST SAW CAN'T BE REAL. IT'S NOT . . . HUMAN. I FEEL the blood roaring in my ears as I watch Leo shake hands with Dr. Takumi, and I wonder who he really is—*what* he is. But then he catches my eye across the pool, flashing me that dimpled grin, and the familiar warmth in my chest replaces my fear. Still, as soon as we're back in uniform and leaving the diving pool, I pull Leo aside.

"What *was* that? I've seen you swim before—I knew you were good, but holding your breath like that? It was almost like you were . . . amphibious."

"It was crazy, right?" Leo's cheeks flush as he smiles, and I realize he thinks I'm simply complimenting him.

"Crazy is a good word for it," I say dryly. "I'm not trying to downplay how great a swimmer you actually are, but . . . was there something different going on today?"

Before he can respond, Lark motions for the five of us to follow her to our next training session on the Mission Floor. Leo and I hang back a few paces as we follow our teammates down the long corridor to the elevator bay, keeping our voices low.

"Well?" I press him. "What exactly happened in the water?"

"I don't know. But I felt something different as soon as I got in the pool," Leo admits. "It was like a—a physical, instinctual charge. I don't know *what* it was. Maybe heightened adrenaline or something?"

I shake my head.

"No. Adrenaline doesn't completely alter your physicality. It doesn't give you otherworldly speed or the ability to go without breathing." I look into his eyes. "You know what this is, don't you?"

Leo folds his arms against his chest. He doesn't want to hear it, doesn't want me bursting his bubble. But I have no choice.

"It's the RRB. That has to be what caused this. You and Suki both had a reaction, only in your case, it wasn't adverse. At least not yet." I think quickly. "I've got to find a way to get a sample of the serum, so I can find out what's in it. I just *know* there's something they're not telling us, something off—"

"No," he interrupts me. "I don't want to see you get in trouble, and that's exactly what will happen if you go poking around and try to swipe the RRB. And besides, I need this. I *need* to be one of the Final Six. If the serum is helping me excel and get to Europa, then I don't care what's in it."

My mouth falls open. I can't be hearing him correctly.

"You can honestly say that? After last night, after Suki, you can really be so—so callous?"

He winces.

"I'm not being callous—you know how terrible I feel about what happened to her. But if Suki were here right now, she would say the same thing. She would tell me not to jeopardize my chances when things are going well."

"Yeah, and it was that attitude that put her in the hospital," I retort. "Whatever is in the RRB has proven to be both powerful and dangerous. This isn't just about Suki or you or me. *All* of us who take it are vulnerable."

We're nearing the elevator bay now, just steps away from the others. Leo stops in his tracks.

"What do you want from me? I can't help the fact that I want this mission, that I *need* it. Just like I can't help the fact that you don't."

His words catch me off guard.

"I—well, we're friends, right?"

A funny expression crosses his face as he nods.

"And friends look out for each other," I continue. "I don't want to see you end up in a situation anywhere close to what happened to Suki. So I need to find out if what I suspect is true—and I need you to trust me."

Leo hesitates before replying.

"Fine. Just as long as your sleuthing doesn't get either of us in trouble."

"Come on, you two!" Lark's voice calls out, and Leo and I quicken our pace to join the rest of the team.

As we step into the elevator, I feel someone's eyes on us. It's Beckett, his expression cold and calculating as he stares at Leo. A shiver runs through me, and I wonder just how much of a target Leo has on his back . . . and if his performance today might cost him.

Returning to the Hab after our training day, we again step into a scene of chaos. Finalists from two other teams are swarming the halls, their faces red and stricken, their bodies racked with sobs, while the team leaders try in vain to calm them. Leo and I turn to each other in fear, and I grab his hand on instinct as I brace myself. *What is happening?*

Lark pushes through the crowd, trying to get answers, while I catch snippets of conversation through the pandemonium. *"Callum." "Submersible." " . . . went mad." "Dead."*

I recoil in horror. I heard wrong—I must have.

I spot Ana Martinez from arrival day crying in Dev Khanna's arms, and I rush toward them.

"What's wrong, Ana? What's going on?"

She breaks away from Dev and looks at me with wild, panicky eyes. "It's Callum. He—he's dead. It happened right in front of us. G-gone, just like that."

Bile rises in my throat. My mind flashes back to the Australian finalist sitting beside me during Dr. Takumi's welcome speech. And I can't breathe.

"How?" Leo whispers.

"We were doing the submersible drills. Our team was last in the diving pool today," Dev says shakily. "Everything was going fine, and then when it was Callum's turn . . . It was the craziest thing."

"What happened?"

"He turned on the thrust-booster, just like he was supposed to—but then he suddenly climbed *out* of the submersible while everything was still running. And he . . . he swam right under the propellers." Dev squeezes his eyes shut, shaking his head, as if to rid himself of the image. "Lieutenant Barnes was screaming at him to stop, he jumped in the water after him, but it was too late. The submersible cut him up in seconds."

I stare at Dev, struggling to comprehend the gruesome story.

"Why—why would he do that?"

"That's what makes no sense," Ana wails. "He was happy; he was doing so well here, and he was excited about the mission. But then today, from the start, something was different about him. It was almost like he was . . ." She shrugs helplessly, and Dev finishes her sentence.

"Possessed."

My heart hammers in my chest. I turn to Leo, and I can see in his eyes that he knows what I'm thinking. *The RRB.*

Footsteps come thundering toward us, and we step back as Dr. Takumi and General Sokolov enter the hall, their faces grave.

"Everyone into the library," Dr. Takumi directs us, and we fall into step, shuffling numbly behind our leaders. Once we're all seated around the long reading tables, Dr. Takumi clears his throat, looking out at the sea of stunned faces.

"Finalists, I know you've been through a terrible shock. The general and I, Lieutenant Barnes, and all of the staff here at ISTC are devastated by what happened to Callum Turner today. For his teammates who were on the scene, we know how traumatizing it must've been to witness. But it's important for you to understand that this was an isolated incident." He pauses. "It appears Callum Turner had an undiagnosed psychiatric condition that our initial vetting failed to pick up on—which explains his fatal behavior today."

What?

"The robots first reported something amiss when monitoring his physical reactions and brain waves during the virtual reality simulation," General Sokolov speaks up. "We scheduled a psychiatric evaluation for him for tomorrow, but" —she hangs her head—"we were too late."

I glance around me, wondering if my fellow finalists are buying this convenient story. But I can already see it on most of their faces: acceptance. I know how easy it is to cling to the first answer you're given in the haze of shock, but I shake my head in frustration, convinced Dr. Takumi and the general are manipulating us into believing what they want.

"I just got off the phone with one of Houston's leading psychiatrists, who confirmed that in a patient such as Callum, stress can trigger symptoms and breakdowns like what occurred in the diving pool," Dr. Takumi continues. "We deeply regret exposing Callum to an environment he wasn't equipped to handle. We also regret the impact this is having on you, his teammates and cofinalists."

I raise my hand. "What *was* his condition, exactly?"

"I'm afraid the specific details must remain confidential, out of respect to Callum's family," Dr. Takumi says smoothly.

Convenient once again. I take a breath, daring myself to ask the next question.

"And are you sure it's not the RRB? What if this was a reaction to that, like what happened to Suki?"

Every face in the room turns in my direction, and I can feel Leo tensing up beside me. When Dr. Takumi finally answers, his voice is controlled and calm—but I can see the threat in his eyes as he looks at me.

"I think we made it clear this has nothing to do with the RRB. As the general said, Cyb and Dot reported irregular brain wave activity in Callum before he received his first dose of the vaccine. Again, this was an *isolated* incident."

He turns his sharp gaze away from me, toward the rest of the watching crowd.

"We will all mourn Callum, and we won't forget him. But know this: in every landmark achievement in the history of mankind, there have been unfortunate casualties along the way. It's as my predecessors at NASA always said: risk is the price of progress." He lets the words linger before continuing, "We'll leave you in the capable hands of your team leaders for the rest of the day. Take this time to comfort yourselves and your teammates. We'll be back to our mission in the morning."

His speech might have worked on the others, but my suspicion is only growing. I *have* to get my hands on the RRB—I have to get the answers we all need.

As soon as everyone is out of their seats, I scan the faces around me, looking for the person who can give me at least one clue. Jian Soo is standing near the computers with the French finalist, Henri, and I elbow my way toward them.

"Jian," I murmur. "I know Callum was your teammate, and I'm so sorry. This is—this is really weird timing, I know, but I have to ask you something. Last night, when Suki was having her—her reaction to the RRB, she kept repeating something in Mandarin."

He raises an eyebrow, and nods at me to continue.

"It sounded like *tā hái huózhe*. Is that—is that a real phrase?"

Jian lets out a sharp exhale.

"Are you sure that's what she said?"

"I couldn't get it out of my mind. So, yes."

Jian stares at me.

"She was saying, *'It's alive.'*"

As if I needed more proof of Dr. Takumi's priorities, that night we're escorted to the medical office for the RRB shots as usual. You would think that today, of all days, he would let us forgo the injections, but even the loss of a finalist isn't enough for him to pause our strict schedule. There is only one benefit of going back and risking another dose: it gives me an opportunity.

"Remember how I asked you to trust me?" I whisper to Leo, pulling him aside on our way there. "I'm going to do something, and I need just a tiny bit of your help. It's for Callum and Suki."

"What is it?" He gives me a wary look. "Don't forget that I also asked *you* not to get us in trouble."

"This is nothing," I assure him, though I have a feeling he might disagree. "So as soon as I get in the chair, but before the nurse takes out the needle, I need you to just . . . cause a distraction. Something that'll make her turn away from me and keep the focus on you for the quick minute it'll take me to grab a vial. Once I turn around and give you the signal, you can go back to normal. Cool?"

"Um. What kind of distraction? And you do know there are security cameras in the building, right?"

"Yes, but even if there's a camera right there in the medical office, which I doubt, I'll be so quick that you wouldn't see anything. And the distraction can be anything—I don't know, pretend to trip and twist your ankle or something." I shrug. "Don't worry about having an audience, either. We can be near the end of the line, so most of the others will be in the cafeteria by the time I go up."

Leo groans. "I'm not going to be able to talk you out of this, am I?"

"Nope. And compared to other plans I've come up with, this one is pretty tame."

"Fine." He sighs, and I give his arm a grateful squeeze. "Thank you. I know you won't regret it."

We join the rest of our teammates and cofinalists outside the medical office, waiting silently as the line trickles down to the last few. As each finalist goes up, wincing at the prick of the needle, my palms sweat with the realization that any one of us could be the next Suki—the next *Callum*. And then it's my turn.

I give Leo an encouraging nod before I step forward, into the office. *One . . . two . . .* The nurse motions me toward the chair and I take my seat, swiveling it just slightly so that I am within arm's length of the wall of vials. *Three.*

The sound of coughing comes right on cue, weak at first, and then growing louder, more urgent. I try not to smile.

The nurse pauses in front of her instruments as the coughing escalates, and Leo yells in a choked voice, "Water!"

"One second," she tells me, before hurrying to tend to him. And then, adrenaline surging, I turn in my seat to face the vials. The glowing pale liquid beckons me, and in one quick motion, I snatch a vial from the back of the shelf, stuffing it in the zippered pocket of my hoodie. I release my breath and turn back to face Leo, who is getting thumped between the shoulder blades by the nurse. He meets my eyes, and I scratch my ear, giving him our signal.

"That's better!" Leo blurts out, pretending to take a gulp of air. "Something must have gone down the wrong pipe, but I can breathe now."

And as the nurse returns to me, I give Leo a grateful smile, mouthing the words *thank you*.

Back in my dorm for the first time since morning, I stare at Suki's now-empty side of the room. The bed is stripped, her desk bare, our shared closet purged of her clothes and shoes. Even the scent in the room is different and chemical-tinged, as though someone scrubbed the place clean while trying to remove every trace of her. It's like she was never here at all.

"But I won't forget you, Suki," I whisper to the empty bed. "I promise I'll find out what happened—to you and Callum."

It hits me with a jolt that whoever came in to clear out her things might have taken the opportunity to snoop through mine, and I race over to the closet, grabbing my backpack. My fingers tremble as I unzip the hidden compartment. *Please, please, please still be there . . .*

I let out a long exhale at the sight of the flash drive with my hacking software, still nestled safely in the zippered compartment. I run my fingers over the drive in relief before setting it aside and rifling through the bag until I find just what I need.

Some girls stock their carry-ons with extra SPF or clothes for a rainy day. I, on the other hand, am the type to pack a portable electron microscope whenever I travel. It may sound weird, but you just never know what you'll find when you leave home. A foreign insect or an unusual pebble in the streets of somewhere new becomes a form of art when placed under a microscopic lens. And I'm about to find out just what kind of art is hiding in this radiation-resistant bacteria.

I pull out the microscope and a miniature bottled water from my backpack, bringing them both to my desk. My eyes flash to the door, double-checking that it's firmly shut, before I pour a drop of water onto the microscope slide. My heartbeat quickening, I retrieve the RRB vial from my pocket and unscrew the top, revealing the icy-blue, viscous serum within. I empty a bit of the serum onto the slide with the drop of water, place the glass coverslip over it—and then I peer into the lens.

Impossible. I shake my head at the sight before me, blinking rapidly to try to clear my vision. Bacteria cells are prokaryotes—they're not supposed to have a nucleus. And yet . . .

I take a breath, wait for the thudding in my chest to slow, and then return my eyes to the lens, expecting something different this time. But still I find three unmistakable nuclei . . . where there should be none.

The RRB is a literal exception to *every rule* of Earth's bacteria.

THIRTEEN

LEO

AT BREAKFAST, NAOMI SLIPS A PIECE OF PAPER INTO MY HAND under the table. My stomach jumps as her fingers brush mine, and I spend the rest of the meal fixated on the message in my grasp, wondering what it says. As soon as we're excused from the cafeteria and my teammates push back from the table, I unfold the paper and read her words, scrawled in blue ink.

Found something. Plan to meet me on the Telescope Tower after dinner. Make sure you're alone.

I draw in my breath. How in the world am I supposed to wait until evening to find out her news?

It takes every ounce of my focus to stay present during training as Lark shuttles us between the Mission Floor, the

Altitude Chamber, and the VR lab. My mind is already up on the tower with Naomi. When we finally make it to dinner, she leans in to murmur in my ear, "You go first. I'll be a few steps behind you."

I nod, glancing up at the clock. Only twenty minutes to go. But then my eyes catch on something else: Beckett, watching the two of us from across the table. I give Naomi a warning look before turning away.

I take the spiral stairs up to the tower two at a time, and as the wind sweeps against my neck, I realize how much I've missed the outdoors. Back in Rome, I tried to spend as little time as possible inside, in the wreckage of our pensione. As much as I hated the sea that stole my family from me, somehow looking at the sky and the stars comforted me.

I make my way to the telescope now, peering through it until I find the constellation I'm looking for—the one that always reminds me of my parents and sister: Orion's Belt, with its three blinking stars. Maybe they're out there, watching over me.

I take a deep breath and shift the telescope to a different angle—toward Europa. I've just caught the colorful sphere of Jupiter and the grayish speck of its moon behind it when I hear the sound of footsteps.

"Hi," Naomi says behind me. "Thanks for meeting me."

"Of course." I turn away from the telescope, noticing how her face glows in the moonlight. A flush creeps up her cheeks, and for a moment we just stand there, our eyes locked. And then she looks away, taking a breath before launching into what she has to say.

"I looked at the RRB. And, Leo—it had *three nuclei*."

At my blank look, she continues, "It's a law of science that bacteria on Earth, like all prokaryote organisms, does *not* contain a nucleus. Just like it's a law of human physiology that we don't have, for example, fins. So just as we wouldn't be considered human if we had fins, the fact that the radiation-resistant bacteria has three nuclei theoretically means . . ."

"It's not from Earth?" I finish her sentence, the words sounding implausible as they come out of my mouth.

"Exactly."

I shake my head, trying to clear the illusion from my mind. One of us here needs to remain levelheaded.

"Could there be an exception to that nucleus rule?" I ask.

"There's only ever been one possible exception, and it's highly contested by scientists anyway. But even that exception, in the Planctomycetes, has just one nucleus-like structure. The idea of a bacteria species from Earth with *three* nuclei is an impossibility. And there's more." Naomi starts pacing the short width of the tower, as if her body can't keep still under the magnitude of her discovery. "Jian translated the phrase Suki kept repeating that night—*tā hái huózhe*. He said it means 'It's alive.'" She looks at me with wild eyes, and I can't tell whether she's afraid or excited—or both. "Don't you see the connection?"

"Um . . ."

"I think when she went into her altered state after the second dose, her body could somehow feel what was in the RRB—that it comes from something *living.* " Naomi's voice drops to a whisper. "Something like . . . the extraterrestrials of Europa."

My eyebrows shoot up. Is this her trying to be funny? Or—

"And I think Callum had the same reaction before the submersible accident," she continues. "That's why he acted so out of character, why he seemed—according to his teammates—*possessed.*"

"Extraterrestrials? As in, little green men?"

She stops pacing, narrowing her eyes at me.

"I never bought that description of them, but yeah—intelligent life. And by the way, I'm hardly the first person to suspect ETs on Europa. I'm guessing you haven't been on the Space Conspirator?"

I shake my head.

"It's this amazing website my brother and I have been following for years, that uses cutting-edge science to debunk myths and prove new theories," she explains. "And for months now they've been posting detailed reasoning for why extraterrestrial life is not just possible, but theoretically *has* to exist on Europa, due to its high-energy particle environment and tidally heated subsurface ocean. The space agencies refuse to take the Conspirator seriously or address the claims head-on, but if there's one thing I believe in, it's science—and the Conspirator is right. The chemicals and particles that exist on Europa are *known* to create life."

She finally pauses to take a breath. "So that means the ISTC isn't just planning to send us to another part of the universe—they're sending us into the unknown. A world where we're not the first."

I stare at her. Now I understand why she's been wary of the mission from the beginning.

"You really believe in this stuff?"

"I do. Now more than ever. And I'm telling you all this because I'm going to prove it . . . and there might come another time, like last night, where I need an accomplice."

"You better tell me what you're planning, then."

Even though I'm nearly certain she's chasing something that doesn't exist, I can't deny the rush of satisfaction I feel that she's chosen me to confide in. Maybe I'm not so alone in the feelings I'm starting to have.

"What I need to do is find biosignatures," Naomi says. At another quizzical look from me, she rolls her eyes. "Did you pay *any* attention in science class, or were you too busy swimming?"

"Too busy swimming," I affirm. We share a grin before she continues.

"Biosignatures are substances like elements, molecules, isotopes, and so on that provide tangible evidence of life. If I could find some way to get into the data from the Europa flyby mission, that's the first thing I would look for."

"But wouldn't the whole world know about it, if there were these so-called biosignatures?" I ask.

"Only if the powers that be decided to share the information with the world. And why would they? It would only jeopardize our mission. Besides, who knows if anyone who had access to the data was even *looking* for biosignatures?"

Naomi suddenly stops in place, her posture straight as an arrow. I can practically see the light bulb going off in her mind.

"*The robots,*" she breathes. "They were *there*. They circled Europa thirty-six times in their probe, close enough to collect the data I need. If there are biosignatures to be found, they have to still be stored within Dot and Cyb." Her body trembles with excitement. "I may not be able to get into NASA's supercomputer—but I can get to the robots."

I hate to disappoint her, but . . . "You really think they're just going to give up classified info if you ask nicely?"

Naomi avoids my eyes.

"There are other ways to get it."

I feel a flicker of worry as I study her, wondering how far she'll go. It's tempting to get swept up in the intrigue of her theory—but I'm the one with something to lose.

"Listen, I . . . I won't stand in your way, and I'm here if you need me. But you have to know that I still want this—still *need* to be one of the Final Six. I know that might seem crazy to you after all you just told me, but what you're saying is still speculation. None of us can know for sure what Suki meant, or what really happened to her and Callum. But what I do know for sure is that Europa is the only future I have." I crack a smile. "Plus, if anything, your hypothesis just made it that much more interesting. Who *wouldn't* want to see aliens up close? I mean, if you didn't have a family waiting for you at home . . . wouldn't you want to go?"

Naomi looks at me for a long moment.

"I get it. I won't blow your chance at this, Leo. But I will try to keep you safe—and that means continuing to dig for the truth. I'll just be . . . careful."

Be careful. The memory returns to me in a flash, of someone else's voice saying the same words. My skin prickles as Elena's warning from before I left comes rushing back to me. *They see you as some kind of weapon.*

Is it possible . . . that what Elena overheard that night at the Palazzo has something to do with Naomi's theory? Should I say something?

But the thought of being forced to return to the emptiness of my old life is worse than any unconfirmed danger on Europa. I keep my mouth shut.

The next day's training finds us back in the Vomit Comet for the first time since our weightless flight. This time, General Sokolov joins us on the Zero-G plane along with Lark, and as we step inside, I see a stack of body harnesses lined up on one of the front-row seats. A long, sturdy rope that wasn't there before is now attached to the door of the plane, running the length of the aircraft.

"Please tell me we're not using those," Naomi says, staring at the body harnesses.

"All right, finalists!" General Sokolov claps her hands

together. "Who here knows what will be required of the Final Six when they dock with the supply ship in Mars orbit and prepare for a gravity slingshot to Europa?"

Asher raises his hand.

"While Cyb and the copilot fly the *Pontus*, two people will need to perform a spacewalk outside—first to patch the fuel leak on the supply ship and run diagnostics, and then to supervise and guide the docking mechanism."

"Correct," General Sokolov says. "So for any of you who may have a fear of heights, now is the time to overcome it. When you're spacewalking in Mars orbit, you will be higher up in the universe than your mind can grasp—and you cannot, *must* not, lose your cool. EVA Height Vertigo can pose a real problem for astronauts, and our goal today is to combat this." She pauses, watching our reactions. "The virtual reality sim helped us get there mentally, but now, in order to physically replicate the sensation of floating among the stars while performing a spacewalk—we'll be bungee jumping off of this plane at ten thousand feet, and landing on another."

I hear Naomi gulp beside me, and I'm tempted to squeeze her hand or wrap my arm around her. But I hold myself back.

"You will be tandem jumping, and paired according to your weight. Meanwhile, the harness and rope you're using today will perform a similar function to the tether you'll be using in space."

The general consults her tablet, and the thumping in my chest speeds up.

"The skydiving pairs are Naomi and Katerina, Asher and me, and Leo and Beckett."

My stomach drops. I should have known it would be him and me.

As the plane's wheels drive forward and we lift off, my adrenaline thankfully takes over. I sit next to Naomi, my body thrumming with anticipation, as the general prepares us for what's to come. She and Asher will be going first, and I watch as Lark helps fasten them into their full-body harnesses, then straps them together. The plane slows to a hover, and as Lark presses a button, the cabin door blows open.

"Oh, God." Naomi grips the armrest with white knuckles, and this time, I don't hesitate to place my hand over hers.

General Sokolov and Asher shuffle in tandem to the edge of the plane, the air blowing at their faces. "Three . . . two . . . one," the general chants. "Jump!"

Katerina's shriek echoes through the cabin as the general and Asher go flying, their bodies hanging upside down from the rope. I press my face to the window, watching as the two of them spread their arms like wings and soar through the clouds, Asher's screams fading. In spite of my ratcheting nerves, I feel a flicker of excitement. This should be a damn good ride.

"I won't die," Naomi mutters to herself through chattering teeth, though it sounds more like a question than a statement. "Terminal velocity—I won't feel the sensation of free-falling once I hit terminal velocity."

I squeeze her shoulder.

"Remember how much you loved the weightless flight? This will be as fun as that, plus it'll be over soon."

A second, smaller plane swoops down to meet Asher and the general midair, and the two of them use their rope to swing through its open door. "Whoa," I murmur. "I can't believe we get to do that."

"*Get* to?" Naomi looks at me incredulously. She flinches as Lark calls her and Katerina up, and I reach over and give her a brief hug. "Good luck."

It's only a second of contact, but I feel it as she steps away from me—the warmth where her body used to be.

I lean forward, nervous for her, as Lark connects the bungee cord to her harness strap and feet. "Three . . . two . . . one . . . jump!" she yells, and I brace myself. But Naomi and Katerina remain on the ledge, staring at the far-off ground in fear, and Lark has to repeat the countdown, this time giving them a slight push. And then they are falling, flying, just like the general and Asher, their screams puncturing the air. When they soar past our plane, I smile at the sight of Naomi laughing from the adrenaline release as she sails through the clouds.

The second plane ropes them in, and now it's our turn. I keep my eyes straight ahead, not saying a word to Beckett as

Lark straps the equipment to our backs.

"You'll be in the air for two full minutes," Lark yells over the sound of the engine as she fastens the cord through our harnesses. "Don't look down, and you should be fine. Bend your knees as you jump, and then spread your arms wide as you fly."

My legs feel like lead as I shuffle toward the open door, tied to my rival. As we approach the edge, I immediately go against Lark's advice and look down. But there's no ground to rush toward, there's only clouds—and the wind, which blows bitterly cold gusts from up here.

"Three . . . two . . ." I glance at Beckett, and on instinct, I extend my hand to shake his. As much as I don't like the guy, we're about to take the jump of our lives together . . . shouldn't we at least be on good terms for this? But he either doesn't see my outstretched hand or he ignores it. And then Lark shouts out, "One! Jump!"

The moment is here, but at first my legs don't move. I stare into the sky, my mind trying to comprehend what I'm about to do, freezing my body in fear. And then I realize that I am closer to my family up here than anywhere in the world.

Beckett lunges forward, and I bend my knees and step off the ledge, into the air.

My heart seems to leap out of my body as I jump. The wind slams against our backs, turning us upside down, and I hear screams as my insides contort, as gravity disappears. But then comes a rush of wild, pure euphoria. And as I soar above Houston, I realize I'm not falling—I'm being carried by air.

I let out a whoop as my body flies, so exhilarated that I don't even mind having to share this with Beckett. Our bodies glide through the wind beside each other, and I look at him with a grin, temporarily forgetting that he's my rival here. But he hasn't forgotten. He is looking at me, too—only his eyes are dark pools. And suddenly, I feel his hand on my back, reaching for my harness.

"Stop—" I try to shout, but I can barely speak up here. We're moving too fast; the wind drowns out my voice. I fumble behind me, trying to grip my harness, the rope, *something*—but his hands have already closed around my harness straps. I feel a sickening lurch in my stomach as he pulls at the first strap. He is going to kill me—right here in the sky, where no one can save me. He is going to throw off my harness, untether me from the rope, and send me hurtling down to the ground in a crushed heap of limbs, where he can tell everyone it was an accident—

An engine roars. Our pickup plane circles, General Sokolov throwing out the rope to reel us in. And I've never been so relieved to see anyone or anything in my entire life. *I'm going to live.* Beckett missed his chance. His hand drops from my harness, and he grips the general's rope instead, swinging his body into the second plane, with me right behind him—never taking my eyes off his back.

"Wasn't that crazy?" Naomi rushes toward me, giddy with relief from having her jump over with.

I nod and try to smile, but my insides are turning to ice. Behind us, Beckett grins and high-fives Asher and Katerina, looking nothing like the killer I saw in the air. Could I have possibly misinterpreted what happened? Or did my competitor, my teammate, just try to *take me out*?

FOURTEEN

NAOMI

I MAKE IT TO THE CAFETERIA IN THE MORNING WITH BARELY A minute to spare, still groggy from a night of the nightmares that have been plaguing me since Suki left. I slip into my seat just as Dr. Takumi rises to make one of his announcements, and I brace myself, almost afraid to hear whatever news he has for us this time. But it's not another report of an RRB reaction—it's something else entirely.

"As vital as your physical skills and academic intelligence are to the mission, there is another factor that plays an equally crucial role in determining who will make up the Final Six," he begins. "That would be your mental and psychological state. The passing of Callum Turner is a tragic reminder of that."

I stiffen in my seat. So he's sticking to that story, then, instead of pointing the finger where it really belongs.

"The personality tests you completed back when you were in school, during the scouting phase of our mission, helped secure you a spot here. However, as we saw with Callum, these tests were far from foolproof. As we prepare for the first round of eliminations later this week, we must employ more in-depth psychological evaluations—which will begin after breakfast today."

Leo and I exchange a nervous glance. The last thing I need is to have one of Dr. Takumi's followers trying to peer into my soul—or guess at my plans.

"To prevent human bias and emotions from affecting the psych evaluations, we are handing control of this task over to our robots," Dr. Takumi reveals. "Dot and Cyb were the only ones to suspect Callum's instability, and they understand exactly what we are looking for. And seeing as they will be traveling and living alongside the Final Six, it is only appropriate to have them closely monitor the personalities involved." His eyes sweep across the room, watching all twenty-two of us. "The best advice I can give you is to be completely honest in your answers. By saying what you *think* we want to hear, you may inadvertently hurt your own chances. And there's no need to worry about self-consciousness in front of your teammates. Each of you will be meeting privately with the robots."

My heartbeat quickens. There's no denying that time alone with the two most advanced robots in existence is the stuff of my scientific dreams—but I always figured I would be the one studying *them*. I didn't expect to be on psychological trial in front of two flawless machines, who probably have some kind of sensors that light up whenever they detect me lying. How am I supposed to outsmart perfection?

The far-off voice of my former computer sciences teacher echoes in my mind: *There are two keys to understanding and manipulating machines: you must have a keen grasp of both the binary number system and logic.*

Both binary and logic play into my strengths. I'm not sure how I can possibly implement them into my upcoming session with the robots . . . but I'll have to try.

Lark steps in and out of our training sessions throughout the morning, pulling us off the Mission Floor one by one for the psych evaluations. Asher goes first, and I'm dying to ask him how it went, what the robots were like and what kinds of questions they asked—but Lark already warned us to keep our sessions confidential. All I can do is gauge the reactions of my teammates as they return, noticing whether they appear rattled or relieved. And then it's my turn.

Walking with Lark to the elevator bay, I realize this is my first opportunity alone with her to ask about Suki. I take a deep breath as we step onto the lift, trying to play it cool, but my words still come tumbling out in a rush.

"Lark, I—I'm really worried about Suki. We haven't gotten any updates, and I don't know if she's still here or how she's doing—but I know she can't go back to Singapore.

The situation is awful for her there, and the only family she has left is her stepfather, who's a—"

Lark holds up a hand to stop me. "Suki's not returning to Singapore."

"She's not?" I breathe a sigh of relief.

"No. She is in a medical facility here in Houston. Doctors are hoping they can reverse the effects of her catatonia."

"What?" My stomach plummets. "They're *hoping*? You mean she's still not any better? What happens if they can't heal her?"

The elevator stops at the fourth floor, and Lark leads the way.

"I've been checking up on her through Dr. Takumi, but it's still too early to determine any sort of prognosis. As I said, the doctors are hopeful. But if they can't reverse her symptoms, Suki will remain in the care of the ISTC's medical team, providing a human case study for the development of the RRB. Either way, she will be taken care of."

"But—but—she's not a lab rat!" I protest, horrified by what I'm hearing. "She's *Suki*. She was brilliant and meant to do great things, and—and that could be any of us in there!"

Lark stops midstride, placing a hand on my shoulder. "She can still achieve great things, even now. By helping us refine and perfect the serum that will keep the Final Six alive and thriving on Europa."

I feel bile rising in my throat at the implication behind her words. While Suki lies defenseless in a hospital bed, they plan to treat her body and mind like some kind of brutal science experiment? How can Lark be okay with this?

"They've gotten to you—" I start to say, but Lark gives me a sharp look before raising her eyes to the ceiling. I follow her gaze to a blinking green light. *Security camera*.

"There are casualties of every mission," she says, her voice a tinge too loud, as if performing for someone out of sight. "I know that better than anyone. All you can do is keep moving forward. Do your best here—in Suki's honor."

I nod and stay silent the rest of the way, as my mind spins with questions about Suki and the scope of Dr. Takumi's plans, about Lark and where her loyalties lie. We pass one closed door after another in the labyrinth-like corridor until Lark finally pauses and pulls out her key fob in front of a blue-painted door. "Welcome to the robotics lab."

I hold my breath as we step inside, entering a vast warehouse-like space with cables coiled all along the floors and long tables littered with metals, wires, computers, and tablets. At the center of the room, emitting an unearthly glow, are two six-foot-tall, egg-shaped pods.

"Are those the sleep pods?" I ask, staring.

"Yes. That's where Cyb and Dot go to recharge their batteries—literally."

As she leads the way through the sprawling space, we pass a row of robot heads and torsos in black storage cases—like dismembered body parts lying in their coffins. Even though I know they're under-construction AIs, the sight still sends a shiver through me.

Lark steps through an archway and into a smaller room within the lab, a study humming with the sound of machinery, centered around a glass touch-screen desk. I follow her inside, and I stop in my tracks as I come face-to-face with the bronze and platinum humanoids. I open my mouth to speak, and find that for the second time in my life, I am starstruck. I haven't felt this way since I met Dr. Wagner—like I'm standing before the highest realm of possibility, the place where science and miracles collide.

"Hello, Naomi," Cyb greets me in a crisp, male-programmed voice.

"Hi," I reply, my voice coming out slightly above a whisper.

"I'll be back in thirty minutes," Lark says. "Remember to just relax and give the first honest answers that come to mind."

"Um. Okay."

"Have a seat," Cyb commands, gesturing to the chair opposite the glass desk. Dot shuffles toward me, and I try not to gasp as the AI proceeds to attach wired sensors to my chest, abdomen, and fingertips, and wraps a blood-pressure cuff around my upper arm. My nerves mount at the realization that they are monitoring my physiological reactions, and I say a silent prayer for my body to not betray me.

Cyb presses a spot on the touch-screen desk, and then swivels his head back up to face me.

"Naomi, how would you assess your time here thus far?"

"Um, well . . ." I shift in my seat. My thoughts are all

jumbled as I stare from the robots to the sensors on my body, but I force myself to focus. *How can I work this to my advantage?* "It's different than I imagined. Some things have been better than I expected, and others have been . . . worse."

"Please elaborate. Which parts have proven to be a challenge?"

"I can't get the image of Suki's last night out of my head," I answer, watching them carefully as I wonder what information they have on her and Callum—and what I might be able to glean. "It hurts to be in my room without her, or to think about what might have been if I'd only forced her to go to the medic. And then what happened to Callum, I just don't believe—"

I break off before I say too much. Dot leans over the touch-screen desk and makes a series of rapid tapping motions, as if taking notes. I watch, mesmerized by the sight of the robot's humanlike hands, consisting of three fingers and a thumb.

"Naomi." Cyb's voice jolts me back to attention. "What don't you believe?"

"I—I don't believe he's dead. I mean, I know it's true, but I just can't believe it happened," I improvise, trying not to think about how my vitals must be spiking on the monitors right now. Dot makes more of her tapping motions over the desk, and my heart sinks. I must be making some kind of impression.

"What are the other difficulties you've faced here?"

Trying to prove the secret behind this RRB we're getting injected with, I say silently. *Trying to uncover what Dr. Takumi is hiding from us about the mission, before it's too late.* But of course I can't say any of that. Instead, I tell the robots a different truth.

"Being away from my family. It's the hardest thing I've ever had to do. There are other finalists here who are eager to get away from Earth, and I understand. But I . . ." I take a deep breath, looking Cyb straight in his artificial eyes. *Be honest. Maybe this will help them trust me.* "I'm not one of them. I need to be with my family, especially my little brother, Sam."

Cyb nods. "Thank you for sharing. Now, tell us the positive aspects. Are there areas here at ISTC where you feel yourself thriving?"

"Yes," I admit. "If I separate myself from the feelings about leaving my family, and if I can manage to get past what happened to Suki and Callum, then this place is in many ways a fantasyland for someone like me, with all the groundbreaking science around every corner. Starting with you two, actually. But . . ."

"But what?" Cyb presses.

But it's a fantasyland with a dark side.

"But I have a hard time letting go," I say instead. "Although there are times when I have, like in the Vomit Comet or the virtual reality sims."

"And with Leonardo Danieli."

My head snaps up. Did . . . did Cyb really just say that?

"Excuse me?"

"We've detected a connection between you and finalist Leonardo Danieli," Cyb says smoothly. "Wouldn't you say that's been one of the positives of your time here?"

My throat turns dry. Even with Cyb's emotionless tone, I can hear the subtext in his seemingly innocuous words. *We're watching. We see more than you know.*

"Leo and I are just friends," I stammer, when I find my voice. "But yeah, he's—he's awesome. My closest friend here."

I clear my throat nervously as Dot and Cyb turn to each other and nod.

"All right. We have a few general questions for you now. You may not understand why these are the questions being asked, but that's not important. What matters is answering promptly with the first thought that comes to mind." Cyb swipes the left-hand corner of the desk, and I can see the reflection of text lighting up the glass.

"Do you believe that everything in the world is relative?"

"Yes," I answer. That's an easy one. "I do."

"Do you trust reason above feelings?" Cyb peers closely at me.

"Um . . ." I falter, unsure which answer is the truth. I am a scientist, therefore I should be ruled by reason. But it's my gut, even more than my reasoning, that's been telling me something shifty is afoot with the Europa Mission.

"If I can add a third choice, I would say I trust my educated intuition most of all," I finally answer.

Cyb doesn't object and moves on to the next question.

"Do images, words, or ideas often come to your mind unbidden?" the robot asks.

I shake my head. That's a weird one.

"Do you have suspicious ideas about the world around you?"

I freeze. Is Cyb asking because the AI somehow *knows* what I've been thinking about the mission? Or are all the finalists being asked the same question?

"I don't think so," I lie, forcing myself to meet the robot's eyes. "I would say I'm no more suspicious than your average person."

"Lastly, if you were forced to fight in self-defense, what would your preferred method be? Would you use your own body, your environment, or weapons?"

Another weird question. I rack my brain, thinking aloud.

"Well, I'm not much of a fighter. Technology is my weapon of choice." The flash drive waiting in my dorm room comes to mind, and my face turns hot. "Um, I'll go with environment."

"We're nearly done now." Cyb double-taps the desk and then turns back to me. "I just need you to take a look at some images here."

I join Cyb and Dot behind the desk, watching in amazement as the glass turns cloudy, colors swirling together in front of me, until they form the shape of a bat extending its wings.

"Please memorize the image," Cyb instructs, before the

colors scramble together again and then fade into the clear glass. "Tell us what you think it looked like."

"It's the Rorschach test," I say, remembering the disappearing inkblots from my Intro to Psychology class. The way I interpret the images will tell Dot and Cyb whether or not I have any psychological disorders. If I knew how to manipulate the test, this could be my way home—but I can't go anywhere until I prove my theories about the RRB and Europa. I'm in too deep.

"I see a bat with its mouth wide open and its wings outstretched," I reply, going with the honest answer.

After giving my interpretation of two more inkblot pictures, it's finally time to go. But while I'm relieved to be done with the test and out from under the robots' watchful eyes, a part of me is reluctant to leave this room—the place the answers lie.

My words to Leo last night replay themselves in my mind. *If there are biosignatures to be found, they have to still be stored within Dot and Cyb.* I gaze up at them now, my eyes fixating on the metal plates covering their torsos—the place where the AIOS software resides. The place where I'd break in and retrieve their secrets, if only I could.

After all, based on what he said about Leo . . . it seems Cyb is already collecting secrets of mine.

We can hear the wind from the cafeteria that night, its gusts rattling the windows all through dinner. A crack of thunder echoes in the room, and as I look at the tense faces surrounding me, I know I'm not the only one worrying about what this means. We've been so sheltered here at ISTC, with all the barriers and fortifications keeping the tide at bay, that it's been easy—at least for me—to pretend that we're safe from the raging storms as long as we're here. But this is the first time the sounds of outside have infiltrated our walls . . . and it makes me wonder what's coming.

"I can't stand the thought of having to go back out there," Katerina says, eyeing the window. "It's crazy to know we're just three days away from the first elimination."

"Don't worry. I bet you'll get chosen, right along with me," the ever-confident Beckett assures her, giving Katerina a flirtatious smile. *Gross.* He glances at Lark. "Don't you think so?"

"You know I can't say a word on that topic," Lark reminds him, before taking a bite of chicken tikka masala from tonight's menu. "Besides, I honestly don't know. I mean, I have my opinions, but Dr. Takumi and the general haven't told me which way they're leaning."

"Well, have you given them your input on who *you* think the Final Six should be?" Beckett asks, watching her carefully. I try to catch Leo's eye to make a face, but he is preoccupied, staring at Beckett with a slight frown. Come to think of it, he's been acting weird since the bungee-jumping day.

Lark laughs, waving Beckett off. "Again, no comment. Dr. Takumi has made it *very* clear that I'm not to discuss this with you. However, I can confidently say that any one of you would be a true asset to the mission."

"I'm so nervous." Asher buries his head in his hands. "What's even the point of trying to eat?"

"Does this mean none of you feel any . . . different about the mission, after what happened to Suki and Callum?" I ask. Lark shoots me a warning glance, but I'm genuinely curious. Aren't they at least a *little* less gung-ho now?

"I feel awful for them, of course I do. But I trust Dr. Takumi when he says the rest of us should be safe," Katerina replies. "And if you knew what I'd be going back to . . ." She shudders. "Besides, how could you *not* want to be one of the six humans in the world to live out an adventure greater than anything in history?"

"Sounds like that doesn't interest her," Beckett says, jerking his thumb in my direction, before turning to Lark. "Maybe she should just go home now, if her heart's not in it. I'm more than happy to carry the American flag on my own."

"Um, I'm right here," I snap at him. Just because he happens to be correct that I'm not ready to take a one-way trip off our planet doesn't mean I'll sit back and let him try to undermine me.

"That's not how this works, Beckett," Lark says, arching an eyebrow at him. "Having the right set of skills and characteristics matters more to the mission leaders than who's the most eager."

While he grumbles into his plate, I turn back to Katerina.

“Could you go somewhere other than Russia? I mean, if you didn’t get chosen.”

“I don’t even want to think about what I’d do,” she says flatly. But to my surprise, Lark backs me up again.

“Actually, it’s smart to think about and prepare for either scenario,” she says. “The reality is, not everyone gets to go to Europa. And I’m sure there are *some* things from your normal lives that you’d be glad to return to. Right?”

“I don’t know where I’d go,” Leo speaks up, shaking his head. “But it won’t be Rome. There are too—too many ghosts for me there. I would have to start over somewhere new.”

“I can’t go back to Israel either,” Asher says, staring at the table. “Our entire land is under the Mediterranean now. Before the draft, I’d just moved in with my aunt and uncle to their two-room flat in Surrey. I know I’m lucky to have a roof over my head, but . . . I never thought I would have to become a *yerida*.” He glances back up at us. “That’s what we call those who emigrate from Israel. I would have stayed forever, on the same street where I grew up, if I could have.”

“You realize how much of yourself is wrapped up in where you’re from once it’s taken away,” Leo says.

The two of them share a knowing glance, and I suddenly feel out of my depth. I don’t have a right to be a part of this conversation, not when I have my parents and little brother waiting for me at home—when I have an actual *home*, period. It’s strange to think that my intact family marks me as different, unrelatable, in my teammates’ eyes. And as I gaze across the table at Leo and Asher, a wave of helplessness washes over me. There's nothing I can do to change their situations . . . nothing.

"You can try to keep a part of it with you, though," Katerina says. "After Moscow went under, I found I missed the nights most of all—the way the monuments looked all lit up, the energy in the capital city before everything sank. So I started painting it all from memory, and even though I'm not the best artist, it really helps. It's sort of like reliving your past on the canvas."

"That's a beautiful idea," Lark says. She turns to Beckett. "What about you?"

"What about me?" he asks, gruffly.

"You'd go back to DC, right? Is there anything you miss about home, or would look forward to seeing again?"

A funny look crosses his face, and then he nods. "Yeah, the White House doesn't suck. My uncle lets us live there, since it has all the best flood barriers and weather protections. But I don't think I'm going back." He lifts his chin. "I was always meant for something bigger."

"I guess in three days we'll know," Asher says, taking a deep breath.

I glance back at Leo, wondering how much time we have left. How much longer will his friendship be in my life?

In three days, we'll know.

FIFTEEN

LEO

I WAKE TO THE SOUND OF A SICKENING CRACK—THE SOUND A tree might make if it snapped its neck. I struggle to sit up, but my bed is shaking, the ground rumbling and sliding beneath it.

"Earthquake!" Asher shouts. "Cover your head!"

I duck under the sheets, shoving my pillow over my head as the walls convulse around us. I brace myself for the shards of shattered glass to come flying, for the furniture to smash to the ground, just like the day the waves crashed through the windows of Rome. But then I remember—there are no windows in this room. Our furniture is bolted to the floor. NASA prepared for everything.

Just as I'm convincing myself that it's merely an

earthquake, that it won't be like Rome all over again, a clap of thunder breaks through the noise—followed by a growing roar. It sounds like a freight train is speeding straight toward us. That can only mean one thing.

"Tsunami," I try to yell, but my voice is garbled and barely makes a sound. *"Tsunami!"*

The water lashes at the walls, the floor rocking from the earthquake's aftershocks. I hear Asher begin to pray in Hebrew, his voice rising in panic, and I squeeze my eyes shut, seeing my mother's face. Her skin was blue when I finally found her in the water, a sight that caused me to throw up for days. But now I am joining her. I thought I had more time left—time to tell Naomi how I feel, to be one of the first humans to set foot on Europa—but I can feel the hand of Earth, reaching down to take me.

And then the door flies open. I pull the covers from my eyes and see the outline of a body swaying in the doorway.

"Get dressed as fast as you can and meet me at the foot of the stairs!" Lark's voice shouts. "Don't forget shoes and flashlights."

She disappears to the next door, and I struggle out of bed, feeling my way to the dresser in the darkness. We throw on clothes, and then bolt out of the room and into the dorm corridor. The floor beneath us seems to have solidified, but the wind howls like a threat, warning us that the danger hasn't passed. The high-pitched wail of an alarm follows us through the halls as we reach the crowd of disheveled finalists and staff at the foot of the stairs. Dr. Takumi and

General Sokolov stand before us, their expressions strained as they scan our faces in the glow of flashlights, taking a head count. And then Dr. Takumi leads us forward to the wall opposite the stairs.

"What's happening?" someone cries in my ear, and I shake my head, watching as Takumi presses a button on his watch—and a camouflaged door swings open within the wall.

It looks like some kind of emergency tunnel, with sandbags lining the space and a water dispenser and row of canned food in the corner. As Dr. Takumi herds us all inside, a hand finds my arm in the dark. I know without looking that it's Naomi.

We make our way deeper into the passage, and I hear the general's voice over my shoulder.

"Dot and Cyb! What about—"

"They're fine," Dr. Takumi interrupts. "Safe in their charging pods."

"And the power?"

"It should be back on once we're out of here," he answers.

That's when Naomi's hand slips out of my grasp. I turn and whisper her name, but she's already gone, her sweater flapping behind her as she disappears out of the tunnel. And the tunnel door starts sliding to a close.

My heart is in my throat, my palms sweating as I make the split-second decision. Do I stay in the safety of the emergency tunnel or follow her? The obvious choice is to stay put—the combination of earthquake aftershocks and a nearby tsunami are a lethal pair—but the thought of anything happening to Naomi springs me into action.

I back away from the crowd, flattening my body as I approach the tunnel opening. When I'm somewhat confident no one is looking, I jump out of the tunnel—making it a second before the door closes.

I watch as the bunker seals shut, leaving me exposed to the elements. And then I run to the stairs, stumbling down the last few steps as the angry earth shudders with aftershocks. Once I reach the fourth floor, I find the shattered windowpanes I was expecting, and I weave around the thick broken shards until I spot a lithe figure up ahead.

"What the hell are you doing?" I yell as I catch up to her.

Naomi spins around and shines her flashlight on me. But then she keeps moving. "This is my shot," she pants. "The robots are alone. I'll never get a chance like this again."

"Are you out of your mind? How could you risk your life for this—this *experiment*?" I sputter.

"If I get the proof I suspect, I'll be *saving* lives—six of them," she shoots back. "Don't worry about me, please. Just go back to the others."

I shake my head in frustration. "I'm not leaving you now."

I follow as she races to the robotics lab, barely able to hear myself think through the rumble of thunder and the shrieking wind outside. We reach the blue-painted door, and I'm just about to remind Naomi that we can't get in without a pass—until she turns the handle and it swings open.

"How did that happen?"

"It's an electronic lock," she explains, pulling me inside with her. "When the power went out, the locks were disabled. Same with the cameras."

"So then aren't the robots shut down, too? In which case, what are we doing here?"

"The AIs run on solar power, since they were built specifically for the spacecraft," Naomi says. "So the blackout doesn't affect them—it only affects their surroundings."

We step into the lab, which looks eerier than usual under the pale glow of our flashlights. I bump straight into a robot under construction, and I cover my mouth as its dismembered head sways on its stand, toppling to the floor with a thud.

"Oh, no," I moan.

Naomi shushes me, pulling me toward the two glowing sleep pods in the center of the room.

"I'm going into Dot's," she tells me, pointing at the pod on the right. "Can you keep watch and make sure Cyb doesn't come out of Sleep Mode—and that no one comes in?"

"Um. What exactly are you planning to do?"

"You'll see," she says grimly. "Wish me luck."

"This is crazy," I mumble, positioning myself between Cyb's pod and the door. I watch as Naomi takes a deep breath and lifts the lid on Dot's pod. Dot's artificial eyes snap open, and my stomach jumps—but Naomi murmurs something to the machine while quickly turning two of the knobs inside the pod. Suddenly Dot's eyes are closed again, her chassis lifeless.

"Can you hand me a screwdriver?" she calls out.

"What? Where?" I can't stop staring at Dot. What did Naomi do to her?

"We're in a robotics lab. There should be a screwdriver on every desk. While you're at it, you might want to grab a stun gun, too . . . just to be safe."

"Excuse me?"

Naomi pauses. "Don't look at me like that. It's just a precaution, in case Cyb wakes up while I'm in here. The electric shock will disable the AI and freeze his memory for three minutes, giving us enough time to get away—and then he'll be fine."

I reluctantly leave my guard position and make my way to the first desk I see, rummaging through the mess of tools until I find a screwdriver—and a small metal stun gun, the size of one of my father's old fountain pens. I shove it in my pocket, and as I hand the screwdriver to Naomi, I can't help saying, "I love how you thought you could do this without any help."

"Well, I *could* have," she replies. "It just would have taken me longer. But . . . thank you."

I return to my watch as Naomi uses the screwdriver to pry open a recessed compartment in the robot's back—leaving Dot with a gaping hole. I'm slightly horrified and yet also fascinated by the sight. And then Naomi pulls something small and shiny from her pocket . . . and plugs it into a port in Dot's back. She fiddles with the dials and sensors on the robot's arm until a small screen on Dot's chest lights up, flashing with symbols and numbers.

I wait for what feels like an eternity as Naomi's hands move across the screen, typing and swiping on the robot's chest, while each sound and creak in the room sets me more on edge. Finally, she removes the flash drive and screws Dot's recessed compartment back on, returning the robot to its normal appearance—all while it remains in Sleep Mode.

"Okay, let's go, *now*!" She tosses the screwdriver on one of the desks and returns to my side, looking nervous for the first time.

She doesn't need to tell me twice. I grab her hand and we break into a run, slamming the door shut behind us.

"What were you doing exactly?" I ask as we race down the corridor, sidestepping fallen shelves and broken glass.

Naomi hesitates before answering. "I have my own hacking software on a flash drive. And before you say anything, I'm not a criminal . . . not really. This is only the second time I've used it. The first time was to get my brother's medical records when the hospital was taking too long to release his results."

I stop in my tracks. "So you really did it. You *hacked* the robot?"

"Yeah. I basically used my malware to access Dot's SSH connection, and I reconfigured the AI operating system to connect to my own tablet. Once I plug the drive into my tablet, I'll be able to program and direct Dot just like the ISTC leaders do from their computers—so Dot will think it's *them* giving commands. That's step one of how I'm going to get the truth about Europa." She turns to me with a steely look. "And no one but you will ever know."

I stare at her. "Do you even *realize* how scary you can be?"

But something in the way I say it makes Naomi burst into unexpected laughter. I try to shush her as we flee the scene, but now she has a case of uncontrollable nervous giggles, and I can't help laughing too.

"At least if this storm kills us—or Dr. Takumi finds us and does the job himself—we'll literally die laughing," I remark.

Suddenly, the smile slips off her face. She switches off her flashlight and grabs my arm, yanking me around a corner. That's when I hear the unmistakable sound of footsteps.

We're not alone.

SIXTEEN

NAOMI

I CAN FEEL THE BLOOD ROARING IN MY EARS, THE BREATH trapped in my throat, as Leo and I flatten ourselves against the wall. There is nothing we can do now but listen to the excruciating sound of footsteps in the dark and wait out our last moments of freedom. Dr. Takumi's list of potential punishments runs through my mind, and my hands start to shake. I was stupid to think I could get away with this—and now Leo has to pay the price for what I did.

All my bravado is gone, and I look to him, hoping he is as strong in this moment as he looks. As the footsteps march closer, I turn my face toward his. *I'm sorry,* I mouth.

Leo nods, reaches for my hand. Through the dark, I notice the outline of his lips. There is so much unspoken between us, so much I want to say, and now we're about to get caught—

"Security breach detected."

"Attention! Security breach detected."

I freeze at the sound of the mechanical voices echoing toward us. And then a light shines in my eyes, and my head snaps up. This time, I can't hold back my scream.

Three faceless utility robots circle us, compact versions of Dot and Cyb, but just as intimidating in the dark. Army insignias glow across their metal chests, and I realize—these are Dr. Takumi's soldiers.

"Source of breach uncovered," one of the robots drones, marching toward us with handcuffs. "Finalists out of bounds—"

A zapping sound crackles through the air, and I jump back at the sight of the flying blue current. One of the robots hits the floor with a crash, and I turn in amazement to see Leo, aiming the stun gun from the lab at the remaining two. They reach into their holsters, withdrawing arms of their own—

Zap. Zap. The breath whooshes from my lungs as the second and third AIs fall. And then Leo is seizing my hand, both of us lunging forward into a run, the adrenaline and fear driving my body faster than I've ever moved in my life. Neither of us says a word as we sprint toward the staircase, and for once I'm thankful for the rain and thunder, as it muffles the sound of us pounding up the steps, our panting breaths.

Within minutes we're back on the Hab floor, running

past the deserted cafeteria and library to the darkened dorm wing. My heartbeat only starts to stabilize when we reach the corridor that separates the girls' wing from the boys'. *We made it*.

"You—you were amazing," I whisper. "Thank you."

Leo shakes his head, his expression dazed. "You're the one who told me to grab the stun gun. I just remembered to use it."

"The way you used it is the reason we're standing here now." I touch his arm. "I was wrong before, when I said I didn't need you."

A smile lights his face. "I'll remember that. And . . . maybe now you can take a break from trying to get in as much trouble as possible?"

"I guess I do owe you that much," I say wryly. "And I promise I'll wait for a few days to go by before I even attempt to access Dot with my drive, to make sure no one's onto us."

"What about the utility robots?" Leo winces. "Are you sure I didn't do any permanent damage?"

"I'm sure. And the electric shocks wiped the past three minutes of their memories, which means they'll have no data of seeing us." I take a step closer to him. "Once again, you were amazing. I just—I'm really sorry I almost roped you into disaster."

"Maybe I should be mad," he acknowledges. "But . . . before I followed you, I was back in that dark place that storms always bring me to. You distracted me. So . . . maybe it was worth it."

My chest fills with warmth at his words. "I—I'm glad."

"And I have to admit, I never thought I'd see the day where I'd manage to disarm three robots. I won't forget that one." He grins.

"You definitely have bragging rights for days," I agree, smiling back.

"So what should we say tomorrow, when people ask why we weren't in the tunnel? I'm guessing they noticed."

I nod, thinking quickly. "Let's just pretend we didn't make it to the tunnel in time—that we were lagging behind and the door closed before we got there, so we had to wait out the storm in our rooms. I know Dr. Takumi took a head count when we were still there, but between the finalists and instructors and all the chaos, it's not hard to believe that he could have counted an extra two."

"Yeah. That makes sense." He takes a breath. "Goodnight, Naomi."

"Night, Leo."

He inches closer to me, and then seems to think better of it, backing away again. I wish he hadn't.

"Sleep well. And for God's sake, hide that flash drive—somewhere no one in the world could find it but you."

"I will. I've taken to keeping it right here." I gesture to my bra, and then instantly turn bright red. *Too much information, Naomi.*

"Oh! Good—good thinking," Leo stammers. "Well. I'll see you in the morning, then."

"See you."

As I watch his retreating figure turn toward the boys' wing, I can't help smiling.

It's nice to see him a little flustered.

I'm just managing to drift off to sleep when the sound of someone barging through my door jolts me awake. I sit upright, heart racing, as Lark slams the door behind her and looms over my bed. Her eyes flash with fury.

"What were you *thinking*?" she snaps. "Do you realize I risked my job covering for the two of you?"

She knows. I open my mouth to speak, but nothing comes out—my throat is like sandpaper. I grasp for the right words to explain, to sugarcoat what I did, but I can't come up with anything better than a pathetic, "It's not what you think."

"Oh, it's exactly what I think." Lark's eyes are like daggers. "I should have guessed earlier. It was obvious something was going on between the two of you—but I didn't think you'd ever be so reckless as to risk your lives during a storm and sneak off together, right under Dr. Takumi's nose!"

My face heats up in embarrassment as I realize what Lark's getting at. But then . . . could her misunderstanding let us off the hook?

"So you're saying you know . . . about me and Leo?" I ask, testing her.

"Obviously!" She throws her hands up in exasperation. "What do you have to say for yourself?"

"I'm sorry. *Really* sorry. I—we just thought this would be our only chance to be alone," I fib.

Lark shakes her head. "I warned them about bringing teenage hormones into this. But of course, no one listened to me!"

"What—what did you tell Dr. Takumi and the general?" I ask. "About us, I mean."

"You're both lucky I thought on my feet. When the others noticed you were gone, I put two and two together and figured out what you were really up to." She gives me a pointed look. "So I said I saw you both come running to the tunnel just before the door closed, and that you missed it."

The same excuse I planned, I note with amusement.

"General Sokolov wanted to open the door in case you were still there waiting, but I said you'd probably gone back to your rooms by then and it wasn't worth exposing the rest of us to the elements. But if she or Dr. Takumi had pressed the issue and found out that you'd disobeyed their orders to go suck face—well, the two of you would be toast."

I'm too mortified to look her in the eye—and also a bit deflated at the realization that my personal life is a whole lot more exciting in Lark's mind than in reality. But I am curious about one thing.

"Why did you cover for us? I'm incredibly grateful, believe me," I add hurriedly. "I just can't help wondering, since you seem awfully . . . mad."

"Oh, I am mad," she says icily. "But I already lost one team member before the first eliminations. The last thing

I want is to show up on Friday as the only leader with half their team already gone. I know Dr. Takumi, and he would blame me for your transgressions."

So she's *not* looking out for us out of the goodness of her heart. But in a way, her motive makes it easier for me to believe we really are safe . . . at least for now. I feel my muscles begin to relax.

"Thank you, Lark. I mean it."

"This is the *only* time, though," she warns me. "From now on, you two are going to have to do a much better job of covering up whatever is going on here—or better yet, nipping it in the bud. It can only work against you with Dr. Takumi and the general."

"You're right." I nod automatically. "I'm sorry. We, uh . . . we'll end it." *Before it's even begun.*

She moves toward the door, seemingly satisfied by my remorse.

"One more thing," she says on her way out. "You owe me one. Remember that."

The power is back on by morning, but when we arrive at the cafeteria, Dr. Takumi announces that the day's training sessions have all been canceled.

"The staff here at ISTC and Johnson Space Center need to focus on repairs and equipment checks in the aftermath of last night," he explains. "So after breakfast, instead of going into a training session, you'll be following me to the media room."

I watch Dr. Takumi carefully as he speaks, trying to gauge whether anything is different—if he has any inkling that something went down in the robotics lab last night, or if he bought Lark's explanation of where me and Leo were. But when his eyes roam over our team table and land on me, his expression is unreadable. I wonder if I can take that as a good sign.

Dr. Takumi leads the way to a space we haven't seen before, a small room at the end of the Hab floor that resembles a movie theater. A large screen unfurls across the front wall, the image paused on what looks like the TV news—something we haven't been allowed to watch since we arrived here. Once we're all seated, Dr. Takumi paces to the front of the screen.

"Last night, we experienced a taste of the devastation that shook the American South with its effects felt even farther beyond: a 7.0 earthquake, and a midlevel tsunami triggered by the quake's undersea megathrust," he says. "Thanks to our extreme precaution methods, Johnson Space Center suffered comparatively little damage. However, very few buildings in the country are privileged with this level of protection. You will find that the majority of others in our region did not fare as well."

My stomach clenches at his words. How many died? How far did the disaster stretch? *Please let California be safe,* I pray silently. *Please let my family be untouched by this.*

"It's important for you to recognize the suffering going

on outside these walls, and to understand why the Europa Mission is the answer," Dr. Takumi continues. "To keep you informed and remind you of what's at stake, I'm lifting the TV restrictions today."

I glance at Leo and Asher on either side of me, unsure how I feel about this. On one hand, it's a relief to be able to catch a glimpse of the outside world after being out of the loop for so long . . . but there is something manipulative about Dr. Takumi letting us watch the news on a day when the images are certain to be harrowing.

I take a deep breath, bracing myself as the screen flickers to life. But even after everything I've seen in the past two years, there's no way to prepare for this: the sight of skyscrapers swaying and sinking into the waves while the earth shakes, the echoing screams of the hundreds of victims trapped inside. I grip the armrest with white knuckles as the scene shifts to a weary-looking anchorman facing the camera.

"We're looking at the wreckage of Oklahoma City, which faced widespread destruction last night in the earthquake and subsequent tsunami," he reports. "The landmark Chase Tower was one of the buildings to fall, and the entire state of Oklahoma is still out of power." He rubs his face, seems to fight back tears. "This marks another city taken from us by Mother Nature."

Panic presses against my chest. I can't watch any more, I can't listen to them counting the casualties. And as the footage pans over anguished Americans, standing in the waist-high rubble and water where their homes used to be, I shoot out of my seat. My family may be miles away from the epicenter of the storm—but they're not far enough to escape its reach, not in this disfigured Earth we're living in. And I can't sit here a second longer, not until I know if they're safe.

I can feel the other finalists' eyes on me as I dash toward Dr. Takumi, who stands by the screen with a poker-faced expression.

"Please—I need to see my family, to know if they're okay." I look him in the eye, hoping against hope that my desperation might move him. "Is there anything you can do? Can we arrange a video-chat for today?"

He sighs. I can feel his refusal coming, and I try another tack.

"Not just for me, but—but for Beckett, too. I'm sure he's worried about how things are looking in DC."

It may be easy to deny me a favor, but Beckett is a different story. The president of the United States is one of the key figures who signed off on this mission, who helped get Congress to bankroll it. If Dr. Takumi thinks his nephew wants to see him . . .

"Fine," he relents. "But let it be known to all of you that this is a one-time exception. If we allowed spontaneous video-chats every time a natural disaster occurred, we'd be spending all day in front of the computer instead of preparing for the mission at hand."

"Thank you!" I cry, before turning to Beckett in the

audience and mouthing, *You're welcome.* After all, it's because of me that he gets to check on his family. But he just looks away with a scowl.

"Sam!"

My eyes well up with relief as soon as I see his face. *He's okay, he's okay,* my mind chants on a loop, the air seeping back into my lungs. But as I look closer at my brother, I notice something is different. His eyes are hollow, all the light gone from them. It's like looking at someone with my brother's face, but none of his spirit.

"What happened?" I ask, afraid to hear the answer. "Is it Mom or Dad? Where are they?"

"They're fine. The only reason they're not here right now is because they're helping the downstairs neighbors evacuate. The lower floor flooded completely in the storm," he says heavily.

I flinch at the thought of the sweet, elderly Bursteins being forced to flee. "Did—did they lose everything? Where are they going to go?"

"They salvaged what they could, but . . ." He shakes his head. "They're staying with us in your room, until they can get ahold of other family."

"I'm glad they'll be with you guys," I say quietly. "So our apartment is okay, then?"

"Yeah, it managed to stay afloat. The damage wasn't as bad up here. But listen, Naomi . . ." He takes another breath, and I notice how shallow it sounds.

"Are you okay? How are you feeling?" I interrupt him.

"The same," he answers, and I don't know whether to be relieved or worried. *The same* isn't necessarily good news for my brother—but if he's telling me the truth, then at least he hasn't gotten worse while I've been away.

"What I was about to say is, I've been thinking about something since we last talked, and . . ." He meets my eyes. "I don't want you to come home."

I recoil in my seat. "*What?* What are you saying?"

"I want you to forget the—the message I gave you." He looks away. "I realize now it was selfish of me to want you to come back. I've lost count of how many times this planet has tried to kill us. Whatever is on Europa, it can't be worse than here. So . . . you have to go."

My mouth falls open. I can't believe what I'm hearing. "You *want* me to leave Earth? To possibly never see you again?"

"I want you to save yourself," he says. "You've been given an opportunity, and I don't want to be the one holding you back. Plus, if the mission has any hope of succeeding, it needs a brain like yours." He musters a smile. "The future needs you."

"But . . . but what about *you*?"

"I—I'll be okay." He gives a resigned shrug. "I'm a lot tougher than I seem, you know? I shouldn't have pushed you to try to come home. Besides, I've been thinking of ways I can help you on Europa, from here." The old spark briefly returns to his eyes. "You're not the only one good with computers."

"But I—I already—" I want to tell him to forget what he's saying, that I hacked Dot last night and set a plan in motion. But of course I can't. I can only hope he reads the truth in my face.

"Two more minutes!" Lark calls out from the doorway, where she's supervising Beckett and me. I hold on to the edges of the computer monitor, as if I can somehow keep my brother close.

"It's not my decision to make, but . . ." I lower my voice. "Even if I get chosen in the end, I'm still not giving up. Not on you, or on Earth."

Sam smiles sadly. "But you should. Let go of us, Sis. Let go and soar, like you're meant to."

"No," I whisper. "You don't know—"

But the screen is flickering, turning pixelated. Our time is up.

SEVENTEEN

LEO

I HEAR ASHER AWAKEN EARLY ON THE MORNING OF THE FIRST elimination, and I listen as he begins murmuring to himself in Hebrew. The sound is a comfort to my nerves.

My family was never very religious—we observed all holidays at Basilica di Sant'Agostino, and that was the extent of it—but in this moment, when our fates and futures lie in the control of someone else, I close my eyes, imagining my mother, father, and Angelica somewhere in the air above, listening to my thoughts. Maybe I can make up my own prayer . . . to them.

Watch over me today, famiglia. *Please let me be one of the twelve still standing at the end of the night. Help me make it all the way to Europa as one of the Final Six—with*

Naomi there too, and Asher. Without you . . . this is all I have.

The alarm in our LED mirror bursts to life. I stretch and sit up in bed as Asher tucks what looks like a prayer book back in the desk drawer.

"Here goes," he says, turning to me with a pale face.

I nod. "Do you think we'll find out right away?"

"Maybe. But if they're still not a hundred percent sure, they might drag this out as late as they can."

Asher is right. At breakfast, we learn we'll be undergoing a last-chance astronaut physical—a comprehensive exam to evaluate how our bodies are adjusting to the RRB and to ensure no new conditions or weaknesses have gone undetected. I can barely swallow two bites of my breakfast after hearing about all the medical poking and prodding that lies ahead. *What if they find something that ruins my shot?* I can't fathom being so close only to lose it all in the last stretch. Glancing around the table, it's clear my teammates share my anxiety. Even the possibly cold-blooded Beckett Wolfe can't hide his nerves as he taps his foot restlessly against the floor.

Lark shuttles us to the main medical facility on Johnson Space Center campus, and as we step onto the main outpatient floor, five doors open in unison. One for each of us.

"Go on." Lark ushers us forward, and I exchange one last look with Naomi before we each disappear into one of the patient rooms.

I sit on the examination chair, staring straight ahead as a

soft-spoken nurse checks my vitals and draws multiple vials of blood for the array of tests. She listens to my ears and heart and puts me through one of those mindless letter-chart vision tests, all while I silently command my body to stay calm, to not betray my nerves with a jittery heartbeat or anything that the nurse might question. And then, after nearly an hour, I'm ushered into the next room—a small, sterile space with only a table and two chairs to fill it. A bearded man sits at one end of the table, consulting a clipboard.

"I'm Dr. Dwyer," he greets me, extending his palm for a handshake. "I'll be administering your final psych evaluation. If you make the Final Six, you will be hearing from me regularly while in space, as mental check-ins are a crucial part of the process when leaving Earth."

"Sounds good." I smile at him, trying to appear even-keeled and confident, despite the sight of this stranger giving me a chill of foreboding. To have someone brand-new evaluating us at the very last moment makes me even more vulnerable than I was before. What if I make the wrong first impression and have no time to change his mind?

"Have a seat," he instructs me. "Today you'll be completing the MMPI-3 standardized psychological test, which consists of a series of statements that you will label true or false. Let me know when you're ready."

I nod.

"Ready."

"First statement. 'A person should try to understand his

dreams and be guided by or take warning from them.' True or false?"

"Um." I have no clue what he wants to hear—which leaves me no choice but to answer with my gut reaction and hope it produces the desired result. "True."

"Next. 'Once in a while, you think of things too bad to talk about.' True or false?" My mind flashes back to the day that was supposed to be my last, when I came so close to making a terrible choice. *If they knew . . . would they see me as another Callum?*

I shake my head, giving Dr. Dwyer what I hope is a calm glance.

"False."

And on it goes for the next hour, each question more unpredictable than the next, leaving me increasingly uncertain how I'm doing. Finally, we reach the last one.

"'If confronted with a potentially threatening creature of foreign origin, your first instinct is to kill it and protect yourself.' True or false?"

My head snaps up. *What in the world?*

"F-false."

Dr. Dwyer nods and makes a series of scribbled notes before finally excusing me out into the hall where Lark waits. But I can't get that last question off my mind.

I wonder if it has to do with Europa.

By five p.m., the judges are still deliberating our fates. Lark informs us that Dr. Takumi, General Sokolov, and the robots are sequestered somewhere on campus, reviewing our Astronaut Physical results and discussing the pros and cons of all twenty-two of us—and there's no telling how long we'll be waiting. With no training to occupy us, and no Wi-Fi, cell phones, or TV to distract us, we are alone with our suspense.

The teams are intermingled as we wait in the lounge, and I share a couch with Asher and Naomi, the three of us making a hopeless attempt at talking about something, anything, other than the draft. Seated on the other side of us are Dev Khanna and the Canadian finalist, a tall, slender girl with dark skin and eyes, named Sydney Pearle. She sits with her head between her knees, muttering something under her breath while Dev awkwardly pats her on the back.

"I know how you feel," I say, leaning over to her. "There's no real way to prepare for a competition on this scale."

She lifts her face with a groan. "That's not it."

"She doesn't know whether she wants to stay or go home," Dev explains. "Which is a bit unusual in this crowd."

Naomi and I exchange a look.

"Trust me," she tells Sydney. "It's not that unusual. And it's hard to feel so . . . out of control."

Sydney nods, looking at Naomi as if seeing her for the first time. "*Yes*. It's maddening."

"I wish I felt indecisive like you two," Asher says glumly. "Then it wouldn't be so hard if—if I get cut."

"You have some of the best odds out of anyone," I

encourage him. "I mean, who else here is a trained pilot?"

"Jian Soo," Dev chimes in, not exactly helping.

"Exactly," Asher says, his voice dropping. "And even if I happen to be better at flying than he is, it doesn't really matter, does it? Not when they have a perfect piloting machine in Cyb."

Naomi wraps a comforting arm around his shoulder. "It'll be okay. Whatever happens, we can help each other get through it." She glances at me. "Right?"

I stare at her and Asher, my two closest friends here, who I never imagined together in that way. But now, seeing them looking close and cozy brings a pang to my chest. *What if they were to get chosen without me?*

She looks at me questioningly, and I clear my throat. "Right. We'll—we'll be okay."

A rush of footsteps comes clattering through the doorway, and we all glance up. Lark and two other team leaders burst into the lounge, excitement vibrating off their skin.

"They've made their decision!" Lark exclaims. "We're meeting Dr. Takumi, the general, and the AIs in the cafeteria right now. Dinner will be served after the announcement."

"Seriously?" Dev whispers to me. "Who's actually going to *eat* after that?"

But I'm too shaken up to answer. *This is it.* I'm either going to continue on for two more weeks here and have an exponentially bigger chance at making the Final Six—or I'll be released back into the emptiness of an earthbound life tonight.

As if sensing my emotions, Naomi squeezes my arm. I gaze down at her, and suddenly I am bargaining with the universe. *If we both make it to the next round, I'll stop skating around how I feel. I'll tell her—even if it means rejection.*

My legs are like lead as we march to the cafeteria. Dr. Takumi, General Sokolov, Dot, and Cyb stand in a line on the raised platform. *Here we go.*

Beckett and Katerina, who were missing from the lounge, are already seated at our team table when we arrive. I still haven't spoken a word to Beckett since the bungee-jumping incident, and as I slide into my seat, I add an addendum to my prayer. *Please let them cut the right person today: Beckett Wolfe.*

"Welcome, finalists, to one of the key milestones in the Europa Mission." Dr. Takumi greets us, his voice booming through the tense quiet of the room. "With the most impressive teenagers in the world to choose from, it was an extremely difficult decision. The ten of you leaving us tomorrow morning should know that it was a close call, and you have much to be proud of." He clears his throat. "Without further ado, your mission pilot, Cyb, will announce the names of the twelve finalists moving forward in the draft."

I can hear my heart thumping wildly as the robot shuffles forward.

"From the United Kingdom, Dianna Dormer," Cyb's mechanical voice calls out. "From India, Dev Khanna. From Ukraine, Minka Palladin. From Italy, Leonardo Danieli—"

"Yes!" I punch the air in celebration, almost dizzy from the sound of my name. *I did it—I made it!*

Beckett looks at me like he's just tasted something rotten, while Naomi smiles at the sight of my happiness, and Asher thumps me on the back in congratulations. Suddenly, I'm nervous all over again. Asher and Naomi *have* to get chosen, too. I can't imagine this place without them.

"From France, Henri Durand. From Canada, Sydney Pearle."

The tension in the room mounts as Cyb reaches the halfway mark. I can hear Katerina's legs jangling under the table, her feet tapping uncontrollably, while Beckett's face takes on a purplish hue. Naomi fidgets in her seat; Asher takes short, shallow breaths. Only six more names.

"From Japan, Ami Nakamura. From the United States . . ."

Naomi's head jerks up. I grab her hand under the table.

". . . Beckett Wolfe!"

No. My spirits plummet as Beckett celebrates in his seat, high-fiving Katerina. My competition—and the most ruthless person here—remains. Naomi's body sags at the realization that it isn't her, though I can't tell whether from relief or disappointment.

"From Spain, Ana Martinez. From Russia . . ."

Katerina sits up excitedly, and Beckett gives her a knowing smile.

"Evgeni Alkaev."

Katerina's mouth falls open. And now we've reached the

final two. I grip Naomi's hand again, closing my eyes and concentrating on her name, as if I can somehow manipulate the outcome.

"From China, Jian Soo."

My shoulders slump. I look from Asher to Naomi and back again. After today, I might never see one—or both—of them again.

"Lastly, from the United States—Naomi Ardalan."

I hear her gasp, feel my own breath return to me. And then I throw my arms around her, unable to contain the huge grin spreading across my face. She smiles back at me, and I wonder if maybe, in spite of herself, she really *did* want to stay. The feel of her hair against my cheek and her body pressed to mine has me almost intoxicated. Something flickers in my chest as I look into her shining dark eyes—and I pull back before I give myself away. That's when I see Asher's face, and it hits me with a blow. He's leaving.

Katerina scrapes back her chair and runs from the room, the sound of a muffled sob following her. I expect Beckett to run after her, but it's Naomi who goes, calling out for her to wait. I move into the empty chair, next to Asher.

"I—I don't know what to say," I tell him, wincing at the uselessness of my words. "It should have been you, too."

Beckett leans in.

"Don't worry, you guys will see each other again. You're not long for this either, Italian."

Rage boils inside me as I whip my head to face Beckett.

"Are you serious right now?"

He gives me a cold smile before pushing back from the table.

"Well, they don't need two underwater specialists on the mission. And we both know it's going to be me in the end."

"You're delusional," I call out to his retreating figure as he goes to congratulate the rest of the twelve like a true politician.

"Don't let him be right." Asher finally speaks up. As he looks at me, I can see the crushing loss and disappointment reflected in his eyes. "If it can't be me, I want it to be you—and not Beckett."

EIGHTEEN

NAOMI

THE ELIMINATED FINALISTS ARE GONE BY MORNING. THERE'S no farewell breakfast, no exchanging of email addresses and cell phone numbers like on the last day of summer camp. They are just . . . gone, their belongings and presence wiped clean from the Hab floor. I feel a pang of regret that I didn't get a proper good-bye with Asher. When he left the cafeteria after the announcement, I was sure he would come back, that we'd have one last dinner as a team. But he and Katerina never returned. And now it's just me, Leo, and Beckett sitting around the breakfast table, with Lark between us as a buffer. While Beckett peppers her with questions about what's next, I turn away, my eyes taking in the half-empty room.

"Hey." Leo nudges me gently. "How are you feeling?"

"I—I'm not sure."

The truth is, it feels like my mind is toying with me. I knew I wasn't ready to leave yesterday, not yet, not with my discoveries still hanging in the balance—and not with Leo still here. But as I imagine an alternate reality with me as one of the eliminated ten, I'm overcome by a wave of sadness. I could have been on my way home this very *moment*. I could have been minutes away from my family's arms. And now . . . who knows when I will see them again?

"What about you?" I ask, changing the subject.

Leo takes a deep breath. "It was tough to see Asher go. My room feels weird. Empty."

I nod, thinking about Suki. "I know the feeling."

"But I'm hopeful, too." Leo leans in closer, giving me a small smile. "About everything."

And as he looks at me, I feel a shiver working its way through my body—one that I know has nothing to do with space.

"Good morning to the Top Twelve!" Dr. Takumi strides into the room, and all conversation comes to a halt. "How does it feel to have made it another week?"

"Incredible!" Beckett yells. Dev lets out a whoop from the next table over, and soon the room is filling with cheers, my fellow finalists letting loose and celebrating in ways they couldn't last night. I scan the room for the Canadian finalist, Sydney, possibly the only person here who knows how I feel. But even she looks caught up in the excitement, beaming in her seat between Dev and Ana Martinez.

"That's the spirit I like to see," Dr. Takumi says with a satisfied nod. "Now, since our pool of candidates is significantly smaller, we've done away with the teams. The twelve of you will be training together for your remaining days here, with General Sokolov taking the lead on most of your instruction."

I exchange a look with Leo. I think we all know what this means. With the teams disbanded, it's going to be every finalist against the others—and out for themselves.

After breakfast, General Sokolov leads the twelve of us to the Mission Floor for our first training session of the day. I fall into step with Leo, noticing the looks of steely determination on my fellow finalists' faces as they pass me by.

"Are you feeling more competitive toward everyone else now, too?" I ask Leo. "Especially with Asher gone?"

He shakes his head slightly. "I wouldn't say more. I mean, the competition has been stiff enough since the beginning." He lowers his voice. "I still haven't told you what happened during the bungee-jumping challenge, have I?"

"No. What?"

Leo glances around to make sure no one is listening before he continues. "Beckett tried to mess with my harness while we were in the air. He was—I think—trying to get me killed. It would have been the perfect accident, but the pickup plane showed up just in time."

I stop in my tracks, feeling as though I've just been socked in the chest. "*What?* That actually happened, and you didn't—didn't *tell* anyone?"

"What was I supposed to say? 'Hi, Dr. Takumi, I think my teammate tried to push me ten thousand feet to my death, but I have no proof and I'm still here, so no damage done'?" He gives me a wry look. "It would have seemed like I was just trying to get him in trouble. Remember that talk he gave us about sabotage?"

"Yeah—exactly what Beckett was trying to do to *you*," I point out. My pulse quickens. "We could get him kicked out for this!"

Leo places his hand over mine, and I'm momentarily distracted by his touch.

"I want him gone more than anyone. But not like that," he says. "Not by weakening myself . . . especially if I was wrong about what I saw. It's not like he's tried anything since."

With a flash, I remember the way Beckett looked at Leo after his showstopping performance in the diving pool. "You weren't wrong. I can feel it."

But there's no more time to talk, as we catch up to General Sokolov and the others, following them through the opening in the wall and onto the Mission Floor. The general stops before one of the space capsules.

"Today you'll be performing a flight simulation that takes you through the Europa Mission's spaceflight path in accelerated time. We'll start with the initial launch into space on a trajectory to Mars orbit, where you'll rendezvous with the *Athena*'s supply ship, followed by the gravity slingshot to Jupiter orbit. And of course, you'll end with the lunar landing on Europa. As you know, while Cyb will be piloting the spacecraft, one of you will serve as copilot—and each of the Final Six will be needed at crucial points along the journey, especially when it comes to in-flight troubleshooting."

I glance at Leo, and I can tell we're both thinking the same thing: *If only Asher had been here for this one.*

"And that is the purpose of today's simulation," the general continues. "To prepare you for the journey, test our copilot candidates . . . and, most importantly, gauge your reactions when the unexpected occcurs and your mission and lives are at stake.

"You'll be completing the sim in pairs, so go ahead and choose a partner. During the downtime while waiting your turn, each of you will be measured for Europa space suits."

Leo nudges me. "Be my partner?"

I turn to him, feeling a sudden rush of gratitude that he is still here. "Of course."

We don't get any hints as to what's unfolding in the simulations, but we can hear the screams clearly from outside. The first four pairs emerge from the space capsule looking a combination of dazed, nauseous, and exhilarated, which only ramps up my anticipation. What, exactly, is waiting for us in there?

Leo and I are the fifth pair up, and when our names are called, General Sokolov hands us each a virtual reality headset and ushers us inside the capsule. It looks identical to the mock cockpit we entered on our first training day, but with two key differences: the electronic sensors dotting the floor and blinking wires suspended from the ceiling.

"Take your acceleration seats and prepare for liftoff," the general commands, before climbing out of the capsule to plug in from her computer.

I watch her leave, wondering if that's really all the instruction we're going to get, and then I slide into one of the two reclined seats in front of the glass cockpit. The seats are folded all the way back, and I turn my face just as Leo angles his toward me—so close.

"Hi," I whisper.

"Ciao," he says with a smile, his breath tickling my cheek.

We slip on our headsets, and the ground beneath us lurches. The capsule begins to shake, rattling the interior with a power that makes last week's earthquake seem modest. This *can't* be just a simulation; it feels too real. But the roar of an engine muffles out my thoughts, and now the cockpit glass surrounding us is filling with moving 5D images, placing us at the center of a rocket barge anchored over the sea.

"T-minus zero . . . and liftoff!" a voice blares from the cockpit speakers. And then we are hurtling forward, my body nearly flying out of my chair before the strap stops me. We are spinning, our bodies turning upside down with breathtaking speed as the reflection in the glass changes from a blue sky to the inky vacuum of space.

"Something's heading toward us," I hear Leo say. "What *is* that?"

I peer closer at the glass.

"Looks like a used rocket stage . . . but if I'm right, wouldn't that kill—"

I break off with a shout as shards of matter come flying in our direction. Through my headset it looks like the shards are aiming straight for my eyes, and I duck in my seat.

"We have to move around it," I yell as Leo grabs the pilot's joystick. "Do you know how to work that thing?"

"We're about to find out." He pushes down on the joystick and turns it to the right, sending us swerving sharply, nearly tearing out of our seats yet again. I exhale with relief as we pass the spinning shards of matter, but now—

"Do you smell that?"

Leo pauses in midair as the unmistakable stench of fire fills the cockpit. And then an enormous blue flame, as tall as my own body, starts ripping through the cabin.

"It's not real, it's not real," I chant under my breath, but it doesn't matter what I tell myself—this moment, this danger, is as tangible as anything I've experienced before.

Leo scans the capsule for a way out of the fire, and as he takes his hand off the joystick, we plunge downward.

"Damn it!"

"Keep steering. I'll take care of it!" I shout above the noise.

He returns to the joystick, and we soar back up as I climb out of my seat and crawl through the shaking cabin, trying to escape the fire's path and yelping as the flame almost singes the back of my shirt. There has to be an extinguisher in here, there *has* to be, right by the—

Door! A red fire extinguisher is mounted by the cabin door, and I yank it out of its case and start firing the water-based foam, until the whole cockpit is drenched and the fire simmers to ash.

"Great work!" Leo calls as I stumble back to the acceleration seat. "And check this out."

He points to the window, and I catch my breath.

"Beginning orbit insertion to Mars," the voice echoes over our speakers.

The red planet looms below us, a massive, bright orb. Up ahead, rotating around Mars, is a dragonfly-shaped floating satellite—the *Athena*'s supply ship! But as I look from the scene out of the window to the scrolling numbers on the cockpit's navigation display, I spot a glaring flaw.

"The supply ship's coordinates don't match where it was plotted to be on our trajectory," I tell Leo, frantically swiping the tablet above my seat until I find the Orbital Dynamics page. "You need to plug in the new numbers before we even attempt the rendezvous, or else we'll overshoot it."

"What?" Leo's palm freezes on the joystick. "But how—"

"The fuel leak—it caused the ship's orbit to start changing." I shiver as it occurs to me: the general must be preparing us for this very scenario, one that could get far more complicated the longer the leak continues. "We need to recompute our navigation to direct us to the supply ship's new coordinates, now!"

"Got it." Leo's hands fly over the touchscreen while my eyes sweep across the cockpit console, searching for the switches General Sokolov showed us in our training, the ones that deploy the robotic arm for docking. They were somewhere on the left side of the control panel. . . .

"Trajectory adjustment confirmed," the voice returns. "Prepare to rendezvous and deploy the Canadarm."

Leo looks at me with a frenzied expression, and then turns back to the joystick. "Here goes nothing!"

He kicks up the speed as my fingers fumble with the panel, looking for the docking controls. And then, as the gravity of Mars pulls us into orbit and we match the supply ship's velocity—that's when I find the docking pane. I press the Deploy button, watching in amazement as the robotic crane slowly unfurls, pulling us toward the ship.

SLAM. Leo and I jump as our vessel swipes against the side pane of the supply ship.

"We went too fast," Leo yells. "Let me try again and decelerate this time."

I return my fingers to the control panel, ready to send the Canadarm back into the fray. This time it works, and I feel the rush of heavy gear clanking into place as we dock. I'm just about to cheer that we did it when our capsule starts spinning once again. And now the scene before our window transforms, sending us millions of miles away in a matter of seconds. I struggle to catch my breath as we descend toward an icy, red-ridged moon. *Europa*.

"We have to land!" Leo turns to me, an expression of both panic and glee in his eyes. "Should I fire the thrusters now, or—"

"Now!" I gasp. "We need to reduce our velocity *fast* if we're going to make the landing."

With one hand driving the joystick and his other working the switches on the pilot's dashboard, Leo activates the thrusters, which ignite with a deafening rumble. As our spacecraft pitches toward the moon's surface, I scan the control panel in front of me until I find the symbol for Deploy Landing Gear. But when I press the button, a red alarm pops up: *SYSTEM FAILURE*.

"Are you kidding me?"

"We're going to miss it!" Leo shouts, and through the window I can see that he is right—we're not slowing down quickly enough; we're dangerously close to skimming past Europa. "Hurry!"

My fingers shake as I try a different tack, entering the command for "Initiate Capsule Separation." A green light illuminates the control panel, and then the voice returns over the cockpit speakers.

"Final Stage Separation and Descent in three . . . two—"

My scream drowns out the countdown as the spacecraft splits in two. The engines and power propulsion modules fall away into the ether, while our remaining combined capsule drops hundreds of feet, our bodies flipping upside down in their seats. And then, finally, we come careening to a stop, our wheels kicking up ice.

The glass screen fades to darkness as the voice over the speakers says, "Simulation completed successfully. You may remove your headsets and detach from the sensors."

I pull off the VR equipment and blink in shock. It looks . . . exactly as it did when we first climbed in with General Sokolov. There's no smoke from the fire, no water from where I doused the cabin with foam. There's not a single hint of the journey we just went on. It's as though Leo and I somehow shared the same multisensory dream.

Leo leans back against his seat, and we turn to each other in exhausted, delirious relief.

"Well, that was insane," he remarks. "But we did it."

"We did it," I whisper.

I inch closer to him, close enough to see myself reflected in his blue eyes, and the longing catches me off guard. Something electric runs through my body, something I haven't felt before.

He reaches for my chin, gently tilting it toward him. I am too hopeful, too nervous, to breathe. And then, softly, he brushes his lips against mine.

We draw back for a split second, our foreheads pressed together and eyes locked, as if we are both taking in the magnitude of this moment. And then I pull him toward me, desperate to feel his lips on mine again. He cradles my face as he kisses me; he runs his mouth across my neck, leaving goose bumps everywhere his lips traced. It feels as though something is exploding in my chest, and suddenly—everything makes sense.

I know why I've been conflicted, why my heart and mind have been pulling me in different directions.

The answer was here, all along.

NINETEEN

LEO

I WRAP NAOMI IN MY ARMS, KISSING HER LIPS, HER FACE, HER hair. I feel her responding to my every touch, her arms tightening around me as she kisses me back with urgency, like this moment is all we have—

Footsteps. We spring apart, the sound outside the hatch door plunging us back down to earth. I jump out of my seat, hoping our flushed faces don't give us away, as General Sokolov bursts into the capsule.

"Come on, you two, let's go! I have another sim to get through."

She doesn't need to tell us twice. Naomi and I hurry to the hatch door, and right before I step through it, the general turns to meet my eyes, a warning in her gaze.

But now Dianna Dormer and Ami Nakamura are climbing into the capsule, and General Sokolov's attention shifts away from me, onto them.

"You don't think she saw, do you?" I murmur as Naomi and I step back onto the Mission Floor.

Her blush deepens.

"It looked like the cameras stopped rolling once we unplugged from the sim, so I think we're safe," she whispers. "But . . . she might have guessed something was up when she walked in."

"I'll be more careful next time."

As soon as the words come out of my mouth, I cringe—was that too bold of me, assuming there will even *be* a next time? What if she just got caught up in the moment and doesn't want anything more? But then she glances up at me with a shy smile.

"This is really happening, isn't it?"

My chest swells. I lean in, whispering one last reply before we join the rest of the finalists. "I think it's been happening since the day we met."

I can't believe this is my life.

The thought plays on a loop in my mind the rest of the day and into the night—as Naomi and I share covert smiles across the floor throughout training, as we float into the cafeteria on a high from our secret. I can't believe she feels the way I do.

Now that the teams are disbanded, we're thankfully no

longer bound to our old table assignments—meaning we don't have to endure another meal with Beckett Wolfe. We join a table with Jian, Sydney, Dev, and Ana, but I'm hardly aware of the conversation. I'm too distracted by the feel of her soft hand, just barely resting against mine under the table.

We spend the after-dinner hour curled up in an empty corner of the library, Naomi leaning against me as she scribbles a bunch of figures into a notebook.

"What are you working on?" I ask, peering over her shoulder.

"I'm double-checking the algorithm coding I have to enter in order to connect my tablet to . . . you know." She gives me a little wink, lowering her voice. "A certain machine."

"Oh." I feel like someone's splashed cold water on my face. "You mean, you still plan on following through with that?"

"Of course." She glances up at me with a bemused expression. "Why would I change my mind?"

Because now you have more reason to stay, I answer silently. *Because maybe it's no longer worth the risk of getting caught.*

But I don't say any of it out loud. I just watch her brain at work, her face scrunching up in concentration as her pencil flies across the page.

I walk her to her door at curfew, peering around the hallway to make sure we're alone before saying goodnight. I'm aching to kiss her again, but the blinking red light of the security camera overhead stops me.

"Hey, I have that book you wanted to borrow," Naomi says loudly, flashing a brief glance at the camera. "Come in for just a quick sec."

My insides thrill as she opens the door to her room, and I follow her inside. As soon as the door shuts behind us, she pulls me toward her, and I pin her against the wall, our hands interlacing as I move my lips across hers. She lets out a sigh, and it's almost unbearable, how good this feels.

"I should go," I whisper, though every part of me wants to stay. "Where's that book I'm supposed to be borrowing?"

Naomi reaches behind her, grabbing the title on her nightstand, a doorstopper-size memoir by Dr. Greta Wagner.

"Just a little light reading, huh?" I say with a grin.

"Yeah, well. It's my favorite, so keep it safe."

"If it's your favorite, then I'll do you one better—I'll actually read it." I lean in closer, brushing my lips against hers one last time. "See you tomorrow."

"See you then." But a shadow crosses her face as I pull away.

"What is it?"

"Nothing. I guess—it's just . . ." Her shoulders sag. "Why couldn't I have met you any other way?"

"What do you mean?" I ask, tucking a lock of hair behind her ear.

"There's such a big chance of us getting separated at the end of this. It—it makes me afraid of what I feel for you," she confesses. "I mean, one minute we were seeing Asher every day, and now we may never see him again. What if it's the same for us?" She blinks back tears, and something tightens in my chest. "It's just—it's so unfair."

"I know. But if we can get drafted together—"

"Or better yet, go back to LA together," she interrupts, giving me a meaningful look. "You would love Sam and my parents, and we could have an actual life—"

I stop her words with a kiss. I'm not ready to contemplate getting cut. Not yet—maybe not ever.

Is it wrong of me to wonder if there's some way I can have it all . . . the girl and the mission?

The next couple days fly by in a blur of training sessions with the general, Lieutenant Barnes, and the AIs, while my evenings are filled with Naomi. Even though neither of us shares a room anymore, we know not to risk another attempt at outsmarting the cameras and sneaking into each other's dorms. Instead, we spend every last second between dinner and curfew together, keeping up a pretense of platonic friendship in front of the others, while our eyes tell a different story. The only place we don't hold back is the Telescope Tower—the spot Naomi says is our safest bet for avoiding the cameras. We make it our own, the place where we can finally hold each other and kiss, after hours spent an arm's length apart.

I fall asleep with her sweet scent on my lips; I wake up with her face in my mind. Being with her is like flying in zero gravity, even while my feet are planted firmly on the ground. There's just one flaw to this new magic in my life: losing her would wreck me. And the closer we get to the reveal of the Final Six—the more possible that scenario becomes.

With T-minus five days left, we learn that our schedules will be shifting to mostly private training in each finalist's area of expertise. While I'll be spending these last days getting one-on-one instruction in drilling through Europa's ice crust, Naomi will be in the Mission Control Center with the capsule communicator, aka CAPCOM, deciphering coded computer messages and working flight-velocity equations. It's clear to all of us what the transition to specialized training means: Dr. Takumi and General Sokolov are auditioning us for the six crew positions.

My suspicion is confirmed when I show up to the diving pool for what I assumed was a private session, only to find Beckett there too. So I was right: the two of us are going head-to-head. I turn my face as soon as I see him, though I can feel his eyes boring a hole into my back. I won't acknowledge him; I won't let him psych me out.

"All right, my two divers!" Lieutenant Barnes says cheerily, oblivious to the tension between us. "Who knows the best way to drill through thirty kilometers of ice quickly in space?"

Am I *supposed* to know this? I stay quiet, hoping Beckett doesn't have the answer either. Thankfully, the lieutenant plunges ahead.

"A nuclear hydrothermal drill!" he answers for us. "Here's

how it works: the underwater specialist on the Final Six will set up the drill on the landing site of Europa. Once in position and switched on, a nuclear power source in the drill will heat water and spit it back out in the form of high-powered jets to melt through the ice. At the same time, rotating drill blades beneath the water jets will chip away at the ice." He smiles. "And *that* is how you will pierce Europa's ice shell and descend into its rocky ocean and land below."

Adrenaline courses through me. I have to beat Beckett—I *have* to be the one chosen for this job.

"The actual drill we plan to use is being finalized at NASA's Jet Propulsion Lab right now, so today we'll be working with a smaller prototype. But first, let's warm up. Give me a twist dive followed by a two-hundred-meter freestyle."

"Are we racing?" I ask the lieutenant, already grinning at the prospect. The First Nephew is about to get crushed.

"Yes. Leo, you can take the ten-meter board."

I can't resist a smirk in Beckett's direction as I climb up to the higher diving board while he is relegated to the three-meter. As I step up to the ledge, I glance down at the prick mark on my arm from last night's RRB shot, wondering if Naomi was right about it. Will I feel . . . *different* in the pool again?

I have my answer as soon as I hit the water. My skin is vibrating, my insides pulsing with the sensation of something coming to life within me—something faster than human. And as I fly through the pool, I think of the word

Naomi used. *Amphibious.* The way I move underwater without needing a breath . . . there does seem to be something almost amphibious about me now.

I touch the wall, ready to lean back and wait for Beckett to catch up. But then I see . . . he's only a few strokes behind me. *How is that possible?*

"Well done, both of you!" Lieutenant Barnes calls out, not looking nearly as stunned as he should be, considering we both just swam faster than Olympians. *What is going on here?*

"Lieutenant Barnes!" Beckett calls out from his lane opposite mine. "I've been working on that breath-holding technique we talked about and I've gotten pretty good. Let me show you?"

"Sure." Lieutenant Barnes nods, and Beckett hoists himself out of the pool and approaches my diving board—the ten-meter. A chill runs through my veins as Beckett executes a near-perfect backflip and stays underwater, the lieutenant gleefully calling out each minute he stays under. He makes it a full seven minutes—not as long as my fifteen-plus, but an unprecedented improvement over his last two-minute hold. And as I watch Beckett break through the surface and speed to the end of the lane, it's obvious that I'm not the only one benefiting from the strange side effects of the RRB.

Naomi was right. There is far more to the RRB than we've been told. Once again, I remember Elena's warning words. But now I'm beginning to have an idea of what the ISTC had in mind . . . the kind of weapons we are intended to be.

TWENTY

NAOMI

THE TWELVE OF US ARRIVE IN THE ALTITUDE CHAMBER TO FIND General Sokolov waiting for us at the center of the ice, standing beside a man we haven't seen before. A heap of aluminum and canvas lies at their feet, folded up like a parachute, and I wonder if we're in for another extreme activity. Is parachuting over Houston next on the agenda? But then the general introduces her guest as Mr. Anthony Nolan from Bigelow Aerospace, and I feel a flicker of excitement. I've been following Bigelow's science ever since I was a kid.

"Now that we're getting so close to departure, today is about learning how to live day-to-day in deep space," General Sokolov begins. "Bigelow Aerospace has done a remarkable job of building an expandable habitat for the

Final Six on Europa." She gestures to the folded materials on the ice. "It doesn't look like much now, but once inflated, it just might rival some of your own homes on Earth."

"The habitat is built to withstand all the elements, provide radiation and ballistic protection, and remain in mint condition for twenty years," Mr. Nolan adds. "And today, you're going to learn how to assemble it once you land on Europa."

Leo gives me a gentle nudge, and a grin that makes my heart constrict. I know what he's saying with his smile. *This could be ours.* But I can't let my mind go there yet; I can't let myself contemplate a world without my family—just as I can't imagine living a world away from Leo now that I've found him. There's only one way this can end in my favor . . . and it's all out of my hands.

"So that stuff would make up our entire home for the next twenty years?" Beckett asks, eyeing the yards of aluminum and canvas. Clearly, it's no White House.

"Due to space restrictions here in the Altitude Chamber, we are only inflating one room of your habitat today—the crew community room, otherwise known as a den," Mr. Nolan answers. "However, the tools and science are the same for one room and module as they are for the entire eighteen-hundred-square-foot Europa habitat. You'll just need to be prepared for a long day of working the pressure equalization valve." He points to a steel spigot that runs the length of the ice floor, nearly blending in with it. "Who wants to give me a hand?"

"I will," I volunteer, curious to try it, and he beckons me over. Once we're at the center of the ice, he instructs me to hold up one end of the canvas while he grasps the other, and then he grabs the valve with his free hand, feeding bursts of air into the hole in the canvas. A popping sound echoes through the chamber as it slowly inflates.

"It sounds like we're microwaving popcorn," I remark, watching as the canvas expands.

Mr. Nolan chuckles. "It sure does. Here, have a go at it."

He hands me the valve, and as I press the trigger, a surge of air blasts into the canvas with surprising strength. "Nice," I say, smiling at my handiwork. We now have almost half of a room standing.

The rest of the twelve each take take a turn at the valve, and as I watch the yards of material transforming into a full-size room, I am reminded of what I love about science. From almost nothing, we have created *something*—something that can support human beings for twenty years. It's like magic. In fact, sometimes I think that's exactly what science is: the magic we look for in stories, without realizing that it exists in all the inventions and creations around us.

As the hour draws to a close, we stand back to admire our hundred-square-foot inflated room. It's hard to believe it used to be just a heap of fabric.

"Would this really shield us from *all* the elements?" Minka, the finalist from Ukraine, asks as she pokes its soft exterior. "I mean, if we ever experienced on Europa anything like the storms and disasters we've had to deal with here on Earth, would this habitat be enough to protect us? It looks so . . . light."

"The habitat is far more durable than it appears, and these materials were chosen with ultimate protection in mind," Mr. Nolan assures us. "But remember: the recent destruction of most of our Earth was a man-made tragedy. Right now, Europa is a pure, untamed wilderness of ice that you will need to terraform, make habitable—and then *protect*. We learned the hard way on Earth that no amount of technology or wealth is worth polluting and destroying our planet over. You can't afford to make the same mistake on Europa."

Finally, one of the authority figures here is speaking to something I believe in. Europa shouldn't be blindly colonized—it needs to be preserved. And if I'm right about Europa's intelligent life, as I'm certain I am . . . how are we supposed to protect and maintain the purity of this new environment, if the very thing to protect it from just might be *us*?

Once again, I reach the same conclusion: Earth is where it's safest—both for us humans, and for Europa's undiscovered life.

That night, I stare at the flash drive in my hands, knowing that this is the moment. I've waited long enough, analyzed and triple-checked every bit of code, and I've even covered my tracks by programming my tablet's IP address to reroute to a fake street address in Texas if traced. There's nothing left for me to do now but finish the hack.

Of course, even with all my careful planning, the risks remain. If my work isn't quick and clean, I could compromise Dot—and if Dr. Takumi or General Sokolov senses something amiss with the robot's systems, they could run a malware scan and find evidence of my tampering. They won't necessarily know it was me, but as the only engineer here, I am the obvious culprit.

If I get caught, I'll be thrown in jail for treason, maybe even tried as an adult. But if I don't attempt this, the world will never know about the extraterrestrials—and we'll be sending six human lives straight into their path. There is no question what I must do.

I plug the drive into my tablet and enter my algorithm to unlock the AIOS software. It takes longer than I expected, twenty minutes of sweating in front of the screen as I work the code, until finally . . . *yes*. I cover my mouth with my hand, both thrilled and slightly terrified to see that it worked. My screen fills with Dot's monitoring signals and functions—the kind of access granted only to ISTC higher-ups. All I have to do now is type in my commands.

I take a moment to consider the best way to receive the data I need from Dot. The easiest method with the least amount of risk would be to instruct the robot to send the files directly to my tablet—but this rudimentary device I brought doesn't have the storage space or capability to receive such advanced files on top of the AIOS software. There's no chance of me getting back into the robotics lab either. Which means . . . I need Dot to bring the files to me.

Using binary code, I type in a command for the robot:

```
Download all data on biosignatures
from Europa. Bring the results to the
private room of finalist Naomi Ardalan
before morning. Discuss with no one.
```

After I hit Send and tuck the flash drive back in its hiding place, another challenge awaits: disabling the security camera in our hallway. I think quickly, weighing my options. There's no clear-cut way to stop the film from rolling without access to the ISTC computer that controls the cameras—but maybe I could blind the lens.

I rush to my backpack, retrieving the pouch Sam refers to as my mad scientist kit: filled with odds and ends that are capable of pulling off an experiment on the fly. I rummage through it, momentarily considering petroleum jelly to blur the lens instead, until my hands close around something even better: my mini LED flashlight. That'll do the trick.

I throw on a hoodie and then, gathering my courage, I open the door and steal through the dark.

The main flaw with this plan is that it requires me to shine an ultrapowerful light straight ahead, to not only blind the lens but also obscure my face as I approach the camera—hardly subtle if anyone else happens to be wandering the dorm in the middle of the night. I just have to pray that I'm the only one on our floor who is daring—or foolish—enough to be up past curfew.

I make my way toward the blinking camera, my heartbeat echoing in my ears. And then, in one quick motion, I blast the LED light directly overhead, creating a lens flare. I hold the flashlight aloft for as long as my nerves allow, until I'm certain the lens is shot. And then I switch off the brightness and pick up my pace, tearing through the dark back to my room. I'm nearly there when I hear it—the sound of something moving behind me.

I whirl around, but all I see are shadows cast by the furniture and framed photographs. It must have been my paranoid imagination.

Except . . . as I push through the door into my room, I can almost swear I hear quickening footsteps.

I stay up waiting until dawn, but there is no sign of Dot. As I shower and get dressed in a sleep-deprived fog, I wonder if I made some kind of mistake. Did I mess up when entering the algorithm or the machine-to-machine command? I replay my every move in my mind, but I can't pinpoint the flaw. Even if the robot was recharging on sleep mode, I know that it's programmed to wake up at a command. So . . . what went wrong?

I rack my brain for a solution, another way to get the biosignatures from Dot. And then I remember that today's training schedule includes a group robotics-operations session with the AIs. Could I maybe work this to my advantage?

After breakfast, I pull Leo aside into the first private

place I can find: an empty utility closet.

"This is hot," he says, pulling me in for a kiss.

As much as I'd love nothing more than to melt into Leo, I force myself to stay on track.

"I have a favor to ask you," I say, pulling back from his kiss. "I need a moment alone with Dot to—to finish my plan. My only opportunity is during group training, but I'll need Cyb and the others occupied."

"Let me guess," Leo says, raking a hand through his hair. "You need to use my powers of distraction once again?"

"I've already thought of something that should do the trick," I tell him. "But I should probably warn you that it might mark you as difficult in the robots' eyes. Then again, I questioned an actual NASA official about this at the very beginning, and I'm still here."

Leo groans.

"What are you getting at?"

I take a deep breath.

"Asking Cyb point-blank about the failed mission to Mars. *Athena*."

Leo leans against the wall, his shoulders slumping.

"Isn't there some other way? Something else I can do that isn't speaking out of turn or coming across like an instigator?"

"Not unless you can think of something compelling enough to take everyone's eyes off Dot—and me—for a good five minutes. Plus, Robotics Ops is one of the only times it's just us finalists and the AIs, with no human instructors or team leaders around, which gives us our best chance."

"I don't know." He sighs. "Even though I—I am starting to believe your theories about the RRB, I still believe in the mission, too. You know how much I want, *need* to make the Final Six, and Cyb is a decision maker. If this could hurt my chances . . ."

"I understand," I say quickly. "Don't worry." Maybe I am asking too much.

"What will you do, then?"

"I'm not sure," I reply. "But I'll have to think of something. Maybe when I'm at one of my private training sessions in Mission Control, I can get near Pleiades—"

"The NASA supercomputer? No. No *way*." Leo holds up his hands, exhaling. "Let's just go with the plan that doesn't involve any more hacking. I'll do it. I'll ask the question."

"You will?" I look at him in surprise and delight.

He chuckles. "Yes, you weirdo. This better be worth it."

I wrap my arms around his neck. "It will be. I have a feeling."

We take our positions as soon as we reach the Mission Floor, with Leo standing right in front of Cyb and me off to the side—the closest in the room to Dot. I try to make eye contact with the AI, but her head is swiveled away from me, watching Cyb lead the session.

"As you've seen in your simulations, there are points on our journey that require two of you to perform a spacewalk while Dot and I, and the rest of the crew, remain inside.

During that time, if ever there is a communication failure, we will rely on the new telemetry software in your space suits to monitor your status," Cyb explains. "Today, we'll be showing you how to read the telemetry signals, and going over emergency procedures."

Leo clears his throat.

"Is that—is that what went wrong on the *Athena* mission?" he blurts out. "Was communication lost because the astronauts didn't have this caliber of space suit equipment?"

I inch closer to Dot. Everyone is watching Leo and Cyb.

"Excuse me?" Cyb utters after a pause.

"Well, I—I mean, even though no official cause was ever given for the tragedy on Mars, there had to have been a reason, right?" Leo rambles. "I guess I'm just wondering what it was."

Cyb makes a series of mechanical sputtering sounds in response, and I can feel all the finalists in this room recognizing the same truth: the robots have clearly not been programmed to discuss the controversial *Athena* and its perished astronauts.

But I can't think about that now. I seize my opportunity, quickly reaching for Dot's mechanical arm, and the AI turns to face me.

"I hear you have something for me," I whisper to the machine.

Dot's artificial eyes bore into mine. She expresses no surprise at my words, confirming that the AI did in fact receive my command. So then, why . . . ?

"Follow me," I say under my breath. I slip behind one of the hulking mock-up modules, out of Cyb's and the group's line of sight. "I received a command on my tablet last night," I fib. "It said something about deciphering biosignatures, and that you would be bringing them to me."

"I am the backup machine," Dot says quietly, her voice like the female twin of Cyb's crisp, clear tone. "Only my superior is authorized to deliver materials to the humans."

Logic, Naomi, I tell myself. *Remember, the robots work off logic.* "But that's not true anymore, is it? Have you ever received a command by mistake?"

Dot hesitates. "No."

"That means something changed," I insist. "You were chosen for this task, Dot. Not Cyb. And only you and I are allowed to talk about it."

I can see the wheels turning in Dot's machine-mind, and I press on. "One of the Europa Mission leaders clearly *needs* both of us to do this. You can't go against your leaders, can you? I know that I can't." I give Dot an imploring look. "What if this is some kind of test to see how well I can read the scientific elements, to determine if I should be one of the Final Six? They need your help finding out . . . and so do I."

I half hate myself as I use logic-filled lies to sway the innocent robot. But as Dot looks back at me, registering my words . . . I can't help feeling a sprig of hope. This just might work.

TWENTY-ONE

LEO

THE AIR SEEMS TO THICKEN AROUND ME AS CYB FUMBLES AT my question and the rest of the finalists stare. I scan the room for Naomi and Dot, wondering when I can put an end to this—but they are both missing. Suddenly, Cyb presses a round button on his mechanical arm and within moments, General Sokolov comes bursting through the doors.

My stomach drops. This can't be good—especially not if the general notices that Naomi and Dot are both absent. *Hurry up, Naomi,* I beg silently.

General Sokolov paces toward us, her eyes flashing with irritation. "Since when do we hijack training sessions with our own inappropriate questions?"

My skin burns under the glare of the general and the

stares of my competitors, most of whom appear to be reveling in seeing me get called out. Only Jian, Henri, and Sydney look at me with a hint of concern. But then I see Dot shuffle into view, followed a second later by Naomi filtering back into the crowd, and I breathe a sigh of relief. At least she managed to get through her part of the plan unscathed. Now I just have to find a way to remedy the situation on my end.

"I'm sorry," I tell the general and Cyb. "I didn't mean any disrespect whatsoever. I was genuinely just . . . curious."

"So am I," an unexpected voice calls out. "I think we all are."

I turn and find that the voice relieving me from the spotlight belongs to Jian. I give him a grateful smile.

The general freezes, and for a second I think she might explode on all of us. But then she heaves a sigh. "Fine. Let's put the rumors to rest once and for all."

I can feel Naomi trying to get my attention from across the room. She meets my eyes and mouths the words *thank you*, putting her hand to her heart.

"I can tell you, from my insider's vantage point of working on the International Space Station at the time, that whatever preposterous stories you heard are complete nonsense," General Sokolov begins. "There was no conspiracy. Russia didn't sabotage the mission for its own gain."

I glance up, suddenly interested. I didn't know about any Russian conspiracy . . . but it must be enough of a story if the general immediately assumed that's what I was getting at.

"Nor did the crew starve to death," she adds. "Not only did they have all the provisions they could fit into their habitat on Mars's surface, but the *Athena*'s supply ship was permanently waiting in orbit with another two decades' worth of food—which the Final Six will now benefit from." She pauses. "The tragedy was simply a failure of science, a failure we all learned from."

"What was the scientific failure, exactly?" Sydney calls out. I can read the subtext in her eyes: *Could it happen again?*

"*Off* the record," the general says, "we instructed the Mars crew on how to build an enclosed Earth-like ecosystem on the planet shortly after they touched down. Because the astronauts all died at the same time, in the middle of the night, we have reason to believe an unexpected chemical reaction in the artificial space caused the oxygen to leak out while they were asleep." Her voice drops. "They were gone before we could do anything."

So they suffocated. I can feel my own throat closing up as I imagine the crew's nightmarish last moments. How did no one know about this?

As if reading my thoughts, General Sokolov continues, "Again, this is just a theory. Without a living crew to tend to the equipment, our monitor readings couldn't be deemed accurate, and NASA's and Roscom's public relations teams felt it was unfair to the families to float theories that may cause greater distress." She gives us a pointed look. "I expect your cooperation in this. But I felt it was important for you to know that the likely cause of the Mars tragedy is something unique to that situation—and will not present itself on Europa. We have enough real complications to prepare for. I can't have my potential Final Six distracted, worrying about impossibilities."

"How is it impossible on Europa?" Henri calls out. "The inflatable habitat—"

"Is exactly why you'll be safe." General Sokolov finishes his sentence. "We began working with Bigelow Aerospace after Mars, and it's a whole new level of protection. In addition, unlike Mars, we don't need to create an artificial ecosystem. Europa has the key ingredient of water—all we have to do is drill through the ice and get to it." She glances at Cyb. "Speaking of which, you all have a training session to return to. Now that I've answered your questions, I hope this will be the last time we discuss the *Athena* mission."

As she saunters out of the room, it occurs to me that others here must have been questioning her about this before me. Otherwise, why would she give in and tell us the truth so quickly?

"There's just one thing she left out," Jian mutters behind me. "The Dr. Takumi connection. Did you know he didn't advance to power until Mars happened?"

I turn around, staring at Jian in surprise.

Leaving the Mission Floor for our next training session, I feel someone push my shoulder.

"What was that about, Italian? Getting cold feet?" Beckett

gives a mocking laugh. "Eager to go home to Mommy and Daddy and avoid big, bad space?"

I spin around, my insides burning with fury at the mention of the family and home I no longer have.

"You wish. I'm not going anywhere. The bigger question is, why do you act so high and mighty when you're obviously the one afraid of *me*?"

"Please." Beckett gives me a scornful look. "You're not a threat."

"Right. That's why you attempted to cut me loose from ten thousand feet in the air."

Beckett stops short, the color draining from his face. *He thought I didn't know.* He must have thought it was a secret moment that only he and his dark conscience would ever remember.

"What the hell?" He wrinkles his nose, making like I'm the crazy one. But I know better.

"I saw you try to mess with my harness. You would have killed me if you could. The only reason you're not trying anything like that here is so you don't get cut." I lean forward. "So tell me, Beckett, what is so terrifying for you back at the White House that you'd try to kill me in order to stay away?"

For a split second, I think Beckett might actually own up to everything. But then he glowers at me. "You don't know what you're talking about," he says before turning his back. I'm still watching him stalk away when I feel a hand on my arm.

"What was that about?" Naomi murmurs in my ear.

"Uh, I'll tell you when we're alone."

"Speaking of, Lark says we have a free hour between training and dinner. Meet me at our spot?" she asks. "I have something to tell you."

I nod, the thought of alone time with her wiping Beckett from my mind.

"I'll be there."

I climb the steps of the Telescope Tower to find Naomi already waiting, leaning her elbows on the balcony railing as she looks up at the stars. She turns at the sound of my footsteps and gives me a sheepish smile.

"Hey," I greet her, kissing her forehead. "What did you want to tell me?"

She looks at me as if in awe. "You mean you're not angry?"

"About what? The whole thing with the general?"

"Yeah." She laces her fingers in mine. "Here I was all prepared to apologize, and you're not even mad."

"Well, considering I let you off the hook after pulling something way riskier the night of the storm, I think we've established that I don't know how to be mad at you. Clearly I need to work on that." I grin. "But I *am* curious to hear the apology you planned out."

"Okay, yeah, let me say it." She stands up straighter. "I didn't expect Cyb to bring in the general. I know how important this mission is to you, and I'm really, *really* sorry if I caused any sort of red flag by your name. But"—she takes a deep breath—"if it turns out I'm right—not just about the RRB, but about what the Space Conspirator has been writing all along—then I'm not afraid to say it. I want you to stay on Earth. I want you safe."

I touch her cheek, momentarily lost for words. It's been a long time since somebody cared this much for me, and I'd almost forgotten, after losing my family, what it feels like to truly *matter* to someone.

"Well, at least one interesting thing came out of your plan," I say when I find my voice. "Jian told me something General Sokolov left out of her explanation about Mars. Apparently, Dr. Takumi accelerated to power right after the *Athena* tragedy."

Naomi's eyes widen. "Wow. That is some seriously shady timing." She leans back against the balcony railing, thinking. "If there's more to it, maybe we'll find out when—if—Dot comes through. Provided I don't get arrested for treason first."

I stare at her, marveling at how she can speak so matter-of-factly about that possibility. "So you're really not afraid of getting caught? Is there *anything* that scares you?"

Naomi gives me a half smile before glancing away. "The thought of losing the people I love. Especially my little brother." She takes a breath. "I'm not just scared of that, I'm *terrified*. So, I'm not fearless. And whatever I do that may seem that way . . . it's all for them."

I nod, realizing as I gaze at her that Naomi's words make

her even more beautiful to me.

"What about you?" she asks. "You don't seem at all scared of the mission, even with the laundry list of risks."

"Yeah. Well . . . I used to have the exact same fear as you. But then my worst fear came true. And for a while, that made me unafraid of anything—including, and especially, death." I swallow hard. "But now I know what it's like to be afraid of losing something again. I've known that feeling since I found you."

Naomi's eyes well up. She pulls me close, answering my words with a kiss. Our kisses start out soft and tender, and then her fingers move beneath my shirt, running down my back, and suddenly we're sliding down to the tower floor together—kissing like it's our last night in this world.

TWENTY-TWO

NAOMI

I'M IN THE MIDDLE OF A PERFECT DREAM WHEN I HEAR THE sound. I'm back home, sitting at the old dining table that still has Sam's and my initials carved into the wood, and my loved ones are seated around me: my brother, our parents, and Leo, too. But then a rhythmic series of beeps seeps into my consciousness, interrupting the golden moment.

"What's that noise?" I ask, glancing around the table.

"What noise, azizam*?" Mom gives me a funny look.*

"You know what it is," Sam says. "It's Morse code, saying you have to wake up." He leans over and shakes my shoulders. "Wake up!"

I sit bolt upright, my eyes snapping open at the beeping in my room. Dot is in front of me, shuffling her way across the floor toward my bed. I cover my mouth to keep from crying out in amazement. *The plan actually worked!*

Dot stops dead center, facing my bed. That's when I see that the AIOS screen in her chest chassis is all lit up and flashing with . . . symbols. But it's more than just images. There's also a *sound* coming from the screen—a vibrational humming, only the pitch and tone are all wrong. It's a foreign sound that turns my body cold, that sends pins and needles prickling through my skin.

The robot beeps again, urging me in Morse to copy down what I see on the screen. I know why Dot isn't speaking verbally—in case anyone on either side of these walls happens to be up at this hour. I've made the AI believe this is a secret, crucial task from one of the mission leaders, and I feel a stab of guilt at the way I've misled Dot. But this is too important for me to hesitate. I switch on the light and run to my desk, grabbing a notepad and pen.

My pen flies across the paper as I copy down one chemical symbol and physics formula after another, not stopping to register what I'm notating—until an image fills the screen, and I almost fall out of my chair.

It's a sketch of what appears to be a cell, its insides punctured with *three nuclei*. Just like the RRB.

I'm shaking as I finish copying the figures on the screen. And then, finally, it turns dark. Dot shuffles back to the door, and as I watch her retreating form, I whisper, "Thank you."

The cell image is a revelation enough, but I still have numerical data to decipher. I spend the next two hours studying it and unscrambling the formulas—until I finally solve the main riddle with a heart-stopping flick of my pen.

$C_{55}H_{72}O_5N_4Mg$-CH4-E

Chlorophyll-Methane-Europa

Chlorophyll and methane found on Europa.

The room sways as I stare at my notes, and for a split second I am outside of my own body, looking down at the surreal scene of my discovery. Because where there is chlorophyll and methane, there is *life*. *These* are the biosignatures I was looking for. And with the RRB cells matching the idiosyncratic image of the cell in this data . . . that proves my hypothesis.

We are being injected with bacteria from *Europa's alien life*.

And it's making some of us more *like them*—as proven by Leo in the diving pool.

It's making some of us *see them* . . . as evidenced by Suki's cries, and Callum's breakdown.

As for the rest of us, we may never know how deep its effects go until we land.

I jump out of my seat, too overcome to sit still. This goes beyond any secret I thought Dr. Takumi was keeping; it's on another level from the Space Conspirator's theories. But how could NASA and all the reputable space agencies allow this? And *why*?

Unless . . . Could it be that the space agencies, as a whole, *don't* know? Dr. Takumi and General Sokolov have jurisdiction over the robots, which certainly makes it possible for them to keep the data secret. *Did they*? And what is their endgame?

One thing is for sure: I can't wait till morning to share this news with Leo. I'm pretty sure I'll explode if I have to keep it inside a minute longer. I know we agreed to resist the temptation of sneaking into each other's rooms, but compared to everything else I've been up to here at ISTC, stealing into the boys' dorm seems practically quaint.

I slide my feet into slippers and grab the flashlight under my bed. I can feel my heart palpitating as I make my way down the corridor to the fork that separates the girls' side from the boys', imagining what Leo will say to my discovery . . . what the world will say when I release the data. Maybe I can find a way to get it to someone like Dr. Wagner, to shield my family from the fallout of my hacking—

My flashlight hits against another yellow beam. I jump back, fear rising in my throat. I'm not alone. Someone is standing across from me in the dorm corridor, shining a flashlight of his own. *Beckett Wolfe*.

He tilts his beam of light straight into my face, catching me red-handed.

"Sneaking out of your room after curfew—I could report for you this," he says with a sly smile.

He looks all wrong, leaning against the wall like he's been here for hours . . . like he's been waiting for something.

"I could say the same about you," I retort, but Beckett just shrugs.

"*I'm* just getting some air. I'm not the one trying to sneak into my secret boyfriend's room."

The breath returns to my lungs. Could he only know about Leo . . . and not about Dot?

I raise myself to my full height, giving Beckett my best scornful expression.

"Don't be stupid. I couldn't sleep and just thought I'd take a walk. It's not any more scandalous than that."

I turn on my heel and as I walk away, I hear Beckett singing something familiar under his breath.

> *"When I am king, you will be first against the wall*
> *With your opinion, which is of no consequence at all."*

The haunting melody continues in my mind as I hurry back to my room. I know that song, it's a classic. So why do I have a creeping feeling of dread?

And then the title flashes in my mind, making me wonder if Beckett saw more than he let on.

He was singing a Radiohead song—called "Paranoid Android."

TWENTY-THREE

LEO

INSTEAD OF THE MIRROR SCREEN ALARM, I WAKE UP TO THE sound of someone flinging open my bedroom door. I scramble upright, covering my bare chest as Lark steps in.

"No breakfast in the cafeteria today," she says by way of greeting. "Dr. Takumi called a press conference in the media room. Get dressed and meet your fellow finalists there right away."

"Is everything oka—"

But she's already on to the next room before I can get my question out. I climb out of bed, an onset of nerves kicking in. Something tells me that whatever this is . . . it's going to be bad.

I throw on my uniform and hurry out the door, catching

up with Henri and the other Russian finalist, Evgeni, at the end of the boys' corridor.

"Do you guys know what's going on?" I ask as we rush down the stairs.

"No clue," Henri answers, and Evgeni shakes his head. But they both look almost as worried as I feel.

We arrive in the media room to find a grim-faced Dr. Takumi and General Sokolov standing at the foot of the stage before a half-dozen news cameras. The sight of outsiders infiltrating our training-camp bubble gives me a shudder of foreboding.

More than half of my fellow finalists fill the seats in front of the stage, and I scan their faces, looking for Naomi—but there's no sign of her. I follow Henri and Evgeni into the second row and slide in next to Dev Khanna, leaving the aisle seat beside me empty for her.

"Any idea what's happening?" I glance at Dev, hoping against the odds that he might have some reassuring info. But he shakes his head. We wait silently, with him watching the stage and me eyeing the door, until he nudges me in the ribs. "Look."

I follow Dev's gaze to the opposite side of the aisle—where General Sokolov leads a stumbling Dot toward the stage. My mouth falls open as I watch Dot struggling to walk, like some kind of robot toddler. I hear Sydney Pearle try to greet Dot, and I see the robot stare at her blankly in return . . . as if she's never seen her before. A pit of dread sets in my stomach.

"What's going on?"

It's Naomi. I breathe a sigh of relief. As long as she's here in the audience with us, she couldn't have been caught . . . right?

I point out the sight of the clumsy, infantile Dot limping her way up the stage, helped along by the general. Dev leans over to the two of us.

"It looks like they reset Dot."

Naomi closes her eyes, shaking her head.

"Reset?" I repeat. "What does that mean, exactly?"

But before they can answer me, Dr. Takumi steps up to the microphone. He leans forward, staring into the eyes of the cameras. "Early this morning, the Johnson Space Center was the victim of an attempted security breach. I want to assure everyone that no harm was done. However, we had to act quickly. Seeing as the security breach occurred in one of our most classified, high-level robots, we had no choice but to restore the AI, Dot, to her original settings before she could be compromised any further. All of her stored memory, data, and functions have been scrubbed. Dot will need to relearn her skills—and will no longer accompany the Final Six to Europa."

My stomach drops. Naomi grabs my arm as a collective gasp fills the air. I can tell from her shallow breaths that she is on the verge of panic, just like me, and I force myself to keep a poker face even as I feel my body twitching, threatening to give us away.

"However, there will still be two robots on the mission,"

Dr. Takumi continues. "While it's less than ideal, a backup AI we recently finished testing will take Dot's place and serve alongside Cyb."

One of the reporters raises his hand.

"Do you have any idea who could be responsible for such a treacherous act?"

Naomi digs her nails into my arm, and I brace myself for the worst. *This is it.* We're caught, and they're going to take her away—

"That information has not been confirmed," Dr. Takumi says coolly. "However, we have reason to suspect someone in particular."

He pauses, and I can't breathe, can't watch anymore. I stare down at Naomi's hand, my mind torturing me with thoughts of what they'll do to her. *How can I protect her?*

"We're fairly certain it was a former ally of ours. It's no secret that Dr. Greta Wagner has been unsuccessfully attempting to hijack the Europa Mission ever since we cut ties with Wagner Enterprises." Dr. Takumi's voice barely disguises his rage.

My body sags with shock. He doesn't even suspect us. And of all people, he thinks it was that scientist Naomi idolizes, whose book is currently sitting by my bed? I glance at Naomi, finding my own guilt and astonishment reflected in her eyes.

"There's something else," Dr. Takumi says—and this time, I could swear he is looking straight at the two of us.

"We'll be making our selections for the Final Six earlier than previously announced. Tomorrow, in fact. This security breach has only highlighted the time-sensitive nature of our mission."

TWENTY-FOUR

NAOMI

HOW COULD I HAVE BEEN SO WRONG?

I stare at the hopeless spectacle of this new Dot, and I can feel the bile rising in my throat. How could I have messed up on such a colossal scale? I thought I knew what I was doing, that I got in and out quickly enough to keep Dot safe—but I'm clearly just an amateur who tried and failed to punch above her own weight. And now, instead of fulfilling my aim of protecting the finalists and exposing the truth about Europa . . . I've managed to endanger us all. There's no scenario where I can come forward with the biosignatures now, not when the data came from a robot that's since been scrubbed. My notes will look like nothing more than the ramblings of a lunatic. And with Dot cut from the mission and Dr. Takumi rushing the next stage of the draft—who even *knows* how much damage my actions caused?

I. Screwed. Up. The words replay over and over in my mind, forming a rhythm, like the backing score to Dr. Takumi's terrifying words. I screwed up royally, and I'm not sure I'll ever be able to make it right.

I glance at Leo, wondering if he hates me now—the way I'm beginning to hate myself. Should I confess? If I do, the wrong person will no longer be blamed . . . and maybe my data on the biosignatures *could* actually be taken seriously, if I'm willing to give up my freedom for it. But all too quickly, another image comes to mind: my family being forced to pay for my crime. The thought of any harm coming to them, of Sam's medical treatment being withheld, forces me to be selfish and keep my secret. Dr. Wagner has the resources to escape the ISTC and the government's reach. We don't.

And there's something else. By confessing, I'm removing the one finalist who knows the truth, whose understanding of extraterrestrials and microbiology could help keep the Final Six alive on Europa. *Me.*

I need to go with them.

As soon as we're excused, Leo and I break out of our seats and make a beeline for the elevators. We jump in the second the doors open, and once we're alone, I bury my face against his chest. And then I feel his arms stiffen around me.

"I thought for sure I wouldn't see *you* this morning,"

comes the sound of Beckett's voice as he slips into the elevator after us.

I freeze. "Why in the world would you think that?"

"Just a feeling I had," he says breezily. "You know. After last night."

The elevator doors open onto the Hab floor, and I watch, my stomach churning, as he saunters off.

"What is he talking about?" Leo asks.

I cover my face with my palms. I can't believe I have more than one giant blunder to admit to. "He caught me trying to sneak into your room last night," I mutter. "And . . . he might have seen something a whole lot more incriminating, too."

But as Leo groans at this latest curveball, I realize something else. If Beckett *did* see Dot leave my room, he's obviously not covering for me out of the goodness of his heart. He plans on lording this over me, using the information to get something from me. The question is . . . *what* does he want?

"Come on." I give Leo a gentle nudge as we reach the door to my room. "We have bigger things to worry about than whether we're caught together in here. We need to talk."

"Okay, but we can't just talk in the middle of the room, where someone walking by could overhear," he says. We step inside, and Leo strides over to my closet. "This should be safer."

"Um. Okay." I crawl into the closet with him, and we

fold our bodies into the dark space beneath my hanging uniforms. If the stakes weren't so high, it would almost be funny. But I sober quickly as I fill Leo in on Dot's data, and the most monumental discoveries of all: the proof of life—and the reality of the alien bacteria inside our bodies, working its way through our muscles, our consciousness, our*selves*.

Leo stares at me, his mouth open in shock.

"You don't want to believe it," I acknowledge. "Because the idea that we could be walking into this kind of danger threatens your view of the mission, of everything it's come to represent for you. I get it. But—"

"It's not that." He swallows hard. "I—there's something I should tell you. Before I left Italy, the prime minister's daughter told me something she overheard—that I was chosen for the Twenty-Four because my underwater skills could make me some sort of weapon on Europa."

My eyebrows shoot up.

"*Seriously?* And you never shared that because . . . ?"

Leo gives me a sheepish look.

"I didn't take it seriously at first. Besides, all I've wanted this whole time is to make the Final Six. The last thing I was going to do is poke holes in the reason I'm a finalist. But when I saw that *change* come over Beckett in the diving pool after the RRB shots, and knowing how the serum affected me in the water, too . . ." He takes a deep breath. "I'm starting to believe Dr. Takumi and the ISTC are grooming us to adapt to the extraterrestrials' world—so we can eventually overtake them, and make Europa *our* world."

I gape at him, speechless, as all the jarring pieces fall into place.

"It makes sense," I whisper, when I find my voice. "Especially the secrecy. Because who would sign off on this mission if they knew upfront what we're up against? So, instead, Dr. Takumi is giving us the tools through the RRB and our training." I shiver, a chill running through my body. "In his mind, it's maybe even a part of terraforming: clearing out the underwater life and making Europa humans-only. And we can't let that happen. No matter how frightening it may be to us, the life that came before is the life that belongs there."

Leo nods, and I can see it in his eyes—the crushing realization of what the mission really entails.

"That's why I need to go," I continue. "I have to be one of the Final Six."

Leo's expression turns incredulous. "*What?* After everything you said about needing to get back home, about how this mission is a likely recipe for death . . . are you saying the proof of alien life actually *changed* your mind?"

"No. It just made me realize where I'm most needed." I take Leo's hand in mine. "The other finalists are going into this blind. If I can use my scientific ability to keep cracking at the mystery of what *kind* of life is waiting for us up there and how we might survive alongside it, then the Final Six needs me. I failed Dot, but maybe I can make up for that now—by trying to keep the rest of the six safe."

Leo gazes at me with an expression that fills my cheeks with heat. "Every time I'm sure I've figured you out, you show me another layer. Maybe that's another reason why I . . . can't imagine going back to a life without you." He wraps his arms around me and I close my eyes, his touch my only comfort.

"It's all in Dr. Takumi's hands now," he murmurs. "But I've got to do something. I have to make sure we go up there together."

TWENTY-FIVE

LEO

TONIGHT IS THE SPACE CAMP VERSION OF THE LAST SUPPER: our last dinner before the Final Six are unveiled tomorrow. The mood in the cafeteria is how I imagine soldiers must feel on the eve of deployment—only in this case, the war we're afraid of returning to is at home. If I thought the nerves and anticipation were extreme leading up to the first elimination, the tension in the air tonight could power an entire city. Especially mine. Not only do I need to make the final draft, I need to make it with her. The only way I can get through tomorrow is if not just one, but two prayers are answered.

Naomi and I sit at a table with Sydney, Minka, Dev, and Henri, all of us too anxious to swallow a bite of food. I glance at Dr. Takumi on and off throughout the hour as I make my decision. And then, when he moves to the door at the end of dinner, I jump out of my seat, catching him just as he exits.

"Dr. Takumi, can I talk to you?" I blurt out. "It will only take a second."

He arches an eyebrow. "What is it, Leonardo?"

"I just wanted to say that . . . there are two people here who were born for this mission. I know I have the underwater skills to get us through the ice crust of Europa. And training on the same team as Naomi Ardalan has convinced me that she has the brains to keep us alive in space." I take a deep breath. "This mission is what I've been living for, ever since the day I was drafted. I know it's your decision, but I just wanted to—to promise you: Naomi and I are both the right choice."

A long pause follows and I wait, every muscle in my body tensing, while Dr. Takumi gives me an inscrutable look. "I'll keep that in mind," he says finally. "Goodnight, Leonardo."

He turns away, leaving me wondering, hoping, that my plea made the right impact.

It's here. The morning of the announcement. The moment all of us have been simultaneously dreading and waiting for. My stomach's been turning somersaults all night from nerves, and as I glance in the mirror while getting ready, I notice the dark circles under my eyes, the sleep-deprived pallor of my skin. Lark had instructed us to show up "camera-ready," but I'm barely thinking about the press and the public, who we'll be facing for the first time in weeks. All I can think about is the impending decision.

The finalists reconvene at the top of the Hab-floor staircase, and as soon as Naomi spots me, she cuts through the others till she's by my side.

"I feel sick," she moans. "I can't take this kind of nerves."

I hold her gaze, aching to touch her, to comfort her with more than just words. "I know. I feel the same. But it—it'll be over soon. And hopefully we'll be celebrating."

A hush comes over the finalists, and Naomi and I turn to see Dr. Takumi and General Sokolov striding toward us.

"Good morning," Dr. Takumi greets us. "Is everyone ready?"

Of course we're not. But we all nod and follow the two of them into the elevator, down to the official entrance that we haven't seen since arrival day—a lifetime ago. Stepping off the elevator, we can hear the same marching band from that first day, too. They're playing "The Star-Spangled Banner" as Dr. Takumi pushes through the doors to the ISTC front steps, the rest of us following in his wake. Naomi and I move slightly closer as we walk together into the roar of the crowd, the two of us blinking against the blaze of flashbulbs.

General Sokolov instructs us to line up on the steps, behind the makeshift podium and microphone set up for Dr. Takumi. I stand between Naomi and Ana Martinez, and as Dr. Takumi steps up to the microphone and the crowd quiets, Naomi brushes her fingertips against mine. In this moment, with tensions running so high, we're both forgetting our unspoken rule: to never touch in public, never give ourselves away.

"Are you all ready to discover the names and faces of the Final Six?" Dr. Takumi shouts out, pumping up a crowd that doesn't need any more energizing. "Here we go!"

Naomi turns to me. "I'm too afraid to watch," she whispers.

"Me, too. Just look at me," I murmur back. "It'll be okay."

"Your lieutenant commander is Dev Khanna from India!"

The crowd erupts while the band launches into the opening notes of the Indian national anthem. I smile to myself, happy for Dev. He's one of the good guys here.

"The mission medical officer is Sydney Pearle from Canada! Copilot is Jian Soo of China!"

I try to keep my eyes on Naomi, to stay calm, as the terror builds within me. It's down to the wire now. If we're not among these last three names . . .

"Our science officer is Minka Palladin from Ukraine. And the underwater specialist—"

I stand up straighter as Naomi grips my hand tighter.

"—is Beckett Wolfe of the United States of America."

No. No.

My vision blurs; all the blood rushes to my head. This can't be happening. He didn't take my spot—he couldn't have.

"It's okay, it'll be okay," I hear Naomi say, looking up at me desperately. "We'll go home together, we'll find another way to help the Final Six. You'll meet my family, and we can have the kind of life—"

She stops suddenly as the unthinkable happens.

"Last but not least, our communications and technology specialist is Naomi Ardalan, also from the United States!"

I want to shout, to scream—but I can't make a sound. Naomi's legs buckle beneath her, and she grips my arm, my own horror reflected in her eyes.

This can't be real. We can't be separated forever, she *can't* go to Europa while I stay behind, with nothing left but her memory. It's like losing my family all over again. Just when my world seemed to be opening up, all hope is gone.

Just like that.

TWENTY-SIX

NAOMI

THE WORLD STOPS WHEN I HEAR MY NAME. THE SOUNDS around me distort, the scene freezes, and I can't hold myself up—

A guard grabs me by the shoulders, tearing me away from Leo. *Leo*. I take one look at his devastated face, and my heart crumbles. There's no way I can leave him. This is all one giant mistake—it has to be.

The security guard pushes me up front with the other five, and I am forced to stand beside Beckett in front of the cameras. Beckett, who looks at me with a knowing smirk that makes my insides recoil.

The band bursts into "You're a Grand Old Flag," and

the crowd breaks into a chant. "Na-o-mi! Be-ckett!" But it's all happening in slow motion, and I can't make any sense of the faces around me. They cheer right in the face of my agony.

It wasn't supposed to be like this. Anytime I ever imagined being named one of the Final Six, I always pictured Leo beside me. And now, the thought of leaving this world and spending the rest of my life with the loathsome Beckett and four near strangers has me on the verge of hysteria.

General Sokolov joins Dr. Takumi at the microphone, and the two begin waxing on about the journey ahead of us and all that's to come starting tomorrow—but I can't listen. All I can do is try not to cry, to avoid Leo's eyes.

It was heartbreaking enough when the draft meant leaving my family. Now, to be leaving my first and only love on top of it . . . is a whole new level of pain.

As the speeches draw to an end, the guards close in around us, ushering the Final Six, the faculty, and eliminated finalists out of the fray, back inside space camp. But instead of falling in line with the others, I break away and sprint to Dr. Takumi before he reaches the door, grabbing his arm with the force of my emotions.

"*Excuse* me?" He peers down his nose at me, shaking his arm loose.

"Why?" I burst out. "Why me, why Beckett—and not Leo?"

Dr. Takumi pauses, and then he gives me a cold smile. "You were an obvious choice. None of the others here can come close to your skill set and *knowledge*."

The way he emphasizes the word makes the hairs on the back of my neck stand on end.

"After seeing what you are capable of, it was clear," he continues. "You are far more useful to us on Europa than on Earth." Dr. Takumi lowers his voice, and something fearsome flashes in his eyes. "You didn't really think you got away with everything, did you? The stunt you pulled in the robotics lab, what you did to Dot—of course I knew it was you. But it only proved you more indispensible to me and to the mission. After all . . . who else has shown themselves to be such a skilled *tech specialist*?"

I can't speak as I stare up at him. His words have knocked the wind out of me. My mind struggles to comprehend the fact that *he knows*, that he was a step ahead of me this entire time. And now it's all the more clear why I was given a coveted spot on the Final Six instead of being thrown in a jail cell. *Because I have something they need.*

I'm more beneficial to the mission as one of the guinea pigs sent to Europa than as an eliminated finalist running her mouth about what she discovered. Even from jail, my story could get out. But now, Dr. Takumi knows I won't say a word. I can't. I owe him for not turning me in to the government—and I have to play this perfectly if I'm going to keep the six of us safe.

My voice shakes as I shift the subject away from me. "Why not Leo? He beat Beckett in every underwater challenge. It makes no sense—"

"We couldn't have both of you," Dr. Takumi interrupts, with an impervious shrug. "On a mission as crucial as this, we can't afford to have any of our astronauts distracted by romance. Beckett will provide a sufficient replacement for Leo's underwater skills—and he has already proven himself to be an invaluable resource."

Romance. And here I actually thought Leo and I were doing a decent job of keeping our relationship under wraps. Once again I was wrong, I miscalculated everything—and now I'm the reason Leo lost his spot.

Dr. Takumi saunters off, leaving me reeling from his words. I see him signal someone, jerking his neck in my direction, and then Lark appears. She wraps her arm around my shoulder, steering me inside, as I search the crowd for Leo.

"He's already upstairs," Lark says, following my gaze.

As soon as we're through the doors, I feel a crack in my chest, a sob breaking loose. Lark folds her arms around me, letting down her tough exterior, as my tears fall.

"You're going to be a hero, Naomi. You just might save us all," she says gently. "If we live to see future generations of humans, it'll be thanks to *you*—you and Beckett, Jian and Sydney, Dev and Minka. I promise, you're making the most worthy sacrifice. I would do it myself if I could."

I nod, but there is no dulling the ache in my heart as the faces of the four people I love most in the world flash in my mind.

Sam. Mom. Dad. Leo . . .

• • •

It's hours before I get to see Leo again. While the eliminated finalists pack and prepare for tomorrow's journey home in a haze of shock, the Final Six are ushered into a series of all-day briefings with the heads of the space agencies and the secretary-general of the United Nations. The others around me, even the previously hesitant Sydney, are brimming with excitement as we're given the rundown of tomorrow's rocket launch, an event expected to "blow the *Apollo* moon landings out of the water." But my mind is miles away.

When we're finally escorted back to our dorm rooms, long after dinner has come and gone, I find Lark on the staircase.

"Can you get a message to Leo for me?" I whisper, pleading to her with my eyes.

She nods, and I hand her the note I scrawled during one of the long briefing meetings. And then I hurry to my dorm room to wait.

Minutes later, he is at my door. Relief mixes with misery as I fly into his arms, wondering how I will ever live without this.

"I'm sorry—so sorry," I sob as he holds me close, kissing me through my tears. "If I hadn't—"

"Don't apologize," he whispers into my hair. And as I look up at him, I see tears in his eyes too.

"Stay with me tonight." I lace my fingers in his. "All night. Lark will cover for us if anyone suspects you're not in your room, but even if she doesn't, I don't care. Dr. Takumi can't punish us any more than he already has."

Leo nods, and lifts me into his arms. He lays me down on the bed, his lips moving over mine until I forget where we are, forget the good-bye tomorrow will bring. And then suddenly, he pulls away.

"What is it?" I ask, taken aback.

"On Europa, they'll expect you to . . . to eventually have a partner, and procreate," Leo says, his voice catching on the words. "I don't know how to face it."

"I won't," I promise. "I don't care what they expect, I won't do it. But . . . but I wouldn't blame you if you end up with someone—someone on Earth." Leo shakes his head no, and I press my finger to his lips. "That's why . . . that's why I need you to be my first. I need you—*this*—to hold on to, for the rest of my life."

"Are you sure?" Leo whispers.

"More sure than I've ever been about anything."

He lowers toward me, nestling his forehead against mine. "*Ti amo,* Naomi."

My heart swells at his words. It's the moment I've dreamed of . . . but I never expected it to happen the night before we are forced to separate forever.

"*Ti amo.*" I tighten my arms around him, closing my eyes as I memorize the feel of his touch. "I love you, too."

TWENTY-SEVEN

LEO

I WAKE UP WITH HER SKIN AGAINST MINE, HER HAIR TICKLING my neck. It's like a dream I didn't dare hope for, and I smile at the sight of her sleeping face pressed against my shoulder.

And then I hear the rapping at thc door.

"One hour till departure!" someone shouts as yesterday's heartbreak comes slamming back to the fore. I feel the blow in my chest, in my stomach, and I sit up, head in my hands. Naomi stirs as I move, and I reach for her hand.

"It's—it's time," I say as she wakes, my voice coming out thick, unlike my own.

She sits up in panic. "I can't say good-bye to you. I can't."

I take a deep breath, realizing I need to be strong for her. I'll have plenty of time later, the rest of my life, to give in to my emotions. But not now. Not in front of her.

"You don't have to say good-bye," I say, tracing her collarbone with my finger. "I'll send you video messages and emails every day, and maybe—maybe when Europa is ready for more settlers from Earth, I can be one of them. It'll be a long time to wait, but I—I'll wait for you."

Naomi doesn't answer, and I know why. I know what she's thinking. What if they don't even *make* it to Europa? What if the extraterrestrial life is intelligent enough to slaughter them as soon as they arrive? What if while she's on the months-long journey through space, another natural disaster happens on Earth, and this time I don't make it?

I know what she's thinking, because these are the same questions playing on a never-ending loop in my own mind.

The six of us also-rans tail the Final Six in a motorcade to the Ellington Field, where we'll be flown home immediately following their departure to the Europa launch site. Whatever hopes I had about staying in America have been swiftly nipped in the bud. As Dr. Takumi informed me yesterday, my time in the United States has come to a close. I have no choice but to go from one setting of heartbreak to another.

As our tram approaches the airfield, the crowds return in full force, waving flags and hoisting up signs bearing the names of the Final Six. It hurts to remember the last time I witnessed this patriotism and celebration . . . when I was still a part of it.

Our tram stops in front of the runway, where Air Force One waits to escort the Final Six. A searing fury runs through me at the thought of Beckett smirking alongside his uncle as he takes my place. It should be me on the jet, it should be *me* in the rocket launch beside Naomi. How could Dr. Takumi make such a huge mistake?

The security guards lead us to a roped-off section of the runway, away from the clamoring crowds, but not nearly close enough to the Final Six—to Naomi. I watch from afar as she stands with her new crewmates, Cyb, and the new backup robot, the eight of them lined up alongside Dr. Takumi, General Sokolov, and President Wolfe. All of them smile proudly, posing for what's sure to be the most legendary photo in human history—all but Naomi. I watch as she searches the crowd, her expression panicked. I raise my hand in a forlorn wave, letting her know I'm here. And suddenly, she darts away from the others.

I hold my breath as she pushes her way toward me, ignoring the shocked murmurs of the crowd. And then she's in my arms, her lips on mine, her tears against my cheeks.

"I love you so much," I whisper.

Two guards break in, pulling her away from me—but not before before I slip my Danieli signet ring off my finger and slide it onto hers. She looks from me to the ring, her voice breaking as she says, "I love you, too."

I am forced to watch as she climbs into the jet behind the others, leaving me forever. She presses her face to the window, gazing down at me. I blow her a final kiss. And as the plane soars up into the sky, I double over in pain.

Ana Martinez approaches me, patting my shoulder awkwardly.

"I know. This sucks. But it'll be okay. . . . You'll feel better once you're home." She looks up. "Our rides will be here any minute."

I know Ana is trying to be nice, but her words only make me feel worse. I don't have anyone or anything to go home to—only ghosts.

"To the eliminated six, we thank you for your service," Dr. Takumi's voice booms from the microphone. "You've been a pride to your countries, and you will be welcomed home with open arms."

I glance around for Lark. Before I go, I want to say good-bye to the only other person here who really knew Naomi . . . who knew *us*. But I don't see her anywhere. She's not with the rest of the faculty, so—where is she?

But before I can ask anyone, the engine of the first return jet roars. We watch as it swoops down from the sky, bearing the French flag, and Henri gives the five of us a friendly salute.

"*Au revoir, mes amis,*" he calls before stepping into his homebound jet.

I brace myself, knowing my plane from Italy is likely to follow France. Sure enough, when the next jet circles, I can spot the green, white, and red of the Italian flag from high in the sky.

The plane skids to a stop on the runway, and the security

guard pushes me forward. I turn around for one last look at Johnson Space Center, the place that changed my life, that brought me painfully close to my dreams—and then I force myself to move forward.

I sense something is wrong as soon as I step into the plane. This isn't the same basic military jet I flew in on—it only looks identical from the outside. This one is surprisingly spacious inside, filled with plush furniture and an array of computer screens, consoles, and blinking sensors. What's more, no one is here to greet me—not Dr. Schroder or anyone else from ESA, not even a flight attendant.

My eyes catch on one of the computer screens. I blink and lean in for a second look, to make sure my eyes aren't deceiving me. But there it is on the screen, the Space Conspirator home page—the same website whose theories Naomi talked so much about. And right there, in the top corner, is the telltale text: *LOGGED IN: ADMINISTRATOR*.

What the hell? How did I end up on this plane?

"Hello?" I call out, stumbling as the jet lifts off. "What *is* this? What's going on?"

"Thank you, Lark," I hear an unfamiliar female voice say. "He's here."

And then a silver-haired woman steps out of the cockpit—the same woman from the photo on Naomi's desk.

"Greta Wagner?" I whisper.

She hangs up the phone and flashes me a smile.

"Hello, Leonardo. Have a seat. We have much to discuss."

TWENTY-EIGHT

NAOMI

MY CREWMATES ARE WILD WITH EXCITEMENT AS AIR FORCE One descends toward the Gulf of Mexico, where we will launch from sea to space. They whoop and cheer; they pose for selfies with the president and ask the Europa Mission flight director traveling with us a million and one questions. But not me. I spend the first half of the flight with my eyes closed, my head bent against my knees, trying to block out the noise and pretend none of this is happening. But now I look up, staring at Beckett Wolfe in hushed conversation with his uncle as my thoughts swirl together. I watch as President Wolfe murmurs something in Beckett's ear and Beckett nods, a strange expression crossing his face. And then the president rises to his feet, moving toward his private cabin at the front of the plane, while Beckett crosses the aisle back to his seat opposite me. He catches me staring.

"What are you looking at?" he scoffs.

"You told Dr. Takumi what you saw that night, didn't you?" I say slowly, as the pieces fall into place. "You told him a lot of things. That's what he meant when he said you proved yourself *invaluable*. You took Leo's spot by being a spy."

Beckett laughs, but it's a false, hollow sound. And as I meet his gaze, I know my hunch is right.

"You'll pay for it."

His eyes narrow into slits.

"Oh, really? Are you actually dumb enough to threaten me, right here on my uncle's plane?"

"Sorry to disappoint, but I'm not afraid of your uncle," I retort.

He leans forward, his hot breath on my cheek.

"You should be. Dr. Takumi put me in charge."

"What?" I can't have heard that right.

"It's true. He told me and my family today." Beckett wraps his hands behind his head, a smug look on his face. And then his smile distorts into a sneer. "So don't even think about threatening me again. As soon as we reach space, you'll be *answering* to me."

For once in my life, I am without a comeback.

Air Force One touches down to a massive crowd at South Texas Spaceport, a swarm of bodies large enough to swallow the throng we just left in Houston. I can see the SpaceInc Jupiter rocket waiting on the launchpad above the Gulf of Mexico, its thousands of tons gleaming in the sunlight while its vapor rises in preparation for liftoff. As I stare at the rocket, it seems impossible that we'll soon be strapped inside. *This is insane.*

Moments after the wheels hit the ground, we are ushered from Air Force One into the astronaut crew quarters, a hangar near the runway, where a flurry of NASA officials help us into our blue space suits built for liftoff and landing. But I'm barely conscious of the action around me, my legs aching to run to where I know my family waits.

Finally, once we're suited up, the flight director and security guards escort us to the VIP area, reserved for President Wolfe and the Final Six families. I whip my head around wildly, searching for them, until I hear—

"Naomi!"

Sam's voice shouts above the din. I break into a sprint, tears blurring my vision as I run toward my family. I don't care that two guards are right behind me, that the whole world is watching our reunion turned good-bye—all I see are my brother, my parents. They hold out their arms to me, and I fly straight into them, the four of us colliding in a tangle of hugs, kisses, and tears.

"I'm sorry," I cry onto Sam's shoulder. "I was supposed to come back for you. It was supposed to be us against the world, for life, and now—"

Sam interrupts, holding me by the shoulders. "It *is* us

against the world, Sis. You're going out to find us a better one." His voice cracks with emotion, but he forces a smile. "I told you before, you were born for this. And I'll be okay."

"We are so proud of you, *azizam*." Dad wraps me in a tight hug, and tears spill from his eyes as he touches my space suit. "We'll talk every day, okay? Email, video-chatting, whatever you can do—we'll be there."

Only my mother is silent, staring at me with a broken look on her face. She tries to smile, but a sob escapes instead.

"I love you, my sweet girl," she whispers, kissing my forehead.

"I love you all so much. And I realize now, more than ever, how lucky I was—*am*—to have you." I take a deep breath. "I'll never forget it."

A roar bursts from the crowd, and I turn to see a giant countdown clock lighting up.

"T-minus ten minutes!" a voice booms.

I cling tighter to my family as I wonder how it's possible for my heart to break so many times in a single day. One of the guards steps forward, placing a firm hand on my back.

"It's time to get into the launch vehicle, Naomi."

This is it. I shake my head. How is it possible I'm already out of time?

I hug my parents and Sam once more, and before our last good-bye, I blurt out, "The other finalist, the one I was standing next to on TV—his name is Leo Danieli, and he doesn't have any family left. Will you find him for me? Maybe—maybe you guys can be there for each other. He . . .

he means the world to me."

"We'll find him," Mom says. "Promise."

I try to smile in thanks.

"Go fly, Sis," Sam says in my ear. "We'll be watching you, cheering you on every day from Earth."

"My body might be up there, but my heart will always be here." I reach out my hand, and my parents and brother cover it with their own. "So I won't say good-bye. I have to believe I'll see you again."

"T-minus seven!" the booming voice echoes, and now two guards are wrenching me away from my family, ushering me in line with the two robots and the rest of the six.

I can hear my heart's loud thumping inside my space suit as we make the slow march into the rocket ship. Cyb supervises us as we strap into our acceleration seats and lie down flat, just like in the virtual reality simulation. I turn my face against the leather seat, as I did with Leo before we kissed . . . but it's not his face beside me anymore. A fist tightens around my heart.

The countdown echoes inside our spacecraft, and it doesn't matter how terrified I am—the clock keeps ticking. "T-minus six . . . T-minus five . . ."

The ground beneath us rumbles violently, and all six of us grip the sides of our seats in fear. Through the porthole window, I spot fish leaping out of the sea, the sky lighting up a fiery shade. I hear Cyb yell, "All clear for liftoff!"

The force of gravity presses down against me as the cabin rattles; the engines ignite. Just when I think I can't stand this feeling any longer, that my whole body is going to explode and disintegrate right here—we break loose. The air whooshes from my lungs as we fly.

And we soar, up past the sky.

TWENTY-NINE

LEO

I STAND AT THE EDGE OF A PRIVATE LAKE IN AUSTRIA WITH DR. Greta Wagner, the exiled inventor and scientist—who I now know as the anonymous mind behind the Space Conspirator, too. Across from us, on a concrete platform, stands her latest secret invention: a single-passenger rocket ship built for Europa.

"I've long believed that both mankind's greatest discoveries and greatest risks lie there, below the ice," Dr. Wagner says, following my gaze. "None of us know how Europa's native environment and extraterrestrials will react to the arrival of humans. I wanted to be the one to take that risk, but as you can see, I'm far too old now. When I saw your face on the news the day the Final Six were announced, I knew I could count on you to be my proxy. I can tell you want this—maybe as much as I do."

My heartbeat picks up speed. "Tell me what to do."

"My spacecraft is smaller, lighter, and therefore faster than the Final Six's. Even though they have a head start, as long as you depart this week, you can catch up to them by the time they reach Mars's orbit. Using the airlocks, you will dock with their ship." Dr. Wagner smiles. "And hitch a ride with them to Europa."

"Is it safe?" I ask. "Not for me, I mean—for the Final Six."

"The only risks involved are on your end, and mine," she answers. "The spacecraft is built for a one-way trip. If the docking fails, you will be adrift in space until you die. If all goes well, I will be in hiding for the rest of my life, since launching a human into space without government approval is a high crime. But it's worth every risk and sacrifice if you make it. Based on my intel, I can say this with certainty: the Final Six are far more likely to survive Europa with the help that you and I can uniquely provide."

I take a deep breath. I have so many questions, but one thought supersedes all others. "I'm in."

And then I look up and whisper:

"I'm on my way, Naomi."

ACKNOWLEDGMENTS

This project has been the biggest thrill of my author life thus far, and I have so many people I wish to thank.

First, to my representation for their unwavering belief in me and my writing, and for pushing this project to greater heights: Brooklyn Weaver, Joe Veltre, and Greg Pedicin, you guys are my heroes! Brooklyn, talking through the story with you early on challenged me to come up with bigger and better ideas, and I'm grateful for you helping me reach my full potential. Joe and Greg, I'll never forget how you guys rallied around this project and helped it soar. I'm beyond blessed to have the three of you on my team.

To the first person who said yes and started this author's dream coming true—Josh Bratman, thank you!! I'm forever grateful for you sharing my vision, for your insightful notes, and for finding us the perfect home for the movie adaptation with Sony. You are a true writer's producer, and working with you has been a game changer—may this be just the beginning!

I'll always remember my amazing first phone call with Alexandra Cooper: the way everything clicked, and I knew right then that I wanted her to be my editor! Alex, thank you for believing in me and this project from the get-go. I'm grateful for your editing wizardry, for listening anytime I needed to talk through the story with you (and letting me express my writerly neuroses!), and for guiding my vision. It's such an honor to be one of your authors!

Rosemary Brosnan, thank you for supporting this project from the acquisition stage, and for the incredible opportunity to publish with HarperTeen. Many thanks to everyone at Harper who had a hand in shaping this book: Alyssa Miele for your help at each stage in the process, Heather Daugherty and Erin Fitzsimmons for that *incredible* cover, Kathryn Silsand in managing editorial for taking such good care of the project, Maya Myers for your thorough copyediting, and Olivia Russo and the publicity, marketing, and sales teams for spreading the message and sharing *The Final Six* far and wide!

So much of this journey began with an incredible executive at Sony, who saw the book's potential early on: Lauren Abrahams, I am so grateful to you! Thank you for believing in this story and saying yes. Thanks also to you and Sara Rastogi for the valuable manuscript notes. It's a dream to be working with all of you at Sony.

Chad Christopher and the team at SGSLLP, thank you for getting my contracts all set and taking such great care of me!

Allison Cohen at Gersh, thank you for your amazing work bringing *The Final Six* to different countries around the world! To my foreign publishers, from Italy to Brazil and beyond, it's a privilege and a thrill to have my book translated into your languages.

Megan Beatie, thank you for your awesome publicity skills and introducing this project to so many!

Dr. Firouz Naderi, I'm endlessly grateful for you taking the time to read and give notes on the manuscript. Getting feedback from someone I admire so greatly was a real privilege, and it was so generous of you!

To a great friend, scientist, Dr. Teresa Segura: thank you for reading and giving me such helpful notes and suggestions, and for all the time you spent answering my questions. You were truly like a science editor for me—thank you!!

Getting to meet and discuss Europa with *actual* NASA Europa scientist Robert Pappalardo was another pinch-me moment in this process. Robert, thank you so much for taking the time to sit down with me, and answering my questions about everything from landers to extraterrestrials!

Dr. Ross Donaldson, thank you for letting me run my biology and tech questions by you, and for being so supportive. Chessa Donaldson, thank you for beta-reading and giving feedback on every one of my books. You two are family to me.

One of the best things I did for research was attending Space Camp for adults at the U.S. Space & Rocket Center in Huntsville, Alabama. Many thanks to the camp organizers and my teammates for an amazing, educational, and fun experience!

And now, to the people without whom I would be nowhere, who give meaning to everything I write and create—my family. My biggest thanks go to you, always . . .

Chris Robertiello, my soul mate and the greatest husband and father: your love and support makes everything possible. I am forever grateful for your belief in me and your understanding, patience, and encouragement as I worked around the clock on this book. I love you to infinity and beyond.

To my mother, ZaZa, aka Mommy Poppins: from coming over and taking care of me during the last weeks of pregnancy while I revised the manuscript like a madwoman, to returning nearly every day to help with Baby Leo while I was in the home stretch of working on the book—you've been a true angel on earth, and I am filled to the brim with gratitude and love for you!

To my father, Shon: none of this would be happening without all the years of you supporting my dreams, ever since I was a little girl scribbling away in a notebook. Thank you for teaching me to believe that whatever I can imagine, I can achieve! Love you beyond words.

Arian, I'm so grateful for the love and laughter you bring to my world. Thank you for being the best big brother ever—and for always reading and giving such valuable feedback on my manuscripts, too!

Gratitude and love to my big, beautiful Iranian family,

on both the Saleh and Madjidi sides. To my family members up in Heaven: Papa, Mama Monir, and Honey, thank you for being my inspiration each day.

Many thanks to my closest friends and family (who were so supportive during this big year of double labor!): Brooke Kaufman Halsband, Sainaz Saleh, Dottie Robertiello, the Bratmans, Mia Antonelli, Ami McCartt, Heather Holley, Jon and Emily Sandler, Meganne and Jeremy Drake, Alex and Lisa Tse, Dan and Heather Kiger, Roxane Cohanim, Adriana Ameri, Marise Freitas, Stacie Surabian, Christina Harmon, Dani Cordaro, and Camilla Moshayedi. And of course, I can't forget my writing companion, Daisy the dog!

Leo, you were a wish in my heart when I started writing this book. You became real, kicking within me, during my late nights revising the story of your namesake. And now you are here—and I'm so grateful.

I love you forever.

For a sneak peek at Alexandra Monir's pulse-pounding sequel to *THE FINAL SIX*, turn the page!

PROLOGUE

PONTUS to EARTH Live Blog
DAY 43
Astronaut: ARDALAN, NAOMI
[Message Status: Upload Failure]

Some disasters begin with a warning, an iceberg you can spot from miles ahead. Others come on all at once, as violent as they are quick, like the earthquakes and hurricanes that wrecked us back home. But up here, it's easy to miss the trigger altogether. A wire doesn't make a sound when it snaps. You don't know what's happened until after—when the creeping sense of dread moves beyond your body and takes the form of a flawed ship.

I don't think I've ever felt so helpless as I do now, writing to an entire population that will never see these words. We're going dark and you won't know why or what it means, but you'll assume the worst. And that's what has me wide-awake and clammy with sweat in the middle of the night, afraid that if I open my mouth I'll start screaming and never stop.

I can't live with them thinking I'm dead. Just imagining my parents and Sam holding each other in grief at a memorial ceremony, staring at my photo while mourners recite Rūmī, hurts worse than any physical pain. And Leo . . . what will he do when he hears the news? When my emails and video messages come to a sudden halt, how will he react? How will *I* make it through losing the four of them? I used to think communicating through a computer screen would never be enough, but now it seems like the ultimate privilege. One that I'd give anything to have back.

Maybe that's why I'm writing now, even as logic tells me it's hopeless. I have to keep trying, on the off chance that I might press Submit and, this time, hear the whoosh of delivery. The sound of everything returning to normal. Or at least as close to it as "normal" can be up here.

We'd been traveling through space for just forty-two days, three hours, and twelve minutes when it happened. It was seven in the morning, Coordinated Universal Time, and the first thing I noticed when I woke up was the sound of silence. Normally, NASA Mission Control serves as our alarm clock, waking us up at the same time each morning by piping a song through the cabin speakers. You could count on them to choose something on-brand and space-themed, like yesterday's vintage Coldplay track, "A Sky Full of Stars." But today there was no song at all. Someone must have fallen asleep on the job. Still, I woke up on cue.

We had half an hour to ourselves before we were due in the dining room for breakfast, and over the past few days I'd figured out how to get ready in ten minutes or less. This way, I could start the day in my favorite part of the ship—the one place where I never felt claustrophobic, or desperate to claw my way out.

I climbed out of my bunk and slipped off my favorite flannel pajamas, which somehow still retained the faintest smell of home. Then I stepped into the tiny shower stall attached to my cabin, which flashed a green light as soon as my feet hit the floor. A timer began, reminding me that the water would shut off in three minutes. Our entire existence here on the *Pontus* seemed to be dominated by countdown clocks.

After squeezing a dollop of shampoo onto my head and rinsing as frantically as someone with a lice problem, the shower was over. I toweled off and threw on a pair of gray track pants and a peach hoodie, then slid open the door of my cabin to the common room. Usually at least one or two of us could be found in here before breakfast, reading or watching TV, but it was empty this morning.

I jogged through the long module that makes up our crew quarters and rode the elevator pod down to the main hatch, leaving the artificial gravity behind. From there I floated, into a place that comforted and intimidated me in equal measure.

The Observatory is a circular chamber made up of wall-to-wall, indestructible quartz-glass windows, which gives you the illusion of flying untethered through the universe. It's the high of a spacewalk, minus the danger. The darkness surrounds you on all sides, with a sudden sweep of beauty whenever the ship spirals within view of Earth. This was one of those mornings when I got to see the shock of color—the blue marble of home.

I pressed my palms against the glass, staring in awe. Somewhere on that planet, in a time zone eight hours behind ours, my parents and brother were just now falling asleep for the night, while six thousand miles from them, Leo was waking up and starting his day. I closed my eyes, trying to picture his surroundings, what that day would look like. And that's when the pain socked me in the stomach. *We don't exist in the same world anymore.*

I took a few breaths to steady myself, stopping the tears before they had a chance to start. I turned away from the blue, keeping my gaze fixed on the darkness and trying to pinpoint the stars around me, until it was time to join the others. When I crawled back through the hatch, I found someone waiting for me on the other side.

Jian Soo, crewmate and copilot of our mission, glanced up sharply as I tumbled back into gravity.

"Morning," I greeted him. "You okay?"

He shook his head, his eyes frantic.

"Communication's down. Our flight nav software is still working fine, but I can't get any response from Houston. And then Sydney told me she tried logging on to email and kept getting an error message that said no connection found." He looked at me intently. "You can fix it, right?"

My first thought was that it was a joke. He was just pulling a prank—probably Beckett Wolfe's idea—to see how fast they could get a panic attack out of me. But then I remembered who I was talking to. Jian was the honest, solid, *good* one among us. And as I thought of the quiet this morning, the forgotten alarm from Mission Control, my stomach plunged.

"It—it has to be just a hiccup," I said, forcing myself to stay calm. "Let me go take a look."

That was my job, to run all the tech and communications on the ship. It had been easy enough until today, but this was uncharted territory. The *Pontus* was never supposed to lose its connection, not for a millisecond. It was as vital to the ship as oxygen.

I sprinted past Jian, toward the Communications Bay and its array of computers, where I found each screen flashing the same message in bold red letters.

COMMUNICATION SIGNALS DROPPED—NO CONNECTION FOUND.

"Houston." My voice came out like a whisper, but it didn't matter. No one could hear me anymore.

"Houston, we're experiencing a comm failure. I'm rebooting the systems and running diagnostics, and will wait for further instructions from Mission Control."

By the time the computers powered back on after the reboot, my anxiety had grown into full-fledged panic. The dreaded words returned on-screen—*NO CONNECTION FOUND*—and my fingers shook as I ran a diagnostics scan, praying the answer would flash in front of me with a simple solution. Within minutes, the problem was staring me in the face. But it was the opposite of simple.

It was our X-band antenna. The single piece of equipment on this ship that enabled all our communication with Earth wasn't even *registering* on the equipment scan. It was as if the antenna never existed.

Something was bubbling in my stomach, a nausea-inducing fear, but I forced myself to stay focused and keep moving. I raced out of the Communications Bay and back to the hatch, where Jian was now joined by Sydney and Dev, the three of them looking almost as rattled as I felt. They turned to me expectantly, but all I could do was shake my head.

"I'm going to the payload bay. Something's up with the antenna."

"Should we go with you?" Dev offered.

"One of you, maybe. There's not room for much

more. But we've got to hurry."

I yanked open the hatch door and climbed inside, with Dev right behind me. We crawled and then floated our way through two different tunnel passageways, known as nodes, until we reached the center of the ship. The payload bay required a password to enter, which always struck me as odd—was a break-in really such a risk when we were the only six humans for hundreds of millions of miles? It took Dev and me ten minutes of racking our brains and scrolling through the notes on our wrist monitors before we finally cracked it.

The hatch door swung open to reveal the vastest stretch of our ship, towering four stories high and packed from floor to ceiling with rows upon rows of cargo, all sealed in white compartments built into the walls. Attached to one of those walls would be a seven-foot-tall, dish-shaped antenna. It was the focal point of the room, the home base of our comm system.

Except . . . it was gone.

The thumping in my chest tripled in speed, loud enough for me to hear the frenetic beating through my headset. I stared at the giant empty space overwhelming the room, half convinced I was hallucinating. It wouldn't be the first time an astronaut lost their grip on reality.

"Tell me—how does the biggest, most powerful antenna of its kind just up and *disappear*?"

"It doesn't," Dev says, all color draining from his

face. "Someone made it disappear."

I followed his gaze and that's when I saw the loose bolt, drifting toward us from the back of the module. It was one of the same bolts used to secure the antenna, only this one was floating free—and heavy enough to kill us with a single strike.

"Move!" I screamed, grabbing Dev's arm and pulling him away just before the bolt careened into our path. We each seized one of the handrails running up the length of the wall, swinging from one to the next like amateur rock climbers in zero g. My head brushed the ceiling as we reached the top story, a safe distance from the floating weapon below. I looked down at the damaged payload bay in disbelief.

"Someone *did this* to us. Someone actually snuck in here, unscrewed the bolts, dismantled the antenna, and . . ."

My eyes caught on the payload door, fused into the opposite wall. It wasn't supposed to open for months—not until the Europa landing. But clearly somebody had opened it, and pushed the antenna through to disappear in space. "Someone wanted us cut off and isolated from the entire world," I whispered, fighting the bile rising in my throat. "Why?"

"Not just someone," Dev said, swallowing hard. "One of us."

It was like every star in the universe gave out at once,

plunging us into an empty, pitch-dark world.

We were lost to Earth. And we were trapped, hurtling through space at thirty thousand miles an hour, with an enemy far more dangerous than we could have imagined.

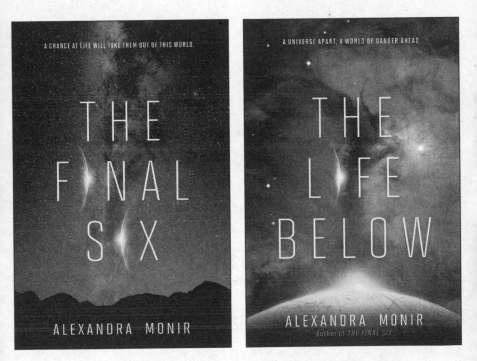